The
Mystery
Guest

A Maid Novel

NITA PROSE

Ballantine Books
New York

Published in the United States by Ballantine Books, an imprint of Random House, a division of Penguin Random House LLC, New York.

BALLANTINE BOOKS and colophon are registered trademarks of Penguin Random House LLC.

LIBRARY OF CONGRESS CATALOGING-IN-PUBLICATION DATA

Names: Prose, Nita, author.
Title: The mystery guest / Nita Prose.
Description: First edition. | New York: Ballantine Group, [2023]
Identifiers: LCCN 2023025958 (print) | LCCN 2023025959 (ebook) |
ISBN 9780593356180 (Hardback) | ISBN 9780593356197 (Ebook) |
ISBN 9780593726433 (International Edition)
Subjects: LCSH: Hotel cleaning personnel—Fiction. | Murder—Investigation—
Fiction. | Hotels—Fiction. | LCGFT: Detective and mystery fiction. | Novels.
Classification: LCC PR9199.4.P7768 M97 2023 (print) |
LCC PR9199.4.P7768 (ebook) | DDC 813/.6—dc23/eng/20230530
LC record available at https://lccn.loc.gov/2023025958
LC ebook record available at https://lccn.loc.gov/2023025959

Printed in the United States of America on acid-free paper

randomhousebooks.com

2 4 6 8 9 7 5 3 1

First Edition

Book design by Virginia Norey
Background art from Daniela Iga/stock.adobe.com

By Nita Prose

The Mystery Guest
The Maid

THE MYSTERY GUEST

To Paul, my father

The Mystery Guest

Prologue

My gran once told me a story about a maid, a rat, and a spoon. It went like this:

There once was a maid who worked for wealthy landowners in a castle. She cleaned for them. She cooked for them. She waited on them hand and foot.

One day, as the maid served her masters a nourishing stew, Her Ladyship noted with a sniff of disdain that she was missing her silver spoon. The maid was certain she had placed the spoon by Her Ladyship's bowl, but when she looked, she saw with her own eyes that the spoon had disappeared.

The maid apologized profusely, but this failed to placate Her Ladyship, nor did it placate His Lordship, who in that moment seethed and raged, accusing the maid of being little more than a petty thief and of stealing their silver.

The maid was frog-marched out of the castle, but not before the stew she had made from scratch was thrown onto her white apron, leaving a shameful blot that could never be removed.

Many years after His Lordship and Her Ladyship died, long after our poor, disgraced maid had moved on, builders who had known her were hired to renovate the castle. When they lifted the dining room floor, they uncovered a nest containing the mummified body of a rat, and beside it, a single silver spoon.

Chapter 1

My beloved grandmother, a.k.a. my gran, worked her
whole life as a maid. I have followed in her footsteps.
It's a figure of speech. I could not literally follow in her footsteps
because she has none, not anymore. She died just over four years
ago, when I was twenty-five years old (ergo, a quarter of a century),
and even before that, her walking days came to an abrupt end
when she suddenly fell ill, much to my dismay.

The point is: she is dead. Gone, but not forgotten, never forgotten. Now my feet follow a proverbial trail all their own, and yet I
owe a debt of gratitude to my dearly departed gran, for it is she
who made me who I am.

Gran taught me everything I know, such as how to polish silver,
how to read books and people, and how to make a proper cup of
tea. It is because of Gran that I have advanced in my career as a
maid at the Regency Grand Hotel, a five-star boutique hotel that
prides itself on sophisticated elegance and proper decorum for the
modern age. Believe me when I say I started at the bottom and

worked my way up to this illustrious position. Like every maid who has ever walked through the gleaming revolving doors of the Regency Grand, I began as a Maid-in-Training. Now, however, if you step closer and read my name tag—aptly placed above my heart—you will see in large block letters:

MOLLY

which is my name, and in delicate serif script underneath it:

Head Maid

Let me tell you, it's no mean feat to climb the corporate ladder in a five-star boutique hotel. But I can say with great pride that I have held this lofty position for going on three and a half years, proving that I am no fly-by-night, but as Mr. Snow, hotel manager, recently said about me in an all-staff meeting, "Molly is an employee who sustains an attitude of gratitude."

I've always struggled with understanding the true meaning behind people's words, but I've gotten a lot better at reading people, even strangers, which is why I know what you're thinking. You think my job is lowly, that it's a position meriting shame, not pride. Far be it from me to tell you what to think, but IMHO (meaning: In My Humble Opinion), you are dead wrong.

My apologies. That came out a bit gruff. When Gran was alive, she'd counsel me on tone and advise me when I'd likely offended. But here's the interesting thing: she's dead, yet I still hear her voice in my head. Isn't it interesting how a person can be as present after death as they were in real life? It's something I ponder with frequency these days.

> *Treat others the way you wish to be treated.*
> *We're all the same in different ways.*
> *Everything will be okay in the end. If it's not okay, it's not the end.*

I thank goodness I still hear Gran's voice, because today has not been a good day. It has, in fact, been the worst day I've had in approximately four years, and Gran's words of wisdom are providing strength for me to face the current "situation." When I say "situation," I don't mean according to the dictionary definition, denoting "circumstance" or "state of affairs," but as hotel manager Mr. Snow uses the term to suggest "a problem of epic proportions with limited solutions."

I won't sugarcoat what is truly an epic catastrophe: this morning, a famous man dropped dead on our tearoom floor. My good friend Angela, head barmaid at the Social, our hotel pub and grill, summarized the "situation" this way: "Molly, a massive bag of shite just hit the whirling fan." Because I like Angela so much, I forgive her use of PPP—Perfectly Polished Profanity. I also forgive that Angela has an unhealthy obsession with true crime, which might explain why she seemed oddly excited about a Very Important Person dropping dead right inside our hotel.

Today was supposed to be a special day at the Regency Grand. Today was the day that world-renowned, bestselling, and award-winning author J. D. Grimthorpe, master of mystery with over twenty novels to his name, was set to make a big important announcement in our recently restored Grand Tearoom.

Everything was going splendidly early this morning. Mr. Snow had put me in charge of the tea, and while that's mostly because he has yet to hire special-event staff to handle tearoom functions, I knew how proud it would make Gran to see me acquiring new professional responsibilities, though of course Gran can't *actually* see me, because she is dead.

Today, I arrived early for my shift and neatly arranged the elegant new room, setting the tea service for fifty-five guests (give or take none), who were bestowed VIP entry passes. The VIPs included numerous LAMBS—Ladies Auxiliary Mystery Book Society members—who had booked rooms on the fourth floor of the hotel days ahead of the event. For weeks, the whispers and conjecture echoed throughout the hotel: Why would J. D. Grimthorpe, a reclusive and fiercely private writer, suddenly want to make a public announcement? Was it just to publicize a new book? Or was he about to announce he'd written his last?

As it turns out, he most definitely has written his last, though I believe this fact was as much a surprise to him as it was to everyone who watched him collapse on the herringbone-patterned floor of the tearoom forty-seven minutes ago.

Moments before he walked onstage, the VIP mystery fans, literary pundits, and reporters were abuzz with anticipation. The room was a cacophonous din of chatter and the high-pitched tinkle of silver cutlery as guests refilled their teacups and popped the last of their finger sandwiches into their mouths. The second J. D. Grimthorpe entered, silence fell. The author stood at the podium, a spindly but imposing figure, cue cards in hand. All eyes watched him as he cleared his throat a couple of times.

"Tea," he said into the microphone, gesturing for a cup, and thank goodness I'd been informed of his teetotaling ways and had asked the kitchen to prepare a cart to his precise specifications— with honey, not sugar. Lily, my Maid-in-Training, who I'd put in charge of all of Mr. Grimthorpe's tea carts during his stay, jumped into action posthaste. With shaking hands, she poured the famous author a cup and raced it to the stage.

"That won't do," he said as he took the cup from her, stepped down from the stage, and went to the tea cart himself. He removed the silver lid of the honey pot, spooned in two enormous globs of glowing yellow honey, then stirred the whole cup with the honey pot spoon, which made a dull clank as it grazed the cup's edges.

Lily, who had rushed forward with the intent to serve him, was at a loss as to what to do next.

The whole room watched as Mr. Grimthorpe held his cup forth, took a long sip, then swallowed and sighed. "A bitter man requires extra honey," he explained, which elicited muffled laughter from the crowd.

Mr. Grimthorpe's irritability has long been a hallmark of his fame, and ironically, the worse he behaves, the more books he seems to sell. Who can forget that infamous moment, which went viral on YouTube a few years ago, when a rabid fan (a recently retired heart surgeon), approached the author and said, "I want to try my hand at a novel. Can you help me?"

"I can," Mr. Grimthorpe replied. "Right after you lend me your scalpel. I want to try my hand at heart surgery."

I thought of that video this morning as Mr. Grimthorpe smiled his serpentine smile, then sauntered back onto the stage, where he gulped a few more deep drafts from his sweetened teacup, then placed it on the podium in front of him and looked out at his adoring crowd. He picked up his cue cards, drew a labored breath, and at last began to speak as he teetered from side to side ever so slightly.

"I'm sure you're all wondering why I've called you here today," he said. "As you know, I prefer to pen words rather than speak them. My privacy has long been my refuge, my personal history a source of mystery. But I find myself in the uncomfortable position of having to make certain revelations to you, my fans and followers, at this critical juncture in my long and storied career—pun intended."

He stopped for a moment, expecting laughter, which followed on cue. I shivered as his piercing eyes surveyed the room, looking for what or for whom, I do not know.

"You see," he continued, "I've been keeping a secret, one that will no doubt surprise you."

He stopped abruptly. He put one long-fingered hand to his collar in a futile attempt to loosen it. "What I'm trying to say is . . ." he croaked, but no other words would leave his throat. His mouth opened and closed, and he suddenly seemed very unsteady, swaying more dramatically from side to side in front of the podium. All I could think about was a goldfish I'd once seen jump from its bowl and lie gaping and apoplectic on a pet store floor.

Mr. Grimthorpe clutched his teacup once again and sipped. Then before anyone could prevent it, he suddenly toppled over, plummeting off the stage and into the crowd, where he fell directly on top of Lily, my most unlucky Maid-in-Training. Together, they landed with a dramatic crash on the floor as the porcelain teacup broke into innumerable razor-edged shards and the spoon on the saucer clattered flatly against the herringbone-patterned floor.

For a moment, silence prevailed. No one could quite believe what had happened before their very eyes. Then suddenly, panic ensued as everyone—superfans and guests, porters and pundits—rushed to the front of the room.

Mr. Snow, hotel manager, was crouched on Mr. Grimthorpe's left, tapping him on the shoulder. "Mr. Grimthorpe! Mr. Grimthorpe!" he said over and over. Ms. Serena Sharpe, Mr. Grimthorpe's personal secretary, was on his right, putting two fingers to the writer's neck. Lily, my Maid-in-Training, was desperately trying to wriggle her way out from under the author. I reached an arm out to assist her and she grabbed my hand. I drew her to me, tucking her in by my side.

"Space! Step back!" Mr. Grimthorpe's personal secretary yelled as fans and VIPs jostled.

"Call emergency services! Immediately!" Mr. Snow demanded

in a most authoritative voice. Waiters and guests, bellhops and receptionists ran off in all directions.

I was close enough to the "situation" to hear what Ms. Serena Sharpe said as she released her fingers from Mr. Grimthorpe's neck:

"I'm afraid it's too late. He's dead."

CHAPTER 2

I am standing in Mr. Snow's office, holding a fresh cup of tea.
My hands are unsteady; my heart is racing. The floor under
my feet tilts like I'm in a fun house, which I most definitely am not.

The tea is not for me. It's for Lily Finch, who I hired three weeks
ago—Lily, who is petite and quiet, with jet-black, shoulder-length
hair and skittish eyes, and who at the moment trembles in Mr.
Snow's maroon leather office chair, tears streaming down her face.
It takes me back, truly it does, to a time when I sat all by myself in
the chair Lily sits in now, trembling as I waited for others to decide
my fate.

It happened approximately four years ago. I was cleaning a
penthouse suite on the fourth floor when I stumbled across a guest
who I thought was sleeping deeply, but even the deepest sleepers
do not give up breathing entirely. A quick check of Mr. Black's
pulse revealed that he was in fact dead—*very* dead—in his hotel
room bed. And while from that moment on I did my utmost to
deal with this most unusual "situation," all fingers suddenly

pointed at me as the murderess. Many in my midst—including the police and an alarming number of my co-workers—assumed that I had murdered Mr. Black.

I am a cleaner, not a killer. I did *not* murder Mr. Black—in cold blood or lukewarm, for that matter. I was wrongly accused. But, with the help of some very good eggs, I was exonerated. Still, the experience most certainly took its toll. It underscored just how hazardous a maid's work can be. It's not the backbreaking labor, the demanding guests, or the cleaning chemicals that present the greatest danger. It's the assumption that maids are delinquents, murderers, and thieves: the maid is always to blame. I truly thought Mr. Black's demise was the beginning of the end for me, but everything turned out just fine, as Gran always predicted it would.

Now, in Mr. Snow's office, I lock eyes with Lily and when I do, I feel her fear like an electric current traveling straight into my heart. Who could blame her for being afraid? Not me. Who on earth actually thinks they'll show up for work one day to host a world-famous author only to have him die in a room filled to capacity with adoring fans and shutter-clicking press? And what poor, hapless maid could ever imagine she'd not only serve the writer upon the moment of his death but also serve *as* his deathbed?

Poor Lily. Poor, poor girl.

You are not alone. You will always have me—Gran's words echo in my head as they always do. If only Lily could hear them.

"A good cup of tea will cure all ills," I say, passing Lily the cup I'm cradling in my hands.

She takes it, but she does not speak. This is not unusual for Lily. She has trouble using her words, but lately, she's been much better at expressing herself, at least with me. She's come so far since her job interview, executed by me and Mr. Snow. It went so poorly that Mr. Snow's eyes grew two sizes behind his tortoiseshell glasses when I announced, "Lily Finch is our strongest candidate for the job."

"But she barely spoke through the entire interview!" Mr. Snow said. "She couldn't come up with an answer when I asked her to outline her best qualities. Molly, why in the world would you choose her?"

"May I remind you, Mr. Snow," I said, "that overweening confidence is not the primary quality to consider when hiring a maid. You may recall that a certain former hotel employee had confidence in spades but turned out to be a very bad egg indeed. Do you not remember?"

Mr. Snow nodded oh so subtly, but the good news is I can read him much better now than I could when I first started as a maid at the Regency Grand Hotel seven and a half years ago. This little nod suggested willingness to defer the final decision about Lily to me.

"Ms. Finch is most definitely quiet," I said. "But since when has loquaciousness been a key skill for a maid? 'Loose lips sink ships.' Isn't that what you always say, Mr. Snow? Lily needs training—which I intend to provide—but I can tell she's a worker bee. She has everything it takes to become a valued member of the hive."

"Very well, Molly," Mr. Snow said, though his pursed mouth suggested he was not entirely convinced.

In the few weeks that I've been training Lily, she's made tremendous progress as a maid. Just the other day, when we encountered our lovely repeat guests Mr. and Mrs. Chen outside their penthouse suite, Lily actually spoke. She used her words in the presence of guests for the very first time.

"Good afternoon, Mr. and Mrs. Chen," she said, her soft voice like wind chimes. "It is lovely to see you. Molly and I have left your rooms in what I hope is a state of perfection."

I smiled from ear to ear. What a joy it was to hear her after so much meaningful silence between us. Day after day, we'd worked side by side. I showed her every task—how to make a bed with crisply cut hospital corners; how to polish a faucet to a high shine; how to plump a pillow to maximum fullness—and wordlessly, she followed my lead. Her work was flawless, and I told her so.

"You have the knack, Lily," I said more than once.

Apart from having a maid's keen eye for details, Lily is also discreet. She moves about the hotel's interior, cleaning and buffing, shining and detailing with stealth-like invisibility. She may be quiet—enigmatic even—but make no mistake: Lily is a gifted maid.

Now, sitting in Mr. Snow's office chair, she places her untouched teacup on his desk and worries her hands in her lap. I feel faint as I look at her. All I can see is myself in that chair. I've been here before, and I don't want to be here again.

How did it come to this?

This morning was sunny and bright when I left our two-bedroom apartment at 7:00 A.M. For two reasons, it was not an ordinary morning. First, today was the day that international bestselling author J. D. Grimthorpe would be making his big announcement during a press conference at the hotel. Second, my boyfriend, Juan Manuel, whom I've been living with in domestic bliss for over three years and whom I've worked with at the hotel for even longer, has been away. He's been gone for three whole days, visiting his family in Mexico, and I must say, absence does not grow fondness in this particular case. More accurately, it grows fungus. Ergo, I miss him terribly.

This is Juan Manuel's first trip home in many years, a trip we've been diligently saving for. Oh, how I wanted to travel alongside my beloved—a trip together, a true adventure—but alas, it was not to be: Juan is in Mexico, and I'm stuck here. For the first time since my gran's death, I'm alone in our two-bedroom apartment. Never mind. All will be well. I'm just glad Juan's seeing his family, and especially his mother, who has missed him for many years as I miss him right now.

Even though he'll be gone only two weeks, I cannot wait until he returns. Life is just better with Juan in it. He texted me this morning before I left for work:

Today will be amazing! IMHO, there's nothing to worry about. Te amo.

I'll admit that his declaration of love elicited a pleasing butterfly sensation in my belly, but his use of acronyms was as consternating as ever.

FYI, I texted back, **I have no idea what you mean.**

I mean I love you.

I understand that part.

In My Humble Opinion, you are incredible, and today will be spectacular, he concluded.

Though I'd desperately wanted to go to Mexico with Juan, duty called, or rather Mr. Snow called, and it instantly became clear I would not be going anywhere.

"Are you familiar with the writer J. D. Grimthorpe?" Mr. Snow asked me on the phone a few weeks ago.

"Indeed I am," I replied, leaving it at that.

"His personal secretary just requested the Regency Grand for an exclusive VIP event during which Mr. Grimthorpe intends to make a very important announcement. And . . . he's requested the Grand Tearoom."

Mr. Snow's breathless excitement traveled right through the phone. This news was serendipitous. When we were rocked by the scandal of Mr. Black's murder, Mr. Snow had the brilliant idea of attracting fresh clientele by returning an old storeroom off the lobby of the hotel to its former glory as a museum-quality example of an Art Deco tearoom. The renovation was nearing completion, and the hotel needed a VIP event to launch it publicly. This was perfect! And even better, Mr. Snow wanted me and my staff to oversee the special event. I told Juan immediately.

"When opportunity knocks, answer the door," he said. "We'll cancel our trip and go another time."

I couldn't bear the thought. "*Mi amor*," I said. "You go without me. We'll go together another time."

"Really?" he replied. "You wouldn't mind?"

"Mind?" I said. "I insist. We can't keep your mother waiting a minute longer."

He wrapped me in a close embrace, then planted kisses all over my face. "One for every day I'll be away," he said. "And a few extras just because. You're sure you'll be okay without me?"

"Of course I will," I said. "What on earth could go wrong?"

And so, Juan got on his plane a few days ago, while I stayed behind and kept myself busy with advance preparations for the Grimthorpe announcement.

This morning, I set out for the momentous occasion with a jittery spring in my step. I was excited and nervous at the same time. As I rounded the last corner downtown, the hotel came into view.

There she was, the Regency Grand, sublimely timeless amongst an urban eyesore of crass neon billboards and stout, modern office blocks. Red carpet graced the short flight of stairs to the hotel's majestic portico. Dazzling brass railings framed the entrance leading to gleaming revolving doors. The lobby was teeming with chatty guests, luggage in tow, as well as reporters and podcasters lugging equipment through the revolving front doors in preparation for the morning's marquee event.

Halfway up the steps on the landing in front of the portico

stood Mr. Preston, the Regency Grand's long-serving doorman, dressed in his stately cap and long greatcoat adorned with hotel crests. "Good morning, Molly," Mr. Preston said as I met him beside his doorman's podium. "Big day today."

"Yes, it is," I replied. "But we're ready for it. Have you seen the tearoom? It's magnificent."

"It is," he replied. "Listen, Molly. I was thinking that just because Juan Manuel is away, it doesn't mean you and I can't get together for our usual Sunday dinner. No point in both of us eating alone. Besides, there's something I've been meaning to speak to you about."

"Sunday dinner sounds nice," I replied. "But let's see how the week goes. It's bound to be a busy one without Juan Manuel around, and I can't promise I'll be up to cooking without him."

Mr. Preston nodded and smiled. "Understood," he said. "I know how hard you work, and I certainly don't want to trouble you."

Sunday dinner with Mr. Preston has been a tradition for several years, and once a week we dine together at the cozy kitchen table in our apartment. The three of us always mark the moment with a toast to another workweek done and dusted. The meals are simple, but as we eat, we regale one another with stories of the week's odd encounters—and let it be noted that at the Regency Grand, odd encounters are frequent occurrences. In fact, just last Sunday, I entertained Juan and Mr. Preston by describing in full Technicolor Room 404, which Lily and I had cleaned earlier that day.

"It was so filled with detritus, boxes, and file folders," I said, "that it looked like a rat's nest. Whoever's occupying that room is hoarding Regency Grand shampoo. There were hundreds of miniature bottles."

"Who needs that many to shower?" Juan Manuel asked.

"The bottles weren't even in the shower," I said. "They were on top of the minibar beside a bunch of snack foods and a big jar of peanut butter sitting open with a stainless-steel spoon sticking out the top."

Mr. Preston and Juan broke out laughing and mimed a toast with bubbly in the form of miniature Regency Grand shampoo bottles.

I leave my memory and look at Mr. Preston now, standing on the red-carpeted stairs. There's more gray in his hair, more lines in his face, but he still manages to do his job so well. I've always had a soft spot for this man. He's been exceptionally kind to me through the years, and he knew my gran. Long ago, before I was even a glint in my mother's eye, Mr. Preston and my gran were beaus—meaning: paramours, a romantic couple—but Gran's parents forbade the union. Mr. Preston eventually married someone else and had a family. Still, Gran's friendship with Mr. Preston endured. She was fond of him to the day she died. She was friends with his wife, Mary, too. But now that Mary is dead and Charlotte, his brilliant daughter who aided me so much after Mr. Black's death, is far away, I wonder if Mr. Preston is lonely. Perhaps that's the reason why our Sunday dinners are so important to him. Lately, he's been even more doting than usual, and I don't know why.

"If things get sticky in there today, just know that I'm here," Mr. Preston said this morning on the red-carpeted stairs. "There isn't much I wouldn't do for you, Molly. You remember that."

"Thank you," I replied. "You're a fine colleague, Mr. Preston."

I said goodbye and made my way through the revolving doors of the Regency Grand leading to the glorious lobby. Even after all these years, the sight of it takes my breath away—the Italian marble floors with their tang of fresh lemon polish, the golden handrails of the grand staircase with its serpent balustrades, the plush velvet settees that over the years have absorbed countless trysts and secrets.

The lobby was positively bustling, and the reception staff, dressed in black and white like neat little penguins, directed porters and guests this way and that. In the middle of the lobby was an enormous sign in an ornate gold frame that I'd polished to perfection just yesterday, making it glimmer, sparkle, and shine:

Today
J. D. Grimthorpe
Renowned Mystery Author
VIP Press Conference, 10 A.M.
Regency Grand Tearoom

There wasn't a moment to lose—so much to prepare. I rushed down the basement staircase into the workers' quarters. Low, tight corridors lit with fluorescent lights led to a maze of rooms, including the laundry, the supply closets, the steamy hotel kitchen, and, of course, my personal favorite, the housekeeping quarters.

I went straight to my locker. Hanging from it in thin, clingy plastic wrap was an *objet* of tremendous beauty—my uniform. Oh, how I love my maid's uniform—a crisply starched white shirt and a slim-fit black skirt made of flexible Lycra allowing for the bend-and-stretch exertions that are a regular part of the job for any hardworking maid.

Without a moment to lose, I changed, then proudly affixed my Head Maid pin above my heart. I checked myself in the full-length mirror, smoothing out a few disobedient, dark strands in my otherwise neatly coiffed bob and pinching my cheeks to bring color to my pallor. Pleased with the effect, I then noticed someone else in the mirror. Reflected behind me was my own double—Lily, the living picture of a perfectly polished maid. She was neatly uniformed, her Maid-in-Training tag was pinned just like mine, adroit and straight, right above her heart.

I turned to face her. "You're early," I said.

She nodded.

"You came early to help me?"

"Yes," she said quietly.

"My dear girl," I replied. "You're a treasure. Let's get to work."

Together, we headed to the doorway, but a pear-shaped figure blocked our passage. It was Cheryl, former Head Maid; Cheryl, who had no qualms about cleaning guest sinks with the same cloth she used for their toilets. She had once been my boss, but she had never been my superior. Mr. Snow demoted her after the Mr. Black debacle and promoted me into her role.

"Cheryl, why on earth are you early?" I asked.

This never happened. She was always late, armed with a panoply of excuses that sometimes induced a rage in me so profound that I wanted not only to fire her but also to *set* fire to her, an uncharitable thought, I admit.

"Busy day today," Cheryl said as she rubbed her nose with the back of her hand.

My shoulders stiffened in revulsion.

"I figure you and your Wisp-in-Training could use a maid with ample years of experience."

Lily stood stock-still and did not speak. She rarely spoke when other staff were present. Instead, she studied the well-polished tops of her shoes.

"How remarkably generous you are, Cheryl," I said. Let the record show I did not mean it. As I've learned, sometimes a smile does not mean someone is happy. Sometimes a compliment is feigned. And while I praised Cheryl's "generosity," I was in fact employing irony, because there are few people in the world as selfishly motivated as she is.

"I have an idea," Cheryl offered. "Lily should clean guest rooms today, and I can help you serve tea at the Grimthorpe event. I've given her a head start by cleaning the Chens' suite."

She may have cleaned their suite, but I knew she'd done so only to steal the tip left by our most generous guests, a tip meant for Lily, not for her.

"Thank you, but no thank you," I said as I pushed through the doorway, forcing Cheryl out of my way. "And, Cheryl," I added, turning to face her. "Wash your hands before you get back to work. Remember: sanitation is our obligation."

I beckoned for Lily to follow me, and we left Cheryl behind.

Once we were down the corridor, one left and one right turn from Housekeeping, I asked Lily to go to the kitchen and check on preparations for the tea reception. "You're in charge of both of Mr. Grimthorpe's tea carts today," I said. "Bring one to his room now. Knock thrice and leave it outside his door. Then have another cart ready for the actual event itself. Make sure the kitchen staff prepares both carts to Mr. Grimthorpe's exact specifications," I said.

Lily nodded, then headed to the snaking corridor that led to the steamy kitchen. Meanwhile, I rushed up the basement stairs and went straight to the Regency Grand Tearoom, stepping past the burgundy cordon that blocked off the entrance.

I stood a moment admiring the splendid sight. The high-ceilinged room featured a domed skylight that bathed everything in a shimmering glow. The walls were clad in green-and-gold Art Deco wallpaper, arches rising triumphantly to empire crown moldings. Round café tables were crisply laid with white linens I'd arranged myself, napkins pleated into rosebud folds, and floral centerpieces spotlighting elegant pink lotus blooms. Simply put, the room was a vision, a glorious return to an era of infinite possibility and grandeur.

My moment of rapture was interrupted by the sound of journalists who'd gathered at the back of the room, running cables and adjusting cameras, murmuring about J. D. Grimthorpe's mysterious motivations for making a most rare public appearance. At the front of the room, Mr. Snow nodded repeatedly at a pretty, binder-toting young woman as she tested the microphone on the podium. Booksellers off to the side of the raised stage were laying a display table of J. D. Grimthorpe's bestselling books, including *The Maid in the Mansion,* the novel that first propelled him to global bestsellerdom. On the cover of the most recent edition was a winding path of blood-red roses leading to a monolithic estate, an ominous light shining in an upper-story window. A tremor ran through me as I eyed the stack of copies. I knew so much about the man who'd written that novel.

Just then, Mr. Snow spotted me and beckoned me to the front of the room. I looped my way around the white-linened tables until I stood in front of him and the young woman.

"Molly," Mr. Snow said. "Allow me to present Ms. Serena Sharpe, J. D. Grimthorpe's personal secretary."

She was wearing a bold blue dress that hugged her figure so perfectly, all eyes in the room were riveted to her. Ms. Sharpe smiled at me, a smile that did not quite reach her feline eyes. Something about her face was sphinxlike, and I could not quite read it.

"I'm Molly Gray, Head Maid," I said by way of introduction.

"Ms. Sharpe is reviewing the final details of Mr. Grimthorpe's appearance," Mr. Snow explained. "I have assured her that no one without a VIP pass will gain entry to this room and that all guests will be served tea and refreshments at precisely 9:15 A.M. in anticipation of Mr. Grimthorpe's entry at exactly 10:00 A.M."

I was not at all surprised by Mr. Snow's precise run-of-show because we'd spent hours reviewing every last detail the day before.

"I do appreciate you accommodating us in your new venue at

short notice," Ms. Sharpe said. "I know such requests put tremendous strain on all staff."

Indeed they had. The builders had rushed to put the finishing
touches on the tearoom's tiled floor; the chefs and sous-chefs had
quickly conjured an elegant breakfast tea menu, complete with finger sandwiches; Mr. Preston had arranged extra hotel security; and
I was tasked with locating in our storerooms fifteen fine silver tea
sets with matching cutlery. Long ago, I acquired quite a talent for
polishing silver, so I buffed every piece myself, right down to the
final spoon.

"It is a pleasure to serve," I said to Mr. Grimthorpe's assistant. "I
hope you find our tearoom pleasing."

"I do," she replied. "In fact, everything's so perfect, I think we're
ahead of schedule. If you're interested, I can send J.D. in early to
sign a few books for staff members."

Mr. Snow's eyebrows shot into his receding hairline. "That
would be wonderful!" he exclaimed as he removed his phone from
the pocket of his double-breasted suit and made a succession of
rapid calls.

Within minutes, an eager group of hotel employees was lined
up behind the burgundy cordon at the tearoom's entrance. Angela,
wearing her black barmaid's apron, was midline, while Cheryl
staked her claim up front. Lily shored up the rear, trailing behind
various cooks, dishwashers, and maids.

"Walk them in, Molly, in an orderly fashion," Mr. Snow said, and
so I guided my fellow employees to line up in front of the book
table, where an empty chair awaited the arrival of our VIP literary
guest.

Ms. Serena Sharpe knocked on a hidden door in the paneling
to the side of the stage. It creaked open, and Mr. Grimthorpe
emerged—lean, lithe, with wild, hawkish eyes, unruly gray hair,
and a measured, confident gait. He took his seat at the signing

table. Ms. Sharpe handed him a black-and-gold fountain pen. The room rippled with murmurs and exploded with recording phones, everyone vying for the best photo.

"Molly, don't forget to line up," Mr. Snow urged. "This is your only chance to get a book signed by the master of mystery himself."

My legs felt like tree stumps, but I urged them into motion, taking my place behind a bellhop who bobbed like an eager gopher in front of me.

I tapped his shoulder. "Did anyone tell Mr. Preston about the staff signing?" I asked.

"Of course," he replied. "He didn't want to come. Said he preferred to breathe fresh air rather than bow down to the author."

"Is that really what he said?"

"Uh-huh," the youth replied before turning his attention to the famous man at the front of the room.

Sweat gathered at my brow as the line dwindled and ecstatic employees rushed off with signed copies of J. D. Grimthorpe's latest book tucked preciously under their arms.

"It's your turn, Molly," Mr. Snow said over my shoulder. "Step up." And so I found myself standing directly in front of the writer himself.

"Your name?" Mr. Grimthorpe asked as he sized me up with raptorial eyes.

"M-M-Molly," I managed.

"A pleasure to meet you. I am J. D. Grimthorpe," he said, as if I didn't already know.

He scribbled my name and his signature in my book, then passed it to me, making eye contact one more time. I waited, but recognition never dawned.

How was it possible that I remembered everything about him but he did not remember me?

CHAPTER 3

Before

In my mind's eye, I return to a memory.

I am ten years old, riding with my gran in the back of a taxi with squeaky faux-leather seats. I grip the door handle tightly as we head out of the downtown core of the city and into the suburbs, where each home seems larger and more exquisite than the last. We are on our way somewhere very special, and I'm performing a well-practiced magic trick in my head, the one where I sketch a recent and unpleasant experience on a chalkboard and then erase it, making it disappear from my thoughts, if not forever then at least for a little while.

Gran, hair tinged with gray, her glasses perched precariously at the end of her nose, sits beside me embroidering a pillowcase. This is a favorite pastime of hers. I once asked her why she likes to embroider.

"To transform the ordinary into something extraordinary," she replied. "Plus, it relieves stress."

She works away with her needle, pulling brightly colored

threads one by one through the plain white fabric. She's completed the first line on the pillow—*God grant me the serenity*—and has begun the line after it.

"What comes next?" I ask her.

She sighs and stops her sewing. "If only I knew."

"It's something about change," I remind her.

"Oh, you mean what's next on the pillowcase. *God grant me the serenity to accept the things I cannot change, the courage to change the things I can . . .*"

"*. . . and the wisdom to know the difference,*" I say.

"That's right," Gran replies.

"Are you sure we can afford it?" I ask, as I wiggle in my squeaky seat and readjust the seat belt digging into my waist.

"Afford what?" she asks.

"This taxi. It will cost us dearly, won't it? Waste not, want not?"

"We can splurge every once in a while, just not all the time. And today, your gran could use a little splurge." She smiles and takes up her needle once more.

"Tell me again what it's like where we're going," I say.

"It's a well-appointed grand estate with rolling lawns, manicured gardens, and many rooms."

"Is it bigger than our apartment?"

She pauses, needle raised. "Dear girl, it is a palatial mansion with eight large bedrooms, a library, a ballroom, a conservatory, a study, and a parlor filled with priceless antiquities. It's the antithesis of our modest apartment."

I still cannot picture it in my head, the scale of it, the grandeur. I try to call up the fanciest house I have ever seen on TV, a home on an episode of *Columbo* with dormer windows, English gardens, and creeping ivy. But it's only when the taxi driver turns one last corner and Gran says, "We're here," that I realize I have never in my life seen a home like this, not in real life or on TV.

The taxi stops in front of imposing wrought-iron gates topped with menacing spears. The gate is flanked by two austere stone columns. Farther along is a gray, three-story security watchtower with dark tinted windows.

"I'll just pop out a moment. The guard will buzz us through," Gran says. I watch with wide eyes as Gran steps out of the taxi, presses a nearly invisible beige button on one of the stone columns, and speaks into camouflaged slats beside it.

She walks back to the taxi and opens my door. "Come," she says. I step out, clutching her pillow to my chest while the taxi driver rolls down his window.

"I can drive you right up, ma'am," he offers. "It's no trouble."

"That won't be necessary," she replies as she opens her purse and fishes out several hard-earned bills.

"I'll get your change," the taxi driver says as he opens his glove compartment.

"No, no," says Gran. "The rest is for you."

"Thank you, ma'am," he replies, then rolls up his window and waves at us both before turning his taxi in a wide circle and heading back down the road from whence we came.

Gran and I stand between the two stone columns of the wide-open gate. In front of us wends a cobblestone path lined with orderly gardens containing verdant bushes bursting with the largest blood-red rose blooms I have ever seen. At the end of the path looms the mansion, three stories, with a smooth, gray façade, eight black-framed windows set in three rows: two, two, and four. The entire edifice reminds me of the eight-eyed wolf spider Gran and I once marveled at on *National Geographic*—well, Gran marveled, while I cringed.

I grab Gran's hand.

"There, there," she says. "All will be well."

It's just another workday for Gran, who has been employed as a maid in the Grimthorpe mansion for a long time, but for me, this is my first visit. Gran has described many details of this mansion over the years—the parlor filled with treasures from Mr. Grimthorpe's book tours abroad or passed down through his patriarchal line; the abstract artwork in the main hallway that Gran calls the "bourgeois blobs"; and more recently, the newly renovated conservatory off the kitchen, with its automated blinds that open and close with just a clap of the hands.

"That's only the beginning," Gran once said when I pressed her for more details. "The lights in the hallway upstairs turn on and off when they sense your presence."

"You don't have to flick a switch?" I asked.

"No," Gran replied. "It's as if the mansion knows you're there."

It sounded supernatural, like magic, something out of a fairy tale. And while Gran has described every detail to me, I've never seen the mansion with my own eyes. No wonder I feel like an astronaut landing on the face of Mars. Regardless, I'd rather be here with Gran than at school, which is where I'd normally find myself on a weekday.

That's where we're coming from, in fact—school. This morning, Gran was called to an early meeting with my teacher, Ms. Cripps, and despite Ms. Cripps's protests, Gran allowed me to attend the appointment. We met my teacher in the principal's office, which I'd visited more times than I cared to remember. Ms. Cripps seated herself behind the principal's large wooden desk, while Gran and I sat in stiff chairs in front of her.

"Thank you for coming," Ms. Cripps said. I can picture her face in my mind, that tight smile that I could not read at the time. I thought her the very picture of politeness. I know better now.

"My granddaughter's education is a matter of utmost importance to me," Gran said, but as I replay the memory, I note Gran's folded hands, how she placed them with purpose on the desk in front of her—a small gesture, both a plea and an assertion.

"May I ask where Molly's mother is?" Ms. Cripps inquired. "Not that I mind dealing with you, but you are one generation removed."

"Molly resides with me. I am her guardian. And she is my legal ward."

I was about to tell Gran she hadn't answered the teacher's question, something Ms. Cripps frowned upon, but as I opened my mouth to speak, Gran's hand came down on my knee, which caused my speech to stop in my throat, though I didn't know why at the time. I tried to work out the connection by humming the Skeleton Song about how the foot bone is connected to the leg bone and so on, but I made it through the entire song without encountering a single lyric connecting my tongue to my knee.

Meanwhile, Ms. Cripps and Gran continued their polite conversation.

"I know you're busy, Mrs. Gray. You are a married woman, correct? A missus?"

"You can call me Ms. Gray," Gran corrected.

"I understand from Molly that you still work. I must say it's impressive at your advanced age."

Gran cleared her throat.

"The issue is this," Ms. Cripps continued. "We're weeks away from the close of the school year, and it's that time when we think about student placement in the year to come."

"I commend your advance planning," Gran replied. "Molly is looking forward to having a new teacher next year, isn't that right, Molly?"

"I can't wait," I said. "I would also like new classmates."

"That's just it, Ms. Gray," Ms. Cripps said as if I hadn't spoken.

"I've come to the difficult decision that the best thing for Molly is to hold her back a year. I'm afraid her progress does not meet our educational benchmarks."

Gran shifted in her chair, looking from me to Ms. Cripps. "I don't understand. Her progress reports indicate good grades."

"Yes, her grades are satisfactory. Her language skills and reading ability far surpass those of her peers. She's often a little too precocious. She corrects her classmates' grammar and schools them on vocabulary."

Gran suppressed a laugh. "That's my Molly."

"But you see, she's . . . different."

"I agree entirely," Gran said. "She's a unique girl. But have you ever noticed, Ms. Cripps, how despite our differences, fundamentally, we are all the same?"

It was Ms. Cripps's turn to avoid the question. Instead of answering, she said, "Molly's social development is subpar. She hasn't made any friends at school. In that way, she's a failure. Ms. Gray, I'd describe Molly's social skills as . . . primitive."

"Primitive," I said. "P-R-I-M-I-T-I-V-E. Primitive." I waited for Gran to approve my spelling, but she didn't say a word. Even though I knew I'd spelled the word correctly, she appeared on the verge of tears.

I wanted to tell her everything was going to be okay and that I knew the word because of the David Attenborough documentary we'd watched together a few weeks earlier. It was about apes, such incredible animals, so often underestimated. They can use primitive tools to problem-solve, not only in laboratory and zoo settings but also in the wild. Remarkable!

"Ms. Gray," Ms. Cripps said, "the other day Molly berated a classmate for chewing with his mouth open. She stands so close to the younger children, it frightens them. She insists on calling the janitor Sir Walter of Brooms. Some days, she hides in a washroom stall and refuses to come out. So you see, she's not at the level of children her age."

Gran straightens in her chair. "I agree entirely. She is *not* at the level of the other children. Molly," Gran said, turning to me. "Why do you hide in the washroom?"

"Dirt," I replied matter-of-factly.

"Dirt?" Gran echoed, and I was so proud that I'd heard it, the delicate curl at the end of her sentence that meant she wanted to hear more.

"At recess, I was invited to play soccer with the other children. I agreed to be goaltender before I noticed the mud puddle stretching from post to post. When I refused to stand in the goal, my teammates held me in place and my shoes filled with mud. When I screamed, they threw mud at me and told me to get used to it. 'Dirt is nothing to be afraid of.' That's what they said."

Gran's mouth opened wide, and she turned to Ms. Cripps wordlessly.

"Kids will be kids. They meant no harm," Ms. Cripps said. "Plus, Molly has to learn somehow."

"On that last point we agree," Gran said. "But certainly Molly docs not nccd to lcarn this way, nor should her peers be in charge of her education."

It was an interesting statement. And I'll admit that up to that point, it had never occurred to me that my classmates could also be my teachers. In my mind I questioned the merits of this educational approach. What was I to learn from having my face periodically forced into the toilet bowl in the washroom, or a glob of spit left in my pencil case? What was I to learn from being called Mental Molly, the Prissy Missy, Clean Machine, and, my least favorite, Oddball Moll?

It's true, I had learned one thing from my classmates, which is that the saying about sticks and stones was all wrong. They had given me ample practice at dodging both projectiles, and even when their missiles met their mark, the bruises faded over time. But words—the sting of them, the stigma—endured forever. Their words sting to this very day.

"Have you ever thought that Molly might benefit from more individualized attention?" Gran asked as she leaned forward in her chair. "Perhaps the school can make adjustments so she feels more comfortable in class. It might be good for her teachers to try new approaches to reach Molly, don't you agree?"

Ms. Cripps chuckled then, and at the time I thought I'd missed a joke. "I've been a teacher for going on seven years after five years of university. I think by this point I know what I'm doing," said Ms. Cripps. "Of course, there are plenty of options for a child like Molly, and I'm happy to send you away with pamphlets about the specialists you can hire to deal with her privately."

"Privately," Gran repeated. "Meaning there'd be a cost."

"Naturally. You don't expect educators to work for free, do you?"

"Of course not," Gran said as she removed her hands from the desk in front of her.

"This is a public school, Ms. Gray. We can't cater to just one girl. I teach a class of thirty-five."

"I see," Gran replied. "I'm afraid a specialist or private school is beyond my means."

"You're a domestic. A maid, correct?"

Gran nodded.

"Molly often talks about you. She wants to grow up to be just like her gran. The apple doesn't fall far from the tree, so they say. She could grow up to be a cleaner. Maybe a dishwasher. That seems like an appropriate career goal for a girl like her."

Gran looked down at her lap. It took her a moment to reply. "I'm having trouble understanding how a child with good grades can be held back a year. I'm not convinced that's the right educational approach. While I appreciate your opinion on this matter, may I please speak with the principal?" Gran asked.

"That's me," Ms. Cripps replied. "It hasn't been announced yet, but the board thought it best to bring in fresh blood, someone . . . a bit more youthful. The old principal is retiring at the end of the year. She's on leave at the moment. Stress leave," she added in a whisper, but I heard it just fine.

"Very well," Gran said, and with that she slapped her thighs, collected her purse, and stood rather abruptly. "Let's go, Molly," she said. "Time is precious."

I followed my gran as she made her way to the door.

"Wait," Ms. Cripps said. "Molly stays here. She's got a full school day ahead of her."

"Ah," said Gran. "I'm afraid you're mistaken. If you're forcing her to repeat the year, then the least I can do is relieve her of having to finish this one. Goodbye," Gran replied. And with that, she marched me right out the door.

In my mind, a warm hand cradles my own, such simple comfort. I'm not in the new principal's office anymore. I'm standing with Gran in front of the Grimthorpe mansion.

"Are we going in?" I ask.

"Yes, we're going in," she says.

"Are they expecting me?"

"No, they're most certainly not expecting you."

"What if they don't want me in the house while you're working? What if they don't like me? What will we do then?"

"My dear girl," Gran says. "We'll tackle the situation the way we tackle everything."

"How's that?" I ask.

"Together," she replies.

CHAPTER 4

Lily and I have been waiting in Mr. Snow's office an inordinately long time. Neither of us has said a word in at least ten minutes. This is, admittedly, more unusual for me than for Lily. I'm pacing the room while she sits immobile in her chair, looking clammy and pale.

It was horrific when Mr. Grimthorpe dropped dead on the tearoom floor and even worse when the police and paramedics hurried in and began yelling, "Everyone out of this room! Now!" A rush of guests made for the exit as the paramedics tried in vain to resuscitate the extinguished man on the floor. I was about to follow the guests out, but Lily had escaped my grasp and was pressed against the wall, raw terror writ so large across her face that even I could read it easily. She was frozen in place, blending into the wallpaper.

"Lily!" I called out. I pushed my way to her. "Let's go," I said as I grabbed her icy hand. Together we exited the tearoom trying not to look at Mr. Grimthorpe's body, limp and lifeless on the floor. "Take her to my office, Molly," Mr. Snow said when he saw us. "The authorities may want to speak to her."

"Authorities." The word sent a shiver down my spine.

With Lily by my side, I cut a path through the crowd plugging up the entire corridor from the tearoom entrance all the way to the front lobby. Mystery-obsessed LAMBS and story-hungry journalists, all with VIP lanyards strung about their necks, were exchanging information in hushed tones—"Is he dead? What happened? What was he going to announce?" But by this point, there were others gathering, too, those who'd heard that something untoward had happened at the Regency Grand.

As we rushed through the lobby, I caught a glimpse of Mr. Preston on the front steps, arms spread, trying to hold back the throng as the flashing red lights of emergency vehicles bounced off the hotel's glossy entrance.

With every step, Lily became heavier on my arm. I got the feeling she was about to collapse right there on the floor. "Chin up, Buttercup. All will be well," I chimed as I gripped her strongly and hurried her through the back corridors of the hotel. In truth, I didn't believe all would be well, but I learned from Gran long ago the importance of a sunny disposition in dark times.

We traversed the maze of corridors and passages until at last we found ourselves outside of Mr. Snow's office. I knocked hard and said, "Housekeeping!" in a trembling but authoritative voice. No one answered, not surprisingly, but it is important to follow protocols. I turned the knob, mercifully finding it unlocked. I led Lily to a maroon guest chair, which she crumpled into like a dropped marionette. She's been sitting there slumped, silent, for over half an hour.

"Lily?" I ask her. "Are you all right?"

Lily looks at me, her pupils larger than I remember them ever being before. "I have a terrible feeling," she whispers. "This could be very, very bad. For me. For us."

Just then, a face appears at the door, a familiar and most welcome face. "Angela!" I call as I rush over to her, slipping out of the office to join her in the corridor. She has a teacup in her hands.

"Here," she says as she passes me the warm cup. "I thought you could use this."

"Thank you," I say. "I can't believe it, Angela. I can't believe he died."

"Neither can I," she replies. "Let's just hope there's a good explanation. But I'm telling you, Molls, this looks bad. Like true-crime bad."

I've always been prone to fainting, and in that moment, my old nemesis—vertigo—strikes again, giving me the horrific feeling that the whole world is turning upside down and there's not a thing I can do to stop it. To keep myself steady, I concentrate on the teacup in my hands.

Isn't it strange how the meaning of a thing can change in a flash? Just a few months ago, Angela introduced me to true-crime podcasts, and I quite enjoyed the experience. Together, we listened to one called *A Dozen Dirty Suspects*, about a string of mafia murders in the suburbs. Angela guessed the killer ten minutes into the very first episode.

"Bam!" she exclaimed gleefully when, in the final episode, the murderer was revealed. "Who's the boss?" she asked as she and her fiery red hair did a jiggy dance to celebrate her clairvoyance.

Just months ago, true crime was an entertaining escape, but now the thought of it makes me feel faint.

"Molly, are you all right?" Angela asks.

I manage a small nod.

"Don't you worry," Angela says. "I've got my ear to the ground. I'll let you know if I uncover any dirt."

"Dirt?" I reply.

"Molly," she says as she lays a hand on my shaking arm. "Dying suddenly like that isn't exactly natural."

"If it's not natural, what is it?" I ask.

"Criminal," Angela says as she fixes me with her somber, orb-like eyes.

"My gran used to say, 'Don't jump to conclusions, lest you trip and fall,'" I tell her.

"My gran used to say, 'Keep your eyes as peeled as your bananas,'" Angela replies. "So that's what I'm doing."

Just then, we hear sobbing from inside Mr. Snow's office. We both peek through the door and see Lily, head in her hands, crying in her chair.

"Is she okay?" Angela asks.

"Truthfully, I do not know," I reply sotto voce. I thank Angela for the cup of tea. Then she nods and leaves without another word or whisper.

I enter the office and put the cup on the side table beside the one I brought Lily earlier. "Here," I say. "A good cup of tea cures all ills. And if it doesn't, have another."

I'm hoping for a smile, a glance, but I receive neither.

For an extraordinarily long time, I trill nonsensically about what a tidy office Mr. Snow keeps, the differences between leather-bound and paperback books, and how I learned from my gran not only tips for polishing silver but also best practices for cleaning leather-bound volumes using a lint-free cloth and saddle soap.

"Molly," Lily says suddenly.

I hurry over and sit on the chair next to hers. "Yes?"

Her eyes are round pools of trepidation. "I'm afraid."

"I know," I say. "But why?"

"Because a famous man is dead. Because they always blame the maid. You of all people should know that."

I take both her hands in mine. I'm about to launch into my best pep talk about how good always triumphs over evil and how the meek shall inherit the earth, but just then, Mr. Snow appears in the doorway.

"Oh, thank goodness," I say. "I'm so glad to see—" My words choke in my throat because as Mr. Snow steps into the room, behind him is someone I had the horrible misfortune to meet some years ago and who I'd hoped never to meet again. She is large, imposing, with broad athletic shoulders. She's wearing a black sweater and black pants, though the fact that she's in plain clothes rather than in uniform does nothing to quell my agitation.

"Hello, Molly," Detective Stark says as she stands confidently in the threshold of Mr. Snow's office.

I know etiquette requires me to say something such as "How lovely to see you" or "What a pleasure to meet you again after you unjustly pegged me as Mr. Black's murderer a few years ago and nearly ruined my life," but I have learned that if I can't control the words in my head, it's best not to open my maw.

"Someone dialed 911 the second Mr. Grimthorpe collapsed," Mr. Snow says. "The police arrived soon after you left the room, Molly."

"And I arrived not long after that," Detective Stark says as she threads her thumbs through her belt loops, tipping back and forth on her heels the way cowboys do in old movies. "Being here is like déjà vu," she adds, looking around Mr. Snow's office.

"I certainly hope not," I say. "If you're here to investigate, it would be preferable to avoid gross miscarriages of justice this time around. As my gran used to say, 'To err once is human; to err twice is idiotic.'"

Mr. Snow clears his throat. "Molly, I understand you're rattled by this morning's events."

Stark enters the room and takes in Lily, slumped and defeated in her chair. "Looks like someone else is rattled, too," the detective says, nodding toward Lily. "I understand that young woman served Grimthorpe just before he died."

"That young woman has a name," I say. "She's Lily Finch, my trusted Maid-in-Training. Please forgive her silence. I believe she's in an abject state of shock."

"May I?" the detective asks as she draws up a chair in front of Lily, then sits before anyone can say "Be my guest."

"I need to ask you some questions," the detective says too loudly. Does she think Lily is deaf?

"Her ears work just fine," I say.

Lily studies her hands, which are white and clenched in her lap.

"She's not the most talkative person, but I assure you she's an exceptional Maid-in-Training," I explain.

"Exceptional at what is the question," the detective replies. "Lily, you understand that Mr. Grimthorpe is deceased. I had a good look at his body just now, and I noted some . . . very strange things. Suspicious things. I hear you prepared his tea this morning."

"How do you know that?" I demand.

"Cheryl told the detective," Mr. Snow replies. "She stuck around at the scene."

"What does Lily preparing Mr. Grimthorpe's tea have to do with him dropping dead on the floor?" I ask.

The detective turns in her chair to face me. "Molly, men don't just die suddenly without a good reason," she says. "They usually require a bit of help." She turns away from me then and leans right into Lily's face. "Lily," she says, "did anyone besides you touch that writer's tea cart this morning?"

Silence.

"Did you see anything out of the ordinary in the hotel today?" Detective Stark asks. "Upstairs or maybe downstairs in the kitchen?"

Lily doesn't answer. Her eyes are glazed and unfocused. The word "catatonic" comes to mind, and I'm tempted to spell it out loud, an old habit, but I resist.

"Detective," I chime in. "The kitchen staff prepared two tea carts for Mr. Grimthorpe this morning—one served before the event and one served during. Lily was charged with delivering both carts. And as for things being 'out of the ordinary in the hotel,' strange things transpire with alarming regularity at the Regency Grand. A few weeks ago, a guest smuggled a pet snake into his room. It escaped and curled up on a lobby chair. Fortunately, I spotted the anomalous coil on an emerald-green settee right before a rather generous-bottomed madam took a seat on the reptile. Did you know that I once caught a pop star filling his toilet with ice to chill champagne? And just yesterday, several fans of Mr. Grimthorpe's were walking through the hotel with falsified VIP passes strung around their necks."

"How did you know they were fakes?" the detective asks.

"Grimthrope," I reply.

"Sorry?"

"The badges had reversed the letters in Grimthorpe's name. Spelling error," I explain. "Very careless."

"Molly has an eagle eye for details," Mr. Snow confirms.

"Hmm," Detective Stark says as her lip curls on one side. I'm reminded of the dog across the street from my apartment. Its lip does exactly the same thing right before it lunges full force at the fence. Perhaps Lily notices this, too, because she suddenly bursts into tears again, burying her face in her hands.

"You're not in any trouble, Lily," I say.

"Bit soon to tell," the detective replies.

"For the record, Lily isn't the only one to touch those tea carts this morning. I touched them, too. I corrected several small over-sights by the kitchen staff. They are short a key employee this week, and I'm sorry to report they are making a few faux pas."

The detective stands and paces the room. After a few complete perambulations, she comes to a halt right in front of me.

"So you admit to touching that tea cart," she says.

"I do," I say as I raise my right hand. "It's my duty as Head Maid to double-check every detail for quality control. And I never shirk duty."

"Was there anything strange about that cart? Or the previous one delivered? Anything askew?" the detective asks.

I think for a moment. "In fact, there was. The doily under the teapot was slightly off kilter, but I straightened it."

"God help me," Detective Stark says as she rubs her forehead with one hand. "I didn't mean it literally."

"I'm sorry?" I say, which I also don't mean literally. I mean: *I don't understand what in heaven's name you want from me.*

"That tea cart," the detective repeats. "I'm asking if there was anything about it that might relate to a man suddenly dropping dead on the tearoom floor."

"Unless the tea was poisoned, I should think not," I reply.

As if on cue, Stark's mouth becomes a smirk and Lily starts up with a fresh round of tears.

The detective turns to Mr. Snow. "I need you to tell me exactly what Grimthorpe said in his big announcement."

"Nothing," Mr. Snow replies. "Before he could say anything of note, he ... he ..."

"Died," I offer. "There's no point calling it anything other than what it was. Mr. Grimthorpe *died* before he gave his speech."

Detective Stark looks at Mr. Snow. "And as the man organizing the event with Grimthorpe, didn't you know what he was going to announce?"

"I'm afraid not," says Mr. Snow.

"Check the cue cards," I suggest.

"Cue cards?" Detective Stark repeats, sounding very much like a trained parrot.

"He had them in his hand when he walked onto the stage. He put them on the podium," I say.

"Really?" Stark replies as she crosses her arms.

I take a moment to reflect on whether this is a rhetorical "really" or if the detective actually expects an answer from me this time. Out of an abundance of caution, I opt for the former.

Detective Stark exhales in a way that my gran might have once described as "overly dramatic." "We didn't find cue cards on the podium," she says. "Or anywhere else in the room."

She turns to Lily. "You need to start talking. Now. And I need you to come with me to that tearoom and walk me through what happened. Is that clear?"

"Detective," I say, as I step between her and my distressed Maid-in-Training. "Lily is not capable of speech at this time. I've experienced similar blockages in the past. In my case, the blockages occurred when people spoke to me in a manner I didn't deserve. I understand this matter is urgent, and since my mouth is fully functional—at least at the moment—I volunteer to accompany you to the tearoom to walk you through this morning's events."

"Nope. Not a chance," the detective replies.

"Now, hold on," says Mr. Snow. "Molly was right there beside Lily. She saw everything. Also, she just identified a missing object that you and your officers failed to uncover at the scene. Molly might be more useful than you think."

"I do have an eagle eye for details," I say.

"Though you miss as many as you spot," Stark adds.

Gran once said that if you don't have anything nice to say, best not say anything at all. It is for this reason that I keep my chin high, my shoulders back, and my mouth firmly shut.

The silence, however, soon becomes deafening.

The detective sighs a few times with her trademark dramatic flair. "Come on, then, Molly," she says. "This better not be a waste of my time."

CHAPTER 5

Before

Do you ever wonder what it would be like to go back to places you remember from your childhood, to see them again through adult eyes? Would they look the same or would they appear smaller, like objects in a rearview mirror, not because they have changed but because you have?

In my mind I hear the mechanical grumble of a black wrought-iron gate closing behind me.

"One foot in front of the other. It's the only way to get anywhere in this life," Gran says. She places her warm hand on my back and urges me up the rose-lined pathway toward the Grimthorpe mansion.

"Are you sure it's not a museum?"

"It's a private residence, my dear," Gran says. "Though I hesitate to call it a home."

"Why?" I ask.

"You'll see."

As we walk, I reach out and touch the soft, satiny petals of the resplendent blood-red rose blossoms.

"Careful," Gran says. "You must always watch out for the thorns."

I retract my hand and find Gran's once more. "Are there other maids and workers in the mansion?" I ask as we reach the halfway point on the long path.

"Not anymore," Gran replies. "Most have been . . . dismissed. There's a gardener and the security guard in the watchtower by the gate. Inside the house proper, they trust almost no one. It's a massive residence, but I'm nearly the only one allowed inside these days."

"Nearly?"

"The point is the house is not exactly brimming with social activity. The Grimthorpes keep to themselves."

"It sounds perfect," I reply.

"You'll soon meet Mrs. Grimthorpe, who demands loyal subservience at all times, but her husband, Mr. Grimthorpe, is largely invisible these days . . . except when he's not."

An eerie tremor runs through me as I imagine a miasma, a human specter, a partially invisible man. "Is he a ghost?" I ask.

Gran chuckles. "In a way," she says. "He's a writer who locks himself in his study most of the time. Mrs. Grimthorpe insists his foul disposition is a sign of artistic genius and that he's above us common folk. We are to serve him and her both without question. Whatever you do, Molly, do *not* disturb his writing. I'd advise keeping a safe distance since he's a bit of a troll, with a temperament that ranges from melancholic to diabolic."

A new image of the man takes shape in my mind—a stout, hirsute bridge troll with red, beady eyes, a hunched back, and a carnivorous underbite. "And Mrs. Grimthorpe?" I ask hopefully. "Does she have children of her own?"

"She does not," Gran replies. "She has devoted her entire life to the welfare of her husband, and to protecting the family's good name."

"Does she at least like children?" I ask.

"I highly doubt it," Gran replies, "but we're about to find out."

We have traversed the long, winding path and now find ourselves in front of the immense front door with its menacing brass knocker in the shape of an angry lion's head.

"Go on, then," Gran says. I take the heavy mandible in my tiny hand, knocking it twice against the hard wood.

High-heeled steps are heard behind the door, then the knob turns. I hurry back to my safe place by Gran's side.

The door creaks open to reveal a woman about Gran's height and age, her face long, her lips a thin, downturned pout.

Gran puts one foot behind the other, lowers her eyes, and curtsies, something I've never seen her do before.

"Flora?" the dour woman says, her voice crackling like a scratchy phonograph record. "What on earth is *that*?"

The woman's squinty eyes turn upon me as I press into Gran's side.

"This is Molly, my granddaughter," Gran says, her voice steady and strong. "I humbly request your permission for her to stay for the day."

"Stay where?" Mrs. Grimthorpe asks.

"Madam, there was an issue at her school today, most unexpected. There's no one else for her to be with while I work, so I'm begging your permission for her to stay here during my shift. She's a good girl. She never makes a fuss. She's . . . she's my treasure."

Mrs. Grimthorpe huffs, then puts her spindly fingers to her forehead as though this news has caused the onset of a terrific fever. "The maid seeking childcare from her employers. Ridiculous in every conceivable way." She shakes her head. "I'll extend my generosity for today, but just know, my beneficence has a limit, and that limit is five P.M. today."

"Beneficence," I say. "B-E-N-E-F-I-C-E-N-C-E. Meaning: kindness, mercy, charity." I curtsy and bow my head, just like Gran did a few moments ago.

"What on earth was all that?" Mrs. Grimthorpe asks.

"Spelling bee," Gran explains. "She's very good at it."

Mrs. Grimthorpe's black-hole eyes drill into mine. "There are rules in this house, young lady. And you shall obey every last one of them."

"I like rules," I say.

"Good. Rule Number One: children are to be seen and not heard. Correction: children are *not* to be seen *and* not to be heard."

I nod, afraid to speak since doing so contravenes Rule Number One.

"Rule Number Two: no shrieking, no yelling, no whining, no running, no sound at all."

I nod again.

"Rule Number Three: you are not—under any circumstances— to disturb Mr. Grimthorpe. He will not take kindly to it, and nor will I. His literary endeavors are of the utmost importance, and his work cannot be interrupted. Do you understand?"

I nod yet again as my fingers tighten in Gran's hand.

"Molly is exceptionally polite and well behaved," Gran says. "She will be content to sit quietly in the parlor."

"And how will she entertain herself?" Mrs. Grimthorpe asks. "Idle hands are the devil's plaything, and I'll not have her destroying the house out of boredom."

"I'll entertain myself with my rich imagination," I reply, realizing too late that I've just broken a rule. I add a "madam," hoping this cancels out my mistake.

Mrs. Grimthorpe sighs, then steps aside, allowing us to cross the threshold to the mansion.

The foyer is grander than anything I've ever seen, with a polished black marble floor inlaid with intricate geometric patterns and a dark oak staircase winding up to a high second story. A full-length gilded mirror on the wall to my left reflects my shocked face back at me. The mirror's frame is so golden that I'm certain it's the magic one from *Snow White*. When I look up, the ceiling is so sky-high that I get a crick in my neck. Hanging from an impossibly thin filament above our heads is a sparkling modern chandelier made of thousands of icy crystal shards. Down the hall, I spot paintings on the walls, and they really are as Gran said—not images of any figures I recognize, but bold, abstract blobs of color that appear thrown onto the canvas rather than brushed.

Mrs. Grimthorpe shuts the door behind us with a hollow thud.

"I'll set you up in the parlor, Molly," Gran says. "You can work on my needlepoint. How does that sound?"

"Get to it quickly," Mrs. Grimthorpe commands. "The conservatory windows won't clean themselves, Flora."

Mrs. Grimthorpe turns on her heel and click-clacks down the hallway, disappearing into the mysterious interior depths of the mansion. Gran gives me a little pat on the shoulder, then leads me through double-glass doors into the first giant room on our right. "The parlor," she announces.

I feel dizzy and giddy as I take it in—the royal-blue high-back chairs, the ornamental moldings that resemble icing on a cake, the classical paintings that fill every inch of wall—ships and shipwrecks, ladies billowing in pretty petticoats, hunting parties advancing on wide-eyed foxes in verdant forests. And finally, on the mantel above the dark mouth of the fireplace, set dead center, is the most striking object I have ever seen. Resting on an intricate tarnished pedestal, encrusted in diamonds and other fine jewels, sits a glowing, pearlescent ornamental egg. It is not large. It would fit in the palm of my hand. It's so hypnotically beautiful I cannot look away.

"Best close your mouth, dear, before the flies get in," Gran says.

I do as I'm told, but I cannot take my eyes off the enchanting object on the mantel.

"Mrs. Grimthorpe claims it's a Fabergé," Gran says. "A precious antiquity passed down through generations. Lovely, isn't it?"

"A treasure," I reply breathlessly.

"I've always loved this room," Gran says. "They've modernized the entrance and some of the other salons, but I love this parlor best of all. Come now." Gran pulls me from my reverie toward one of the royal-blue high-back chairs. "You sit here and work on my pillow. You can stitch the little pink-and-blue flowers. Remember how I showed you?"

I do remember. The needle is a rabbit—you loop it down the hole, then once it's under, you tie a knot to keep it safe.

"I best hurry to the conservatory. If you think Mrs. Grimthorpe's grumpy now, believe me, you won't want to see her if I don't start those windows soon."

Gran does a funny thing then. She crouches in front of me and grabs my hands. "I'm so sorry," she says as her eyes fill with tears. "You deserve better, but I don't know what else to do."

I have no idea why she's upset. My stomach curdles as I watch her tears fall. "Don't cry, Gran," I say. "Don't you remember what you always say about me finding my happy place?"

"Once you find it, all will be well?"

"Yes," I reply. "And, Gran?"

"What?" she asks.

"I just found it."

* * *

After Gran leaves the parlor, I spend a long while sitting in that royal-blue high-back chair, taking in every fine detail of the majestic room, studying and memorizing, recording each object in an imaginary ledger in my mind. This way, even if I never return to the Grimthorpe mansion, I can always revisit it in my memory.

This is a technique I learned on a school field trip to the national gallery not so long ago. Though I was laughed at by my classmates and scolded for reading every descriptive tag on every exhibit, I didn't care. Nothing mattered more than what I was building in my mind—not just a happy place but a happy palace.

Once I've enumerated every painting, tapestry, and piece of art in the Grimthorpe parlor, I re-create the details with my eyes closed, and only after I have a complete picture stored do I pick up Gran's needlepoint pillow. I start with a pink-and-blue flower, but before long, my eyelids feel heavy. I rest Gran's embroidery in my lap and allow my eyes to close.

"Teatime!" I hear, and my eyes startle open. It takes me a moment to remember where I am. Gran is standing in front of me. I check the clock on the coffee table and am shocked to see that the minute hand has made more than a full rotation.

"I see you got some rest," Gran says. "No wonder you're tired, Molly. You've had quite a morning."

Beside her is a cart on wheels containing a steaming pot of tea, a robin's-egg-blue teacup on a delicate porcelain saucer, a basket of fresh-baked currant scones, clotted cream in a pretty pink bowl, lemon slices in a yellow one, cucumber finger sandwiches on a side plate, crusts removed, and one ornate silver spoon.

"Who is all this for? You said the Grimthorpes never entertain guests," I say.

Gran laughs. "I assure you they don't. This is all for you."

I can hardly believe it. On Saturdays, Gran prepares us a special tea with crumpets, which we eat at our small secondhand kitchen table in our cramped apartment. Once, for my eighth birthday, Gran bought clotted cream, which was so delightfully delicious I've never forgotten the taste. I asked if we could have it every weekend, but Gran shook her head. "I wish we could," she said. "But the cost is too dear."

Now, Gran prepares my tea just the way I like it—two lumps of sugar and a splash of milk. She fills a side plate with delectable treats and places it on the bowlegged side table next to me. She folds a clean cloth over the arm of my chair, presumably for crumbs and spills.

"Won't you join me, Gran?" I fully expect her to pull up a chair. I can't wait to tell her all about my mind palace, how I've committed every item in this room to memory, from the pheasants in the hand-woven rug to the assortment of fine jewels on the Fabergé egg, just in case I never come back to this glorious mansion.

"Molly, I can't join you. I've got more windows to clean," Gran says. "But I'll check in on you later. Today is dusting day—so dust we must. Later, you can keep me company while I clean this room. Would you like that?"

"Yes, Gran," I reply.

Her hand grazes my cheek. Then she leaves the room.

I marvel once more at the tea cart. I prepare one scone with clotted cream and marmalade, then another. I devour both, washing them down with tea that tastes like citrus and roses steeped in sunshine. I pour myself a second cup using two hands, just like Gran taught me. I'm proud of myself for not spilling a drop.

I try to pace myself, chewing every bite at least twenty times, but before long, the basket of scones is empty and all that's left on the sandwich plate is a sprinkle of crumbs. I return my dishes to the tea cart. It's then that I spot the cloth Gran left on the arm of my chair. It gives me an idea. Why should I spend my time enjoying tea and embroidering when I can make myself useful?

Do a good deed for someone in need. Gran taught me that.

I pick up the cloth and start by wiping the crumbs from my chair. Then I continue Gran's chore by dusting and polishing the side table until it shines. I move through the room, wiping every surface, not just tabletops and chairs but also the frames on the wall, at least the ones I can reach. I dust the clock on the coffee table and the leather-bound books on it, too. I dust trinkets and statues, lamp bases and shades, windowsills and sashes.

There's only one item in the room left to polish—the stunning but tarnished Fabergé egg. I pick it up off the mantel and carefully carry it to my chair. I sit and rest the precious *objet* in my lap. It's heavier than it looks and even more beautiful up close. The arching legs of the pedestal are decorated with intricate garlands, the fine diamonds and opalescent pearls on the egg itself are inlaid in perfectly symmetrical rows. The gold pedestal may be dull and discolored now, but I know just what to do to fix that.

I grab a couple of lemon slices from the tea cart and squeeze the liquid onto the stained legs the way Gran showed me when we clean our secondhand silver at home. Using her cloth, I rub and polish, I buff and scour. When I'm finished, my hands and fingers are tired, but there is not a single spot on that golden pedestal that doesn't glint and glimmer. I bring the egg to the mantel and put it back on its base, where it shines like a miniature sun.

That's when I hear it, a raspy voice behind me. "What have you done?"

I jump and turn around.

Mrs. Grimthorpe stands at the entrance of the room, one bony finger pointing at the glowing Fabergé. I hear rushed footsteps, and then Gran appears at the threshold as well. She looks at the cleaning cloth and the bowl of lemons I left on my chair.

"Molly," Gran says. "What are you doing?"

"I thought I'd get a head start on your cleaning chore," I reply.

"Dust we must. I'm polishing, too. The Fabergé was so dirty, Gran. I don't think it has ever been cleaned."

I'm expecting Gran to compliment me on my initiative, but instead she puts one hand over her mouth.

"You wretched girl!" Mrs. Grimthorpe shrieks, thereby breaking her very own Rule Number Two about raised voices in the house. She turns to Gran. "She's just stripped the patina off a priceless antiquity!"

"I didn't harm it," I say. "Look, it shines."

"You're an imbecile!" Mrs. Grimthorpe screeches, her bony finger still pointing at me as though I'm a five-legged toad or a two-headed calf, or some other unnatural abomination.

"She was only trying to help," Gran offers.

"She's a half-wit! She destroyed the value of a Fabergé! If I told Mr. Grimthorpe about what you just did, young lady, you and your grandmother would both be frog-marched out the door."

"But Gran didn't do anything," I say. "It was all me."

"Hush," Mrs. Grimthorpe orders. "Do you not understand what it means to *be quiet*?"

This is exactly the kind of conundrum that cracks my brain in two. How am I to stay quiet when asked a question?

Gran intervenes. "Madam, I can restore the patina. There are tricks any good maid knows. Mr. Grimthorpe need not find out. Don't dismiss me. You know how hard it is to find reliable help these days. As you always say, *Things can and will get worse.*"

"You'll never find a better maid than Gran," I say. "Not ever."

Mrs. Grimthorpe looks from Gran to me through angry, slitted eyes. "Your grandmother is loyal, sometimes to a fault. Unlike *other* maids who have passed through this house, at least she understands duty. But you, young lady, do not."

"Please," says Gran. "Molly made a mistake. That's all."

"If your granddaughter is to make it in this world, she needs to learn there are consequences for her actions," Mrs. Grimthorpe says. "The girl must be punished."

"I agree entirely," Gran replies. "She deserves a harsh punishment. The most severe."

"Gran!" I say. I'm shocked that she should suggest such a thing when she knows I was only trying to help. But when I look at Gran, she puts two fingers to her chin, our secret signal meaning everything will be okay and that I'm to follow her lead. I stop speaking instantly.

"What I propose," Gran says, "is that Molly work to pay off her debt to you. Children must learn their lesson, and what better lesson to learn than hard work, don't you agree?"

Mrs. Grimthorpe's face changes. "Hard work?" she repeats. "What exactly do you have in mind?"

"Molly will put her talents to good use. She will clean. At no cost to you."

Mrs. Grimthorpe smiles, but it's not the kind that reaches her eyes. "I suppose the punishment does fit the crime. She'll polish the silver in the silver pantry," she commands.

"All of it?" Gran asks.

"All of it," Mrs. Grimthorpe replies.

"But that will take weeks!" Gran says.

"Yes," Mrs. Grimthorpe answers. "It will."

Gran looks at me in a peculiar way that I cannot comprehend. She's glowing as brightly as the Fabergé. "Come, Molly," she says. "Let's go to the room where you will endure your severe punishment."

My head is spinning. I don't understand anything that's happening, but I follow Gran and Mrs. Grimthorpe as they lead me out of the room and down the long corridor deeper into the labyrinthine belly of the mansion. We pass a massive ballroom on the left, a formal dining room on the right, a billiard room, and more than one washroom. Finally, the ample corridor opens into the largest, cleanest, most magnificent kitchen I have ever seen, with floor-to-ceiling windows overlooking a glass conservatory and gardens beyond that are so green and manicured they look like something out of a fairy tale.

"Keep up, child," Mrs. Grimthorpe says as she stomps to the far end of the kitchen. She opens a door and flicks on a light. The room is twice the size of my bedroom at home, with floor-to-ceiling shelves filled with silver chargers, silver plates, silver bowls, silver teapots, silver platters, and countless sets of silver knives, silver forks, and silver spoons. This cannot be. How can one couple own so much silver? Have we just entered a pirate's trove or a dragon's secret lair?

"This is the silver pantry," Mrs. Grimthorpe announces. "The silver is tarnished. Filthy, all of it. I once fired a maid because she refused to polish it, said it was a waste of time. Apart from other ridiculous assertions, she also claimed the lye in the polish ruined her hands. Well, I never."

"Gran," I say. "Why is it you haven't polished the silver?"

"Because your grandmother has other duties," Mrs. Grimthorpe exclaims, "including taking care of the entire mansion and seeing to the copious needs of my husband. Do you understand that it's a privilege just to be near an artistic genius such as he? By serving him, we serve creativity itself."

I nod repeatedly to show understanding, then I raise my hand the way I would in the classroom when I have a pressing question.

Mrs. Grimthorpe sneers. "What is it now?" she asks.

"Does this mean I get to come to this mansion every day instead of going to school? And does it mean I get to clean this silver?"

I look at Gran, and she gives me the chin signal again. I stay statue-still and press my lips shut.

"You are a terrible, undisciplined child," Mrs. Grimthorpe says.

"But I hope that unlike those who've come before you, you will turn out better. In my beneficence, I'm offering you a second chance. For the foreseeable future, you're to come here every day and work to make amends for the harm you've caused to one of Mr. Grimthorpe's priceless antiquities. You'll recompense me by cleaning and polishing all of the silver in this pantry."

I cannot believe my good fortune! I start to jump up and down on the spot. I look at Gran, who appears to be eating her own grin.

"This is so delightful," I say. "But I have one more question." I look at Mrs. Grimthorpe, then ask, "May I begin cleaning right away?"

CHAPTER 6

Detective Stark marches out of Mr. Snow's office, leaving Lily and Mr. Snow behind. I follow her as instructed, but she stops suddenly when the corridor opens in two directions. I nearly stumble into her backside.

"Which way to the tearoom?" she asks.

"That all depends," I reply. "Would you prefer the more scenic route through the lobby or the fastest route through the back corridors?"

"Just get me there as quickly as you can, will you?" she replies, accompanying the statement with what I detect is a generous side serving of sass.

"Very well," I say. "The early bird catches the worm." I turn left and lead the detective through the back corridors, turning once more left then right then left, until we reach the Grand Tearoom, where caution tape is affixed across the entrance. A deep sense of unease haunts me once again, a growing apprehension about everything that transpired this morning. When I look inside the room, I gasp out loud at what I see.

"You get used to it over time," Stark says.

She's referring to Mr. Grimthorpe, whose body lies stiff in a black bag in the middle of the tearoom floor. Two uniformed officers are zipping the bag closed. But Mr. Grimthorpe's corpse is not the cause of my shock. It's the state of the room that's disconcerting. After all my hard work, it's now in utter shambles. The tablecloths are tea-stained and askew, the dishes jostled and toppled. The tiles under my feet are sticky. Here and there, finger sandwiches have been trampled and mashed into the floor. It's a wonder nothing is broken besides Mr. Grimthorpe's teacup, the shards scattered haphazardly around his body bag.

"As you know, Detective," I say, "I've encountered death before." What I don't say is that I'm not terribly upset that Mr. Grimthorpe is dead and that sometimes fate has an uncanny way of delivering exactly what's deserved. I also don't mention my connection to the man in the body bag. If I've learned anything from *Columbo* and from past experience, it's that living acquaintances of the dead quickly become suspects, and that's the last thing I want to be right now.

I look about the room once more and feel utterly crestfallen. I was so proud of the way we'd transformed it from a dusty, old storage room to a dazzling, new event space. It's then that it strikes me—how a room is just a container. Any space can be poisoned by the memory of what occurred within it. A tearoom, a library, a parlor . . .

I suddenly feel unsteady on my feet. The whole world tilts on an angle. Behind me, I hear sobs and sniffs.

"Is he really . . . dead?" a quivering voice asks.

Detective Stark and I turn.

Gathered in the corridor is a gaggle of middle-aged women

pressed so tightly together it's hard to tell where one woman ends and the next begins. They're all wearing VIP lanyards and identical buttons over their hearts that read J. D. GRIMTHORPE'S #1 FAN.

"Who are you?" Stark asks.

"We are the LAMBS," says a tall woman with curly gray hair at the front of the group. I recognize her immediately as the president of the LAMBS because of her small red flag. For days, she's carried it, herding her brethren around the hotel, hoping to catch a glimpse of the famous writer himself, score his autograph, or, better yet, snap a selfie by his side.

"They're a fan club," I explain to the detective. "Ardent readers of mystery novels who specialize in the study of Mr. Grimthorpe and his *oeuvre*."

"We're not *just* a fan club. We are aficionados of mystery," a different, rather buxom gray-haired woman says as she points to the #1 FAN button fastened to her lumpy brown sweater. The sweater is either made entirely of cat hair or so covered in it that the material underneath is largely invisible.

"Dead or alive, in sickness or in health, we devote ourselves to the master of mystery," a petite woman sporting silver-gray hair with bright fuchsia highlights says from mid-huddle. "In our hearts and memories, J.D. lives *in perpetuum*."

"Meaning: forever," I say, recalling the moment when I first learned the phrase.

Several if not all of the LAMBS begin to sob in unison. A packet of tissues appears from somewhere in the huddle and is passed from one fan club member to the next.

"You're a detective?" the tall, curly-haired president asks Stark as she points her red flag at her.

"Yeah," Stark replies.

"Do you know the cause of death?" asks another woman mid-huddle.

"That's what I'm here to find out," Stark replies.

"Was it murder?" the petite woman with the shock of pink hair asks.

"I haven't ruled out anything," Detective Stark replies.

"I can help you," the cat-hair-sweater lady offers. "I'm an expert on J. D. Grimthorpe."

"I've already got more help than I want," Stark replies as she looks at me. "And what I require from all of you right now is privacy. I'm going to ask you to clear the vicinity immediately."

The president nods. "Of course. LAMBS—give the detective space." She raises her red flag to rally the others. "Detective, we're here if you change your mind and want background information," she offers as she guides her group away from the tearoom entrance.

"Please don't forget us," says the tiny, gray-haired woman with the fuchsia highlights.

"I couldn't if I tried," Detective Stark replies.

The flag-bearing president leads her flock down the corridor and out of sight.

Once they're gone, Detective Stark raises the yellow caution tape hanging across the entrance. "Go in, Molly," she orders.

"How kind of you," I say as I duck under the tape. Detective Stark follows after me.

The two male officers who were zipping up the body bag saunter our way.

"Findings?" Detective Stark asks.

"Urticaria around the mouth, angioedema under the eyes."

"Meaning: swelling consistent with organ failure or sometimes cardiac arrest," I say. "But what really causes a heart to stop? That's always the question, is it not?"

The officers turn my way as though seeing me for the first time. "Who the hell is she?" the taller one asks.

"Molly. She's just a maid," Detective Stark replies.

"Molly the maid? You've gotta be kidding me," says the shorter one.

"Wish I were," Detective Stark replies sotto voce, but not sotto voce enough to escape my ears.

"What's a maid doing at the crime scene?" the tall one asks.

"Are you assuming this is a crime scene?" I ask. "When you assume, you make an A-S-S out of U and ME." For some reason I cannot fathom, Detective Stark rolls her eyes, while the mouths of both her officers fall slack.

"Ignore her," Detective Stark says. "She's my problem. Just get back to work."

"But I need to clean this mess up," I tell the detective. "It will take some time to return this room to a state of perfection."

"Not a chance. No cleaning," Stark says.

I realize only then what a foolish impulse this was.

The two officers go back to the mess at the front of the room.

Stark removes a small notebook from her pocket. "Okay, let's get this over with. I want you to describe the room as it was before the event. Can you tell me who and what was where the moment before Mr. Grimthorpe took to the stage? No detail is too small. Do you understand?"

"I understand perfectly," I reply as I turn back time to this morning and call to my mind a portrait of the tearoom in its full glory, populated with guests awaiting Mr. Grimthorpe's entrance.

"At a quarter past nine, all the guests were seated. Porters, waiters, and maids stood on the sidelines. I was right there, near the front of the room, right beside Lily. The photographers and journalists were behind us."

"And that table?" Stark asks.

"The booksellers were behind it. And Lily was manning Mr. Grimthorpe's tea cart."

"Is that his cart there?" She points to a cart at the front of the room.

"It is," I reply. "I mean, it *was* Mr. Grimthorpe's tea cart."

"Boys!" Detective Stark calls out. "That one's the Grimthorpe cart." They nod and begin inspecting it with gloved hands.

"Was Grimthorpe in the room when you entered?" Stark asks.

"No. He was behind the hidden paneled door in the wall. Ms. Serena Sharpe, Mr. Grimthorpe's personal secretary, knocked. Then Mr. Grimthorpe emerged. The room went pin-drop silent as he walked onto the stage and placed his cue cards on the podium."

"Right. The cue cards. Boys!" she calls out. "Did you locate any cue cards?"

"No, ma'am," the tall officer replies.

The other shakes his head.

"And what happened next, Molly?" Stark asks as she scribbles on her notepad.

"Mr. Grimthorpe cleared his throat and asked for a cup of tea, which Lily poured for him and rushed to the stage."

"We'll be testing the tea in that teapot."

"No need," I say. "It was English Breakfast. I know that for a fact."

"I mean testing for toxins, Molly. Do you get that? We want to know if someone, like that half-wit in Mr. Snow's office, put something in the writer's tea."

"There's no need for name-calling," I say. "And as for Grimthorpe's tea, there most certainly was something in it: honey."

"Honey," Detective Stark repeats.

"Yes. From the honey pot I placed on the tea cart earlier. As I mentioned, right before the big event, I inspected the tea cart myself and realized there were qualitative faux pas. Mr. Grimthorpe takes his tea with honey, not sugar. I straightened an off-kilter doily, then switched out the sugar bowl for a honey pot."

"Boys!" she calls out again. "Locate the honey pot on that cart."

The gloved men search for it but fail to find it.

"It's got to be there," I say. "A high-quality silver pot with a small cutout in the lid for a Regency Grand spoon." I march over to the cart, but when I arrive, all I see is a bare doily on the silver tray.

"The honey pot is gone," I say. I look about the room. There are sugar bowls on every table but no other honey pots because they're not a part of our regular tea service.

"How strange," I say. "Mr. Grimthorpe walked off the stage himself to add more honey to his tea."

"Did he drink from that cup that's broken on the floor?" Detective Stark asks.

"Most definitely. We all saw it. He took several sips right away and a few more when he got back onstage. Then he put the cup down and started to speak. He was about to reveal a secret—he said as much—but before he could, he began to sway, appearing almost inebriated. Suddenly, he tipped forward and then crashed onto the floor on top of poor Lily."

"And his teacup went flying," Stark notes.

"It did," I reply, eyeing the shards on the floor. "And so did the spoon and the saucer."

Detective Stark walks over to the broken cup and saucer on the floor, gingerly crouching by the shards. She turns to her officers. "Boys, did you bag a spoon from the floor?"

"No," says the tall one, and the other shakes his head.

She writes something down, then turns a page on her pad. "What happened after Grimthorpe collapsed?" she asks.

"Everyone rushed to the front of the room. There were calls for help, people jostling. I pushed my way forward, then I extricated Lily from underneath Mr. Grimthorpe. Mr. Snow and his personal secretary, Ms. Serena Sharpe, were trying to revive him."

The detective's head jolts up from her pad. "Where do you suppose she is now, that secretary?"

"In her room, perhaps?" I offer. "It adjoins Mr. Grimthorpe's on the second floor."

"Adjoining rooms? With her boss?" the detective says. She turns to her men. "Did it occur to either of you to detain and question the personal secretary?"

The two men avoid her eyes.

Detective Stark snaps her notepad shut. "Time to hustle," she says as she marches toward the exit.

"Where are you going?" I ask.

"To find Serena Sharpe."

I follow the detective out of the tearoom, past the hotel lobby, to the elevators, where several guests are waiting to board.

"You're dismissed. Go do whatever it is you do here," Detective Stark announces as she presses the Up button with a good deal more force than is necessary. "But don't leave this hotel yet, Molly. You hear? And don't let that sidekick of yours go anywhere either."

"Very well," I reply. "And how exactly do you intend to enter Ms. Sharpe's room if she isn't there? Did someone furnish you with a key? Mr. Snow, perhaps? And I presume you have a warrant, since you can't just enter a guest's room at will . . . unless, of course, you're a maid," I say as I hold up my master keycard.

Stark surveys the guests in our midst. Is it a trick of the light, or do I detect a tomato-red hue traveling up her neck to the apples of her cheeks?

"Fine," she mutters under her breath. "You can come with me. And should anyone ask, technically, you'll be the one entering that room, not me, got it?"

"As you wish," I reply.

Then something happens that has never occurred in all my years as a hotel maid. The elevator doors open and guests standing near us step back, allowing the detective and me to enter first. When we do, they don't even follow us in. I can hear them whispering to one another: "Who's the woman in black? She looks like a plainclothes detective! Does this mean Grimthorpe was murdered?" The doors slide closed, and I push the button for the second floor. Stark and I ride in silence until the elevator doors ding open.

"This way," I say, leading Detective Stark to Ms. Sharpe's suite, number 201. I knock on the door while the detective waits a few paces back. "Housekeeping!" I call out in a firm but authoritative voice. "For once, I'm not here to clean your room. Rather, I have someone who wishes to speak with you."

We wait, but there's no reply. I turn to Detective Stark. "Strictly speaking, and according to my very own rule book, only Ms. Sharpe's maid is allowed to enter the room, and that is not me. But I'll make an exception just this once."

"I'm eternally grateful," Detective Stark replies, though the way she says it makes me question her sincerity.

I buzz in with my keycard and prop the door open. The detective remains outside, but her head juts in, pivoting this way and that. I know what she's doing because I do it, too. She's memorizing the details of the room, saving them in her mind's eye to be studied later.

The bed is freshly made, tight hospital corners folded just so. The water glasses on the table are fitted with sanitation covers. The carpet is freshly vacuumed in Zen-garden rows, the pile perfect and pristine. Not only has this room been recently cleaned but also Ms. Sharpe is clearly gone. There's no suitcase anywhere, no personal items at all on any surface.

"Is everything okay, Molly?" I hear behind me. "Did we polish everything adequately?"

I turn to see Sunshine and Sunitha, two senior maids, standing by a cleaning trolley in the doorway beside the detective.

"Have either of you seen Ms. Sharpe?" I ask the maids.

Sunshine shakes her head. "Reception said she checked out. We were told to clean this suite and Mr. Grimthorpe's adjoining one. He's checked out as well."

"That's one way to put it," Detective Stark says.

"He's dead," I explain to the maids. "Very dead."

Sunitha's mouth falls open. Sunshine's eyes pop wide.

"You hadn't heard?" I ask.

"We're short two maids, Molly, because you and Lily were assigned to the tearoom. This is actually Lily's room to clean, but Cheryl told us to do it. We haven't left this floor all morning," Sunshine explains.

"Can I look through your trash?" the detective asks.

Sunshine and Sunitha exchange a look that can only mean they suspect this giant of a woman dressed head to toe in black of lunacy, perversion, or a medley of both.

"She's here to investigate," I say. "Please produce the bagged garbage from this room."

Sunitha nods and rummages through her trolley to extract a small white garbage bag, which she passes to Detective Stark.

"Got any gloves?" Stark asks.

Sunshine grabs a fresh pair of disposables from the trolley and passes them to her.

The detective puts them on, opens the bag, fishes around for a bit, then produces something from the bottom, a crumpled note on Regency Grand stationery. She smooths it out as I read over her shoulder:

> *You are an angel.*
> *Regards,*
> *Your Chiefest Admirer*

The penmanship is perfect, written with a fountain pen, judging from the finely tapered curlicues and loops. It looks so familiar, and yet I can't quite place it.

"Is it Mr. Grimthorpe's handwriting?" the detective asks.

"Definitely not," I reply. I can tell that much immediately.

The detective stares at me, her brow furrowed. "What makes you so sure?"

My mind races. My heart pounds. The edges of the room start to darken. "I know because . . . because he signed books earlier, for me and for many others," I blurt out. "This handwriting is not a match."

"Hmm," Stark replies.

Sunshine and Sunitha have been following the conversation between us as though it were a tennis match, but trained as they are to serve guests rather than question them, they ask nothing about what in good heavens is going on.

"Ladies, did Sharpe leave anything else behind in this room?"

"Yes," Sunshine says. "Those." She points to twelve red, long-stem roses in a glass vase perched atop her maid's trolley. "Molly, we kept them. It seemed like such a waste to throw them out. We wanted to ask you—is that okay?"

I immediately sympathize with the conundrum faced by my well-intentioned maids. On the one hand, *A Maid's Guide & Handbook to Housekeeping, Cleaning & Maintaining a State of Pinnacle Perfection* (an official rule book I conceived of and wrote myself) states that items left behind by guests shalt be delivered unto the lost and found at Reception. However, a subclause also says that if and when items left behind by guests are deemed discarded rather than forgotten, said items may be acquired by maids for personal use.

"You may keep the flowers," I say. "Waste not, want not."

"What about Mr. Grimthorpe's room?" Stark asks. "Was there anything left in it?"

Sunitha shakes her head.

"Nothing in the trash?"

"Nothing in the room at all," Sunshine offers. "No suitcase, no garbage, nothing. Just a downturned bed."

"So her boss dies suddenly and she hightails it outta here, just like that?" Detective Stark squints. She folds the note from the rubbish and puts it into her notepad, then walks over to the trolley, dumps the garbage bag she's holding into the bin, and discards her rubber gloves.

"That will be all," she says as she starts down the hall.

"Where are you off to?" I ask, trailing after her.

"To the station."

"So your investigation is finished?"

She turns suddenly, and I almost face-plant right into her.

"It's far from finished. You better hope for your sake—and for the sake of your little sidekick—that everything in the tearoom comes up clean."

"Oh, it will," I say. "Everything will be spotless once I'm done."

"I don't mean cleaning, Molly. I mean the toxicology reports. I mean the tea on that cart."

"I'm well aware of what you mean, Detective. Are you aware of what *I* mean?"

Detective Stark puts her hands on her hips. "Let me just ask you this very directly. Do you know of any maid or other hotel employee, be it yourself or someone else, who had a reason to hate Mr. Grimthorpe?"

I hesitate because I don't know how to answer. The truth is that I do know of a maid who had a reason to hate Mr. Grimthorpe. But I also know that maid is dead.

—

CHAPTER 7

Before

I recall it in my mind and can relive it as though it were yesterday. It's the night after the first day I spent working beside Gran at the Grimthorpe mansion. I'm back at our apartment. Gran has tucked me in and given me her usual caution about bedbugs and sleeping tight. I close my eyes and fall into the deepest, most exquisite sleep of my life.

For the first time in a long time, I'm not plagued by nightmares about the tortures that await me in the schoolyard the next day. Instead, my dreams sparkle and flash, visions of silver and Fabergé eggs dancing in my head. I wake up in the morning refreshed and excited about spending another day at the Grimthorpe mansion.

Gran and I set out at quarter to eight. No expensive taxi today. Instead, we are powered by our own feet, and then a city bus and then another bus. On the long commute, I tell Gran the big revelation I had before falling asleep the night before. "I've made up my mind. I know what I want to be when I grow up."

"What's that?" Gran asks.

"A maid, just like you."

"Oh, I don't recommend it," Gran says. "The job has many hidden perils. And I think you can aim higher, what with that sharp mind of yours."

"What do you mean 'aim higher'? I want to be a maid," I say.

Gran sighs and pats my hand. "Very well. For now, you can be my Maid-in-Training at the mansion. How does that sound?"

"Like heaven," I reply.

An hour later, we arrive at the mansion gate. Gran buzzes the hidden intercom to announce our arrival, and the invisible gatekeeper in the tower opens sesame. We're walking up the cobblestone path flanked by fragrant roses. At the entrance to the mansion, a contorted face I did not notice yesterday stares down at us from above the door.

"Gran, is that Mr. Grimthorpe?" I ask.

"No," she says with a little laugh. "That's a stone gargoyle, though I admit the resemblance is uncanny."

I step up to the door, grab the heavy lion mandible, and knock hard three times. The knob turns, and Mrs. Grimthorpe appears in a beige blouse and a gray skirt, her mouth a tight pucker.

"Good morning, Mrs. Grimthorpe," I say. "I'm ready to polish and shine," I say, proud of my new distinction as Gran's official Maid-in-Training.

Mrs. Grimthorpe does not reply but steps aside to allow us to enter. She crosses her arms and stares at us as we stand in the foyer. Gran removes a cloth from the front vestibule and instructs me to take off my shoes. She vigorously wipes the bottoms of both of our pairs before placing them inside the closet separate from all the other fancy shoes.

Mrs. Grimthorpe sniffs, then leads us down the main corridor, past the bourgeois blobs, and into the house. We arrive in the glorious, sun-filled kitchen, which smells like lemons and spring-fresh air.

"I have shopping to do and errands to run in town today," Mrs. Grimthorpe announces. "The gatekeeper will drive us to town. Flora, you'll accompany me and carry my bags. The girl will stay behind and work."

"Madam, I can't leave Molly," Gran says. "Who will look after her?"

"Surely she can look after herself. Also, Mr. Grimthorpe is upstairs in his study and Jenkins is right there in the garden."

I look out the floor-to-ceiling windows and spot a ruddy-faced man with bulbous eyes and a back as straight as an exclamation point. He's staring at us as he slices through the hedges with razor-sharp clippers.

Mrs. Grimthorpe checks her watch, then says, "Chop, chop, Flora. Set the girl up in the silver pantry while I gather my things." Then she click-clacks down a corridor and out of sight.

The minute she's gone, I feel Gran's hands come down on my small shoulders.

"Molly, I don't want to leave you here by yourself."

"I don't mind," I say. "I'll be fine."

"Will you? Sometimes I just don't know what to do," Gran says, her eyes crinkling up in that way that makes my stomach hurt. This happens sometimes between Gran and me. I feel what she feels; her emotion passes through my skin and burrows right into my being. I make a mental note to look this up in the anatomy book at the library, because even if the Skeleton Song doesn't say it, there must be an explanation for how Gran's eyes connect to my stomach.

"When in doubt, clean inside and out," I tell Gran. It's a jingle that, like so many others, we sing together when tackling cleaning chores at home.

Gran hugs me to her, then holds me at arm's length. "If you need anything while I'm gone, you go to Jenkins the gardener, okay? I know he looks a fright, but he's soft as a jiggly pudding. I'll tell him to watch over you. You're not to disturb Mr. Grimthorpe upstairs for any reason, do you understand?"

Before I can answer, I notice a woman marching up the path toward the side door of the mansion. She's wearing a blue kerchief tied around her head and matching blue gloves. She waves at us through the window and nods at Jenkins before continuing on her way.

"Gran, who is she?" I ask.

"Oh, that's Mr. Grimthorpe's personal secretary. Mrs. Grimthorpe forbids her from mixing with the rest of us—says it's to preserve the privacy of Mr. Grimthorpe's work. Come," Gran says. "To the silver pantry."

I trot beside Gran to the room I dreamt about all night long. It's exactly as I left it, filled to the rafters with silver heirlooms, all in need of attention. On the large table, the pieces I cleaned yesterday twinkle like bright stars.

Gran rummages through a cupboard, removes two pairs of rubber gloves, a large jug, and a wide-mouthed basin. She turns to me, hands on her hips. "I can't have you polish all of this silver using elbow grease alone. At some point, your arm will fall off."

Yesterday's exertions used all the grease from both of my elbows, so they do feel a tad stiff, but as of yet I don't think I'm in danger of dismemberment.

Gran dons gloves and carefully pours liquid from the jug into the basin.

"This is silver polish, Molly. It contains minute amounts of lye, which is corrosive to the skin. In the olden days, when I was a Maid-in-Training, we mixed the solution ourselves. Once, a maid I worked with quadrupled the lye in the recipe and left the basin by the back entrance of the estate. His Lordship walked in with dirty hands after a hunt. He saw the basin and plunked his fingers right in. Had I not doused his flesh in water immediately, the acid would have eaten clean through his bones."

"What a terrible accident," I say.

"Terrible, yes. An accident? I've never been quite sure."

"What do you mean?" I ask.

"Fate, Molly," Gran says. "It works in mysterious ways. That's why it's important to treat others with respect at all times," she says as she passes me a pair of gloves. I put them on.

"This modern polish is not like the rough stuff we used years ago. It's very gentle, but you are still to wear rubber gloves when you work."

Gran picks up a tarnished silver candlestick, dips it in the solution, and wipes it with a cloth. After a bit of buffing, the silver is polished to a high shine.

"It's magic!" I say, clapping my gloved hands.

"Flora!" we hear from somewhere deep in the house. "Chop! Chop!"

Gran peels off her gloves and places them neatly beside the basin. She plants a kiss on my forehead. "I'll be back faster than you can spell 'serendipitous,'" she says and then rushes out of the room.

I listen to Mrs. Grimthorpe ordering Gran about at the entrance. Then the door shuts with a hollow thud, and I know they are gone.

This is it, I think to myself. I'm on my own in the mansion—no Gran. Rather than frightening me, the prospect fills me with pride at my newfound responsibility. I spell out "serendipitous" five times, then come to the conclusion that Gran meant what she said figuratively (meaning: not really) rather than literally (meaning: precisely and exactly).

In the silence, a new sound echoes through the hollow mansion.

Rat-a-tat-tat-tat.

It's the sound of typing. So many noises bother my ears, but I don't mind this one because it's rhythmic and predictable. It must be the woman in blue, Mr. Grimthorpe's personal secretary, typing in an office somewhere deep within the mansion.

As I look around the silver pantry, a feeling of rapture overtakes me. I'm on my own. In a mansion! I'm a grown-up entrusted with grown-up responsibilities. I skip around the room, then put on my apron and my fresh rubber gloves.

Dip in the brine, then polish and shine.

I get to work, polishing piece after piece, placing each glimmering object in a perfect line on the table. As I work, I imagine I'm setting it for a regal banquet hosted by Gran, also known as the Duchess of Apron, and me, Maid Molly of Fabergé.

Our guest list is the crème de la crème. Robin Hood is seated at the head of the table in a green crushed-velvet suit. By his side is Columbo in a brand-new trench coat, his hair combed neatly for once, just as Gran would like it. Across from them are Badger and Mr. Toad, then Sir David Attenborough in a safari suit, a wobbly Humpty Dumpty in short pants and suspenders, and Sir Walter of Brooms, my school's janitor, and the only person there whom I liked.

There are still a few seats to fill, so I populate them with the Scarecrow, the Lion, and the Tin Man from *The Wizard of Oz.* I add the Cheshire Cat, who is curled up on a chair smiling and smiling at the far end of the table. There's one empty chair left, and that one is for me. I'm wearing a pristine white gown with cap lace sleeves and petticoat ruffles to my ankles.

I call for a toast by tapping my porcelain teacup with a freshly polished silver spoon. The high-pitched tinkle is a delight to my ears. "To Gran," I say. "And to my finest storybook friends. Thank you for being loyal and true, from the first page to the last."

We drink tea and eat scones with clotted cream. We have a spelling bee, and I spell "stupendous" correctly on the very first try. We are the True Silver Knights of the Table Rectangular, kindred spirits, the only friends I'll ever have.

A small sting rips me from my daydream. A single drop of silver polish has landed on my forearm just above my glove. I rush to the sink, where I douse the burning spot in cold water. It relieves the sting, but when I turn back to the tea party, my friends have vanished into thin air.

"Wait, come back!" I say, but my imagination fails me. I look down at my tatty apron, no ruffles and cap sleeves, just the threadbare truth.

It's then that it strikes me. I realize with some urgency that I'm in need of a washroom. I take off my rubber gloves and exit the silver pantry. Yesterday, Gran showed me the washroom I'm to use. It's not the visitors' powder room near the entrance, which Gran calls the "gold de toilette." And it's not the washroom off the kitchen, the one with the massive whirlpool tub. And it's certainly not the washroom upstairs. I'm to use the servants' washroom, which is downstairs in the basement, where the walls are dank stone and where every nook and cranny houses a hairy spider with terrifying, beady compound eyes.

"It has the bare necessities," Gran said yesterday as she pulled the cord on the naked bulb and led me down the creaky, slippery stairs.

Now, I stand in front of that basement door just off the kitchen, steeling myself to open it and descend, but my legs are stuck to the floor. I cannot move.

Knock, knock, knock, I hear.

I nearly jump out of my skin. I turn to see Jenkins's protruding eyes staring at me through the glass of the kitchen windows. He shakes his head several times and says something I don't understand.

"I can't hear you," I say. "I don't know what you're saying."

Jenkins moves from the window to the glass door. He opens it, but he doesn't step inside. Rather, he shoves his head through and whispers, "You don't have to go down there."

"I do," I say. "I need the washroom." I remember what Gran said, how Jenkins looks a fright rather than like a pudding, which would be preferable. He's covered in little scratches, presumably from rose thorns, and he carries a menacing array of sharp tools in the leather belt around his waist. The sight of his razor-sharp clippers sends a shiver down my spine. Still, he's better than spiders. And he's my only hope right now. "Please, sir," I say. "Will you accompany me to the cellar?"

"I wish I could, Little Mite," he says, "but I'm not allowed inside the house. Dirty workman and all that business. If the Madam caught me, she'd tan my hide. Then she'd kick me to the curb. Just use another loo. If you're neat about it, Mrs. Grimthorpe will never know," he says with a wink.

I nod and swallow.

Jenkins closes the door quietly, then removes the hedge clippers from his belt and begins to savage a hedge by the window.

I breathe deeply a few times to steady myself. Gran told me explicitly that the main-floor washrooms are off-limits, and the last thing I want is to anger Mrs. Grimthorpe by breaking the rules and thereby cause the tanning of my own hide, which sounds horrifically unpleasant.

I head to the front of the house and stand under the icy shards of the modernist chandelier. Perhaps if I use an upstairs washroom, evidence of my presence will be attributed to Mr. Grimthorpe or his secretary. I tiptoe up the main staircase, the treads creaking under every footfall. The stairs wind to a small landing with a window and then up another flight to the second story. I make it to the top and am peering down a long, cavernous corridor wallpapered in a dark design that's meant to be brocade but looks to me like hundreds of squinty eyeballs watching my every move.

I traverse the hallway, and the lights overhead turn on as if by magic. I pass bedroom after luxuriously appointed bedroom, taking a quick peek in each—the four-poster bed in one; the brass bed in the next that looks straight out of *Bedknobs and Broomsticks*. At last, I find a washroom. I close and lock the door behind me. After taking care of my necessities, I lather and bathe my hands under water from the gold taps, then I dry them on a hand towel so plush it might be a cloud. I unlock the door and exit, much relieved.

I know I should creep down the stairs and get back to work on the silver, but as I stare down the hallway, I see that a door is open to an expansive room that takes my breath away. It's the library, which Gran has described to me before, but nothing could have prepared me for the sight of it in real life. Even from a distance, I can see that it's filled with floor-to-ceiling bookshelves and sumptuous leather volumes in red and blue, gold and green.

There are times when my feet have a mind of their own, and this is one of them. They tiptoe all the way down the hallway, the overhead lights beckoning me forth. Before I know it, I'm standing on the threshold of the awe-inspiring library. There's a velvet chaise longue in a corner by the window, and beside it a reading lamp, the shade held by a brass nymph frozen in mid-frolic. A tall ladder with wheels on the bottom leans against the far wall. It can reach the highest volumes all around the room.

Entranced, I step past the threshold. Some of these books I've heard of or seen at the public library. Others are new to me, including the ones with J. D. Grimthorpe's name on the spines—*Dead Man's Secret, Poison & Punishment, The Mystery Guest*. I reach out and

trace a shelf of jewel-toned leather volumes with my fingertips—
The Count of Monte Cristo, Grimms' Fairy Tales, The Turn of the Screw. I
want nothing more than to fish out a book, curl up on the chaise
longue, and lose myself in the pages.

Rat-a-tat-tat-tat.

The sound of typing again, much closer now. It's then that I see
it, a thin shaft of light coming from a crack in the bottom of the
nearest book-lined wall. I move closer to the beam.

Then I hear footsteps. Someone is walking on the other side of
the wall.

"Confounding! Rubbish, all of it. A pox on every word!" It's a
man's voice, a dark and husky growl. The footsteps become
stomps, and then something thuds against the floor. I can feel the
vibrations beneath my own feet.

A shadow falls across the shaft of light on the floorboards. I
take a few tentative steps closer, but as I do, the boards creak beneath my feet.

"Who's there?" I hear, a thunderous boom.

To my young ears, it's unmistakable—the ornery, bloodthirsty
voice of a troll.

"Answer me!" the troll demands.

I begin to tremble because I can see him in my mind's eye—
hunchbacked and hairy, with protruding fangs and bloodshot
eyes. He'll pick me up by the strings of my apron and pop my wrig-
gling body straight into his gaping, voracious mouth.

I don't move or run away or even investigate further, because
Gran always says that curiosity kills cats, and in this case, I do not
wish to be a feline.

The room goes quiet, and I'm terribly relieved. But then my feet
disobey me again. Suddenly, I'm creeping forward and crouching
down. I can't stop myself. I'm lying horizontally on the floor so I
can look through the ominous crack in the wall and into the room

next door. I'm on my side at eye level. I pull myself, closer, closer to the crack until . . . an eye—a steely blue troll's eye—is staring back at me from the other side of the wall.

"AHHHHHHHHhhhhhh!" I scream, which sends adrenaline coursing through my entire body. I hurry to my feet and run out of the library and down the long corridor just as I hear the front door of the mansion opening and Mrs. Grimthorpe ordering Gran to bring in all the bags from outside.

I hurtle down the main staircase, taking the steps two by two until I'm standing breathless at the entrance, trying to appear perfectly ordinary in every possible way.

"Molly?" Gran says as she puts an armful of shopping bags on the floor. "You look like you've just seen a ghost."

I cling to the banister in a valiant attempt at normalcy. "Not a ghost," I reply. "Not that exactly."

Chapter 8

In my dream, I'm foraging in an enchanted forest just down the path from our gingerbread cottage.

A strange-looking sheep asks me what I'm doing. "Collecting medicines for Gran," I reply.

"You better hurry before it's too late," the sheep says as it trots down the path.

When I arrive at our cottage, Gran is tucked in bed, the sheets pulled tight to her chin. "I've got your medicines. Everything's going to be okay."

"You're too late," Gran replies. Only then do I realize it's not Gran in bed but Mr. Grimthorpe the troll, wrapped in a sheepskin and wearing a white bonnet on his head.

"No!" I scream. "You're dead! Go away and never come back!"

He starts to laugh, a deep, maniacal laugh. Just as he's about to reach his claws out to grab me, I wake up to my phone ringing on my bedside table.

I'm not a child in a nightmare but a grown woman in her own bed.

I swipe to answer the call. "Hello?" I say breathlessly.

"Molly?" Juan Manuel replies. "You sound like you've been running."

"I was asleep," I say. I feel sweaty and confused.

"I'm sorry to wake you, *mi amor*. I just wanted to wish you a good morning and to remind you to rise, polish, and shine."

He's quoting Gran. I've told him how she used to say this every morning as she pulled my curtains open when I was a little girl. "Rise, polish, and shine!" her voice trilled, bright and cheerful like a singing sparrow. She died before Juan Manuel could ever meet her, and yet in ways I'll never fully comprehend, parts of her live on in him just as they live on in me. This truth adds solace to all of my days.

"How was the Grimthorpe event, Molly? Did you slay it?"

"Did I what?" I ask as I sit up taller in bed. It takes me a moment to realize he's not referencing Mr. Grimthorpe but using one of those newfangled expressions he loves so much. "For the record," I say, "I've slain no one."

Juan responds with a laugh. "Did yesterday's event go okay?"

I don't want to avoid the truth, but I know if I tell him a famous writer died in the Regency Grand Tearoom, he'll be worried sick. Knowing him, he'll be on a plane back here before I can say Jiminy Cricket, and that would be so unfair. I can't expect Juan to be there for me every time something goes awry. Besides, I'm perfectly capable of handling this situation myself. After all, I *am* a Head Maid.

"Mi *amor*, are you there? Is everything okay?" he asks.

"Who said things weren't okay?" I ask. "Was someone from the hotel in touch with you?"

"No," he replies. "They're not allowed to contact me. Mr. Snow told the kitchen staff he expects them to figure things out for a change rather than come to me every time things go wrong."

"Exactly right," I say. "We all rely on you far too much. It's high time you had a good, proper break."

"But you do miss me, don't you, *mi amor?*"

"Of course I do," I say. "You have no idea how much." Sadness suddenly rises in my throat, and I quickly swallow it down before it escapes. "I'd better go now. Lots of cleanup to do at the hotel."

"I'm sure you'll sort it out. You always do."

We say our heartfelt goodbyes, and I hang up.

I jump out of bed, sleep and dreams forgotten. I bustle about the apartment getting ready for my day. I have no idea what it will bring, but as Gran used to say, *Embrace the possibilities. You never know what might happen.* I just hope that we'll soon be able to chalk up the untimely death of Mr. Grimthorpe to natural causes and get on with doing what we do best at the Regency Grand—providing our guests with the finest customer service in a sophisticated venue that befits the modern age.

Within the hour, I'm walking briskly in the sunshine toward the hotel's scarlet stairs. Mr. Preston, in cap and greatcoat, is standing on the carpeted landing helping some tourists with directions. He points a young couple to the next street over and they hurry down the stairs to their destination as though everything is normal, as though our hotel did not experience a seismic upheaval just the day before. As I stare at the entrance to the hotel, my knees start to shake.

"Molly!" Mr. Preston calls out the moment he spots me.

I walk up the stairs to meet him.

"My dear girl, I've been thinking about you all morning. What a horrendous shock you must have had yesterday. Are you all right?"

"Mr. Preston, I'm not the one who died. It stands to reason that I'm fine," I reply, though I don't quite believe my own words.

"Thank heavens for that," Mr. Preston says. "I'm just glad you survived yesterday's ordeal without getting too rattled. Good riddance to the writer, I say."

"Good riddance?" I reply. "That's not very charitable."

"I reserve charity for those who deserve it," Mr. Preston replies. "And that man did not deserve it."

A strange tingling sensation stirs in the depths of my belly. My gran used to get feelings like this. She called them her "intuitions."

"Mr. Preston," I say. "Did you know Mr. Grimthorpe?"

"I'm not sure anyone knew him, least of all himself," he replies.

"You don't actually think someone inside this hotel could have killed him, do you?"

"A man like that? Anything's possible."

Just then, some guests arrive in a taxi. "Molly, be careful in there today," Mr. Preston says. "There are things going on around here that I don't quite understand, and until I do, you best be vigilant."

It's an odd thing to say in a conversation replete with oddities, but Mr. Preston has not been himself lately. He keeps insisting on meeting me for dinner, which makes me wonder if he's all right. He's more distracted and tired than usual, too. He's asking the valets for help and taking breaks with greater frequency these days.

"There's no need to worry about me, Mr. Preston," I say. "I'll be fine. If anything, you should worry about yourself."

He nods and starts down the stairs. I head the other way, pushing through the revolving doors into the stunning lobby of the Regency Grand. It's a hive of activity even though it's not yet nine. Visitors gather in close huddles on every jewel-toned settee. The morning scents of coffee and fresh lemon polish commingle in the air.

A line of new guests waits at Reception as bellhops call back and forth, tackling the sudden surfeit of suitcases that litters the lobby. I've seen this before, of course, the day after the infamous Mr. Black died in our hotel. That morning, our hotel was filled to capacity. Every lookie-loo in town had suddenly checked in to be part of "the scene," all of them asking the same question: had Mr. Black died of natural causes or was something more sinister at play in the Regency Grand? It's no different this time. Yesterday, a world-renowned writer dropped dead on the tearoom floor, and today the lobby pulses with conspiratorial energy as guests and staff members exchange salient bits of gossip about who knows who and who knows what. It's worrisome, all this chatter about potential suspects and possible criminals in our midst.

I take a sharp right away from the lobby and rush downstairs to the housekeeping quarters, where my freshly dry-cleaned uniform hangs in clingy plastic on my locker door—a new beginning. I quickly put it on and am fastening my Head Maid pin above my heart when something in the corner of the low-ceilinged room makes me jump.

"Lily!" I say. She's standing stock-still in the shadows by her locker. "You frightened me half to death. My dear girl, what are you doing here today? I didn't expect you, not after yesterday's commotion. Why didn't you call in sick?"

"Because I'm not sick," she whispers. "And there's something I have to—"

At that moment, Cheryl enters, dragging her feet in that slovenly way that makes me want to chop them off.

"There you are, my little wallflower," Cheryl drones as she spots Lily hiding in the corner. "Aren't you just 'polished to perfection.' You'll clean the whole second floor today since Molly's being called elsewhere."

"What are you talking about?" I ask Cheryl.

"Oh, didn't Mr. Snow tell you? He needs you in the Social. Something about waiters not showing up. That makes *me* your supervisor today, Lily. Mr. Snow's orders." She points to the lopsided pin fastened above her substantial bosom. "Look who's back to being Head Maid."

Turmoil bubbles inside me. I cannot decide whether to straighten Cheryl's lopsided pin or simply slap her across the face. "I'm sure this is some misunderstanding," I assure Lily. "I'll speak to Mr. Snow about this posthaste."

"Knock yourself out," Cheryl mutters.

Gran used to say, *There's no point boxing with buffoons,* so I unclasp my Head Maid pin and tuck it neatly into my locker. "Have a lovely day, Lily," I say to her before walking out of the change room without another word to Cheryl.

Up the stairs I trot, feeling hotter than a boiling kettle.

I make my way to the lobby, where Mr. Snow is standing by the reception desk wearing a black velvet waistcoat and a neat paisley cravat. Beside him is Angela, her blazing red hair in a tizzy.

I head straight for them. "Am I or am I not the Head Maid at this hotel?" I ask Mr. Snow.

He sighs, then straightens his cravat. "It's only for today, Molly. Angela's short three servers, so we're in quite a pickle. We need your help in the restaurant. And with you away from the guest rooms, I had to put someone in charge of the maids."

"And you chose Cheryl?" I say. "Why didn't you consult me about the running of my very own department? Has the world officially turned upside down? And what happened to the waiters? Did they call in sick?" I ask.

"Called in afraid is more like it," Angela replies. "Seems they're worried there's a murderer on the loose right here in our hotel."

"That's absurd," Mr. Snow says. "Patently ridiculous."

"Is it?" Angela replies. "If podcasts have taught me anything, it's that the worst things happen in the safest places."

Mr. Snow's lips pucker as though he's sucking on a lemon.

"Also," Angela says, "don't you think it's a bit weird that

Grimthorpe's personal secretary bolted out of here yesterday right after her boss kicked the bucket? I mean, I'm glad she's coming back today, but still . . . it's messed up."

"How do you know Ms. Sharpe is coming back today?" Mr. Snow asks.

"Duh," Angela says. "The banker's box right behind you has her name on it."

Mr. Snow adjusts his glasses, setting them more or less straight on the bridge of his nose.

"By the way, you look some fit today, Mr. Snow," Angela says. "Doesn't he look sharp, Molly?"

"Indeed," I say. "Is there a high-end wedding in the hotel? Or a banquet? Mr. Snow, why are you so dressed up?"

Mr. Snow's eyes search the lobby again, looking for what or whom, I do not know.

"Mr. Snow?" I repeat.

"What's in the box?" Angela asks.

He looks at her with trepidation. "A few trifles," he replies. "Odds and ends left behind after all of the commotion yesterday." He flattens a palm over the lid of the box behind him.

"Cool. I like trifles," says Angela as she grabs the lid and removes it in one fell swoop, causing Mr. Snow's hand to plummet to his side. "Get a load of that, Molls!" Angela says as she peers into the box.

Inside is a very old edition of Mr. Grimthorpe's bestselling novel *The Maid in the Mansion*, which, unlike the ones for sale at the event yesterday, features the original cover art—an iconic mansion door and an eye looking through the keyhole. Beside the book is Mr. Grimthorpe's fountain pen, which I recognize from yesterday's signing, as well as a black monogrammed Moleskine and a sealed Regency Grand envelope labeled *Serena*.

"The note to Serena is from me," Mr. Snow says. "To thank her for her patronage."

"Serena? Surely you mean Ms. Sharpe," I say. I'm about to launch into a diatribe about the proper protocols for addressing guests, but before I can commence my lecture, Mr. Snow interrupts.

"Let me make one thing abundantly clear," he says. "Serena is as innocent as a spring lamb."

"No one in this hotel is *that* innocent," Angela replies. "Not even you, Mr. Snow." She picks up the novel and flips through the pages until she finds the copyright page. "Dang! It's a first edition," she says. "This has gotta be rare."

"Yes. It is," Mr. Snow concedes. "We had it in a display case out front to promote Mr. Grimthorpe's announcement, alongside the other mementos in the box. Anyhow, Serena has asked for everything back."

"Well, well. Speak of the devil," Angela says.

Just then, Ms. Serena Sharpe pushes through the gold revolving doors of the Regency Grand. She is radiant, ethereal, though her outfit—a form-fitting black velvet dress—makes it clear she's in mourning.

Ms. Sharpe looks around the lobby and spots Mr. Snow waving frantically in her direction. She makes her way over to us. Up close I can't help but notice the fatigue—or is it sadness?—writ large in the dark circles under her enigmatic blue eyes.

"My dearest Serena," Mr. Snow says. "How are you doing?"

"To be honest, I'm still in shock," she says. "I can't quite believe he's gone."

"That's completely understandable," Mr. Snow replies. "You have my deepest sympathies, and should you require emotional support during this difficult time, please know you can count on me."

I cannot believe what happens next. Mr. Snow lays a hand on Ms. Sharpe's bare arm. I'm about to point out that this is a violation of all hotel rules outlining appropriate guest-to-employee conduct—rules that came from Mr. Snow himself—but before I can do so, Ms. Sharpe extricates herself from his hand.

"I wanted to ask," she says. "Do you have an update about how Mr. Grimthorpe died? Did the police reveal anything?" Her voice is shaky and unsure.

"I'm afraid not," says Mr. Snow. "The autopsy results will take a day or two, so I'm told."

"Actually," I say. "Yesterday, Detective Stark was looking for you, Ms. Sharpe. She wanted to know what Mr. Grimthorpe was about to announce before he died."

"Oh, I'm aware," she replies. "The detective left a half dozen messages on my phone."

"Perhaps you can ring her back," I suggest.

Ms. Sharpe's face turns to stone. "I'm heading to the station now, as a matter of fact," she says stiffly.

Just then, something flits at the edge of my vision. I turn and spot Lily in the darkest corner of the lobby. She's holding a feather duster and standing under the grand staircase between two emerald settees. Why on earth is she in the lobby when she should be upstairs cleaning guest rooms?

"Exactly how long have you worked for Mr. Grimthorpe?" Mr. Snow asks Ms. Sharpe.

"A little over a year," she replies. "He hired me as his personal secretary after his previous secretary passed away. I have no idea what I'm going to do for work now that he's gone."

At exactly that moment, Cheryl enters the lobby pushing a discolored woolly mop. Why on earth is yet another maid in the lobby when she should be upstairs? Clearly, Mr. Snow is thinking the very same thing because he's looking at Cheryl with utmost disdain. He's opened his mouth, but before he can call out to her, a piercing sound assaults our ears. My hands spring up to cover my own. It takes a moment to realize the fire alarm has sounded. All around me, guests and employees jostle and start.

I feel a hand on my arm. It's Angela, guiding me to the hotel entrance. Throngs of guests surround us, all of us pushing through the revolving doors. Before long, we're standing outside on the plush scarlet staircase, where the shrieking alarm is not nearly as deafening.

A sea of humanity gathers around us.

"What's going on?"

"What happened?"

"Is there a fire?"

In the midst of the chaos, Mr. Preston calls for calm and ushers people down the staircase toward the safety of the sidewalk.

As suddenly as the hubbub began, the alarm ends. Mr. Snow rushes through the revolving doors and calls down the stairs: "All is well! A false alarm! Please, you may reenter the Regency Grand."

Audible sounds of relief are heard all around me.

"That was exciting," Angela says.

"It was far from exciting," I reply. "It was stressful and agitating."

"Come on," Angela says. "It's over now. Let's go back in."

I follow her up the stairs and through the revolving doors. We make our way to the reception desk, where we were standing earlier.

Mr. Snow rushes over. His eyes search the lobby. "Where did she go?" he asks. "Where's Serena?"

"Your guess is as good as mine," Angela replies.

It's then that I take in the reception desk behind us. It appears that Ms. Sharpe is not the only absentee. The banker's box containing the rare first edition is gone.

Chapter 9

Before

I am transported back to the tiny kitchen where Gran and I enjoyed so many meals together when I was a child. It's the morning after I looked into the steely eye of the troll that lives behind the wall in the Grimthorpe library. Was I frightened? Yes. Did I run? I did. But the troll did not eat me. I did not turn to stone or melt on the spot. I faced the monster, and I survived.

I swing my little legs back and forth under our worn country kitchen table. Gran brings over two steaming bowls of cinnamon porridge. I take in the scent that to this day I equate with goodness and home.

"Gran, if you were rich, what would you spend your money on?" I ask between warm mouthfuls.

"A private school for you, with kind and patient teachers. And a small house we could call our own, with no bills or landlord, and two easy chairs by the fireplace."

"When we're rich, can we have tea with clotted cream every single day?"

"Every single day," she replies.

"Tell me again, Gran. What happened to my mother?"

It comes out of nowhere, and it takes her by surprise. She puts down her spoon. "Your mother left us," she says.

"I know that," I reply as I try to conjure a memory of her face, but I draw a complete blank. All I can envisage is the framed photo of her that Gran keeps in the living room. That photo was taken when my mother was only a few years older than I am now.

"Your mother had demons," Gran says. "She got lost in the labyrinth, as people sometimes do. By the time I realized she'd been wooed away by a fly-by-night, it was too late to save her."

I think about the troll in the mansion. He seems not nearly as frightening as my mother's demons or the winged fly-by-night that wooed her away. You can fight monsters you can see, or you can run away from them. But the invisible ones are inescapable.

I swirl my spoon around in my bowl. "Gran, what happens if you die?"

Her eyes grow two sizes. "My dear girl, I'm not going to die."

"That's a lie," I say as I plunk down my spoon in protest.

"You're right. I will die one day. But not soon. And besides, even when I'm gone, I won't leave you. You won't see me, but I'll be there with you, always."

"Like a ghost?"

"Yes. Like a friendly ghost haunting you for the rest of your days. And reminding you to brush your teeth when you're done with your breakfast." She smiles and grazes my cheek with her palm.

I pick up my empty bowl and place it in the sink, then rush down the hallway to our tiny washroom, where I brush my teeth as instructed. A few minutes later, I meet Gran by our front door.

"To the mansion we go," she says. She's crouching down, tying her right shoe. When she's finished, she gazes up at me. "Molly, promise you'll tell me if you're unhappy at the mansion?" Her eyes are scrunched and glassy.

"Unhappy? Gran, I love it there. I love to clean."

"You certainly made a good impression on Mrs. Grimthorpe with all that silver you polished yesterday. She called you 'obedient and compliant,' which from her is as high a compliment as they come. She has a surprise for you today."

"A surprise?" I ask. "What is it?"

Gran stands and pinches my cheek. "You'll have to wait and see."

Together, we head out on our long commute. I spend the entire journey imagining what surprise a woman like Mrs. Grimthorpe could have in store for me. Used gray pajamas? A lump of coal in a darned stocking? A hairy spider in a jar?

But when Mrs. Grimthorpe opens the heavy front door to the mansion, she announces it right away. "Your grandmother and I had a chat the other day while we were shopping. We've come to a conclusion," she says.

"About what?" I ask.

"About you," Mrs. Grimthorpe replies, as her eyes narrow to pinpoints, sticking me to my place like a butterfly affixed to a board. "Mr. Grimthorpe and I have always maintained that bad habits can be broken, and that a mannered, well-educated child is preferable to a lazy ragamuffin."

"R-A-G-A-M-U-F-F-I-N. Meaning: a gadabout?"

"Or a ne'er-do-well," says Gran.

"The great unwashed," Mrs. Grimthorpe adds with grave finality.

"What Mrs. Grimthorpe is saying," Gran explains, "is that all children—and even adults—are capable of learning; it's just that some need to learn in their own ways, and an institution, such as a school or other facility, is not the place for everyone."

"But no person, be they adult or child, should waste a chance at betterment," Mrs. Grimthorpe adds.

"Including you, Mrs. Grimthorpe?" I ask.

Mrs. Grimthorpe's hands spring to her waist and her pointy elbows jut out dangerously. "I'll have you know," she huffs, "that there are two women standing before you who have sacrificed greatly for the betterment of a loved one, and someday, you will come to understand that, though it's clear that at present your mind is so filled with childish poppycock there's not much room for anything else."

"What Mrs. Grimthorpe is trying to say," Gran cuts in, "is that you did such a good job cleaning the silver yesterday that she, in her *infinite kindness,* wants to *reward you.* Isn't that what you're getting at, Mrs. Grimthorpe?"

Mrs. Grimthorpe's face contorts as though paying me a compliment might very well send her into paroxysms. "We have a library upstairs," she eventually says. "It is filled to the rafters with books. Mr. Grimthorpe and I have always maintained that books can rehabilitate anyone. I understand you enjoy reading."

I nod repeatedly.

"Very well. From now on, you will polish and clean for half the day, and you will read for the other half. If you can't attend school, then the least you can do is self-educate."

I can't believe what I'm hearing. It sounds too good to be true. I look at Gran for confirmation. She smiles and nods.

"Follow me," Mrs. Grimthorpe says. "To the library."

"Oh, I know where—" I stop myself just in time. "Yes, madam," I say.

Mrs. Grimthorpe heads up the main staircase, which creaks and groans under every footfall. I trail close behind her. At the first landing, I look out the window and see the lady in blue walking toward the side of the mansion just as she did yesterday.

"Where's her office?" I ask Mrs. Grimthorpe.

"Whose office?" Mrs. Grimthorpe asks as she pauses on the landing.

"Hers," I say, pointing to the elegant lady in the blue kerchief and gloves pushing through the side door.

"That, young lady, is categorically and conclusively none of your business. Understood?"

In the interest of keeping the peace, I nod and keep my mouth firmly shut.

Mrs. Grimthorpe starts up the next flight of stairs and I follow behind her. Once we make it to the landing, we head down the long corridor that I've traversed on my own once before. The lights overhead track us as if by magic, turning on as we pass and illuminating the damask wallpaper. How strange that the pattern, which was full of watchful evil eyes the last time I was here, has transformed into a refined and pleasing paisley. We pass bedroom after bedroom after bedroom—but no office—until at last we're standing at the threshold of the breathtaking library.

Mrs. Grimthorpe enters and pulls back the heavy velvet draperies from the long window on one wall. Daylight streams in and dust motes dance like sprites in the air. My eyes turn to the crack in the wall near the floor in front of me. There's no light beam coming through today, and not a sound can be heard on the other side of the wall. For a moment, I wonder if my mind played tricks on me yesterday. Maybe there's no troll after all. Maybe it was all a figment of my overactive imagination.

"What you are seeing in this library is one of the finest private collections of leather-bound rare editions you will ever encounter in the English-speaking world," Mrs. Grimthorpe says. "Mr. Grimthorpe has personally studied every facet of every book in this room, and each one has inspired his literary pursuits. He is an erudite man who has earned his sterling reputation through serious scholarship. It is a privilege for a girl like you to even be allowed to step into a room like this. Do you understand?"

"Yes," I reply. "I understand."

"Your grandmother seems to think you're a gifted reader, though I suspect her of being prone to overweening filial blindness and general hyperbole."

I scan the shelf on the wall in front of us for a dictionary in which I can look up several of the words Mrs. Grimthorpe just used. I spot one and reach for it.

"No!" Mrs. Grimthorpe snaps. The caustic force of her rebuke sends me hurtling backward.

"You are not allowed to take any books from the fourth wall," she commands. "You may take books from this wall, that one, and the other, but you are never, ever to touch the wall in front of you. Is that clear? Those volumes are precious collector's items, and I won't have you ruining them the way you ruined our Fabergé."

I stare up at her pinched face, which resembles a crumpled paper bag. I can't find my voice, so I nod in response.

"You may read in here for a few hours. After tea, you will return to your duty of polishing silver downstairs. Make use of your time, Molly. A good mind is a terrible thing to waste. Opportunities for self-improvement are precious."

With that she turns on her heel, marches down the damask hallway, and descends the main staircase as the lights above dim in her wake.

Once she's gone, I survey the luminous library. I can't believe my good fortune. How is it that I'm allowed to sit here and read? I walk over to the far wall, one of the three I'm allowed to touch. I run my hands along the spines. *Murder on the Orient Express, The Hound of the Baskervilles, Great Expectations.* I pry out *Great Expectations* with my index finger and carry the heavy indigo tome over to the chaise longue, where I sit down, crack open the cover, and begin.

I'm acquainting myself with an unfortunate young orphan named Pip when I hear it—creaking footsteps from beyond the fourth wall. There's an audible click, and then light spills through the crack in the wall, throwing a long shadow on the floor in the library.

Rat-a-tat-tat-tat.

The sound of a typewriter yet again.

"Bloody bugger and tarnation! Rubbish and gibberish!" I hear, the growl of a hungry troll on the other side of the forbidden wall.

I put down my book and tiptoe toward the voice. I know I shouldn't. I've been told not to touch that wall, but I lay my hand on the Oxford dictionary and press my ear against the *Atlas of the World* so I can hear the troll more clearly. No sooner does my hand make contact than something gives way. The wall springs open.

"AHHHhhhhhhhhh!" I scream as I jump back in surprise.

"Wahhhhhhh!" I hear in deep echo.

Before I can even process what's happened, I'm standing in front of a lean, rickety man seated at a colossal mahogany desk between two looming stacks of Moleskine notebooks. His salt-and-pepper hair is wildly unkempt, his steely blue eyes are drilling into mine with a look that, if I'm not mistaken, betrays either cannibalistic intent or abject confusion.

My hand trembles on the Oxford dictionary, but I cannot let it go because the entire bookcase is in fact a hidden door that I'm propping open with my hand.

"Who in the dickens are you?" asks the being before me as he clutches a black-and-gold fountain pen, wielding it above his head like a knife. I cannot quite tell if he's going to stab me or take notes, but when I look at his hand, I notice I'm not the only one trembling.

"Speak!" he booms. "What are you doing here?"

I fear my very life depends on my answer, and yet I'm not sure what to say.

"I'm . . . I'm sorry to have interrupted you," I say. "I mean no harm."

"Who are you?" he growls. "To whom do you belong?"

"To my gran?" I say. "She works here."

"The maid?" he asks.

"Yes. The maid. I'm her granddaughter. My name is . . ." I suddenly remember that Gran expressly forbids me from telling strangers my name.

"Call me Pip," I say, punctuating this with a wobbly curtsy.

"In that case," he replies, "I shall expect great things from you."

I look at him for a moment, afraid that doing so might convert me to dust. "Are you a troll or a man?" I ask, my voice trembling.

"How refreshing. Never have I been asked that question so directly. I'm a bit of both, I suppose," he says. "I'm what's known as a misanthrope."

"Misanthorpe," I repeat. "M-I-S-A-N-T-H-O-R-P-E."

"Incorrect. You've confused it with Grimthorpe. You've reversed two letters."

I look carefully at the being before me. He's thin and lithe, with no facial hair at all. His skin is pale and smooth. His teeth are straight and clean, not pointed, bloodthirsty fangs. His hair is unruly and might be possessed, but he himself is dressed neatly in a button-down blue shirt, pressed slacks, and monogrammed corduroy slippers. My eyes flitter around the spartan room, taking in the details. There's a reading chair in the corner piled with newspapers. There's the desk, with the looming piles of black Moleskines stacked on top. There's also a bookcase on the far wall, every spine sporting the name J. D. Grimthorpe. Though the study is far from tidy, there are no bones of children or other small mammals strewn about. There is no evidence whatsoever of overt monstrosity.

"You're not a troll," I say. "You're a man. You're Mr. Grimthorpe, the very important writer who should not be disturbed."

He crosses his arms and scrutinizes me. "Is that what she told you? My wife?"

I nod.

"Well, then," he replies. "What an enormous privilege for you to be in the presence of such hallowed greatness." He stands from his desk and offers a bow. "I suppose she also told you never to come into my study." He slaps his pointy pen down on his desk, much to my relief. Then he walks in front of his desk and perches on it, right between the teetering stacks of black monogrammed Moleskines. He glares at me with his two steely blue eyes, one of which I saw yesterday through the crack under the door, though I can't be sure which eye it was.

"I didn't mean to disturb you," I explain. "I heard a voice. I didn't know your study was behind the wall. I was sitting in the library reading a book."

"Reading? What were you reading?"

"A book about a child with no mother or father, just like me."

"Ah yes. I see. *Great Expectations*. Precocious."

"Precocious," I repeat. I know this word. I've been called it before. "Meaning: clever, intelligent. Ahead of one's peers."

"Evidently," he replies.

He starts to pace in front of his desk, occasionally glancing at me with those piercing eyes. "So you like to read," he says.

"Yes, I do," I reply. My knees are shaking, but clearly they're not connected to my mouth after all, because despite my terror, I'm still capable of speech.

"*Why* do you like to read?" Mr. Grimthorpe asks.

He's so tall and knobby it's as though he's formed entirely of acute angles, and yet he moves with stealthy grace. He awaits my answer to his impossible question.

I search my mind for what to say and eventually an idea bubbles to the surface. "Reading helps me understand things," I say. "And people. I also like to visit other worlds."

"Don't like the one you're in?"

"Not always, no."

"Hmm." He huffs as he rests an elbow on one of the Moleskine stacks on his desk. "So the misanthrope and the child have something in common."

Suddenly, his face clouds over like the sky before a summer rain. It takes me a moment, but I work up the courage. "I told you why I read," I say. "So why do you write?"

He scratches his head, pauses. "I write to prove that I can, and to exorcise my demons. My name will live in infamy the way the names of all those writers in my library do—*in perpetuum*."

"Meaning?"

"Forever," he replies.

"But you're already a very famous writer. Isn't that enough?"

His arms cross against his spindly chest. "Has anyone ever told you that you have a disturbingly acute ability to rub salt in a wound?"

"My gran says that must be done to clean it."

"Hmm. She's said the very same thing to me," he replies. "They don't know you're in here, do they? Your grandmother and my wife?"

I shake my head.

"They won't like it. The Great Writer is not to be disturbed. He's mercurial. Unpredictable. An angry, middle-aged, newly teetotaling creative tyrant with a penchant to fly off the handle for no good reason. Furthermore, he's busy redefining the mystery genre for the contemporary age."

"So you're writing a new book?"

"Of course I am. What on earth do you think all these Moleskines are for?" He grabs one from the looming pile, strides my way, and places it in my hands.

I gingerly open the notebook to a random page. It's filled with messy, smudged scrawl. I focus on the words, but I can't make head or tails of what's written. It's either penned in another language or written in some kind of code I can't decipher.

Before I can ask about this, he snatches the notebook from my hands, slams it shut, and places it back on the teetering stack.

"It's not easy, you know," he says. "To conceive a masterpiece, a book that withstands the test of time." His voice has lost all its growl and bite. He suddenly resembles a petulant, overgrown child. I'm reminded of the moment when I first laid eyes on the Fabergé in the parlor downstairs—a jewel-encrusted treasure concealed under centuries of grime, and yet I saw it for what it was.

"It's a matter of polish," I say. "With most things, especially masterpieces, it's about removing the tarnish to reveal the shine."

He stares at me through narrowed eyes. He takes two loping steps my way, then crouches to meet me at eye level. He's an arm's length away, and yet I'm not afraid. Not anymore. I see him for what he is. He's not a troll or a monster. He's just a man.

"Are you a child philosopher?" he asks. "A court jester? The palace fool? She who can say what others don't dare to?"

"Gran says I have wisdom beyond my years."

"The maid who knows all. There's shine under her tarnish, too." He hoists himself to a stand. "You're welcome to visit me anytime, provided you don't get underfoot."

"Your feet aren't nearly as large or hairy as I imagined they'd be," I reply. "Mr. Grimthorpe, may I ask you one more question?"

"Ms. Pip, you may."

"Where is the woman in the blue kerchief and gloves? Your personal secretary."

"In her office, doing my bidding," he says.

"Does she type up your Moleskines? I always hear someone typing."

"Naturally," he replies.

"And is that all she does?"

That's when it happens. His face clouds over again and his eyes turn to slits. "Who exactly do you think you are? Of course that's all she does! Now get *out!*" he roars.

I'm glued to my spot. I want to run, but it's as though I've been turned to stone.

"Did you hear me or are you an imbecile? I said get OUT!" he growls.

My feet untether from the floor, and I rush out of the room, the secret door slamming shut behind me and becoming a wall of books once more. I stand breathless and alone in the library, my heart pounding in my ears. I have no idea what I've done wrong or in what way I've caused offense.

"Molly?" I hear. It's Gran's singsong voice, echoing up the stairs.

"Sorry to interrupt your reading, but can you come downstairs? It's teatime!"

"Coming!" I call down.

I grab my book from the chaise longue and put it back on the far shelf. I take one last look at the shaft of light spilling onto the floor from the hidden study behind the wall. Then, with a sick feeling in the base of my stomach, I rush out of the library and hurry to the safety of tea and my gran.

CHAPTER 10

We're back in the hotel lobby—Mr. Snow, Angela, and me. No more fire alarm. Order is restored.

We're staring at an empty space on the reception desk, a void that less than an hour ago was filled with a single banker's box containing a first edition of Mr. Grimthorpe's most famous novel; his fountain pen; a black, monogrammed Moleskine; and a thank-you note to Ms. Sharpe.

"The box," I say. "It was right here . . . and now it's gone."

"You see?" Angela says. "You can't be too careful these days. There are criminals everywhere."

"There is nothing criminal about any of this," says Mr. Snow. "Clearly, Serena was in a rush. And she left with the box she came here for. Angela, there's no need to turn everything into a conspiracy."

Just then, Cheryl pushes through the revolving front doors of the Regency Grand, her sloppy mop knocking awkwardly against guests as she shuffles our way.

She stops when she reaches us and leans on her mop. "Damn fire alarms," she says. "We should get rid of them."

Mr. Snow removes his glasses and massages the bridge of his nose. "Cheryl, in a safe hotel, the guests sleep well." He's quoting directly from *A Maid's Guide & Handbook,* and to hear him repeat my words fills me with overweening pride. But Cheryl's eyes roll so far back into her head, it's a wonder she doesn't choke on them.

"Where's Grimthorpe's little lady?" she asks.

"That is not how we address guests in this hotel," Mr. Snow replies. "And shouldn't you be upstairs cleaning guest rooms? I have no idea what you're doing in the lobby at all."

"The same goes for Lily," I say. "As her temporary supervisor, you should be looking out for her. I don't know why she was here earlier."

"She wasn't," Cheryl insists.

"She was. Right by the stairs." I point to the now-empty spot by the staircase where Lily stood with her duster.

"Hmm," says Angela. "Right by the lever for the fire alarm."

Mr. Snow claps his hands together. "All right. That's enough. Doesn't anyone in this hotel have a job to do? Off you go. Molly, you're to assist Angela at the Social, and as I assured you, it's just for today."

Cheryl smirks, then drags her sloppy mop toward the elevators while Angela and I head to the Social Bar & Grill.

Once we're out of earshot, Angela grabs me by the shoulders and rather brusquely tucks us both under an alcove.

"What on earth did you do that for?" I ask.

"Molly, I need to tell you something," she says, as she whisks stray strands of hair away from her wide, round eyes. "We're not as short-staffed as I said. I needed to get you away, to warn you. You're in trouble, do you understand? We *all* are."

"What are you talking about?" I ask.

"I heard that detective speaking to her officers yesterday. They think there was foul play involved in Mr. Grimthorpe's death. They interviewed the kitchen staff last night and the Social staff, too. They've put together a list of potential suspects even before they've gotten the autopsy results. They were naming names."

"Mine?" I ask.

"Uh-huh," she replies.

"Did they name anyone else?" I ask, afraid to hear the answer.

"Your delicate flower," she answers. "Lily."

My eyesight starts to blur. It's always like this—whenever living proves too much to handle, a dark veil is thrown over me, removing me from the present.

"Molly!" Angela says as she shakes my shoulders. "Don't you dare pass out on me now. Don't worry. I've got a plan."

"A plan?" I say to the triplicates of Angela swaying before my eyes.

"To stay one step ahead. I'm telling you, I've been preparing for this for my entire life."

Truly, I haven't a clue what she's talking about, but at least the world has stopped spinning for the time being. "What have you been preparing for?" I ask.

"Murder. Crime. Suspects, motives, and alibis." She shakes her head as if this is the most obvious statement in the world. "Sometimes bad shit happens for a good reason, Molls, you know what I mean?"

"I do," I say. "My gran used to say the same thing . . . minus the fecal expletive."

"Molly, I'm a bartender. People tell me everything. And what they don't tell me, I overhear anyhow. You know those crazy cat ladies, the number-one fans who've been stalking Mr. G?"

"The LAMBS," I say. "And they're not cat ladies—well, not all of them—they're book ladies, aficionados of mystery."

"Whatever. They'll be at the Social for breakfast any minute, and if anyone knows the truth about what happened to Grimthorpe, it's them. They've been stalking him ever since they got here."

"So?" I reply. "What exactly are we supposed to do? Interrogate them over breakfast?"

"Yes. Well, kind of. *You* are going to interrogate them over breakfast. It's all set up."

"Angela," I say. "Have you lost your mind?"

"I haven't." Angela sighs. "Look, you gotta trust me. Yesterday, a man died unexpectedly in our hotel. Shit keeps disappearing around here, and just now, Snow was getting googly eyes around Grimthorpe's personal secretary . . . though I'm not so sure she's really a secretary, if you know what I mean."

"For the record," I say, "I have absolutely no idea what you mean."

"Never mind. Remember yesterday when you were outside the tearoom with the detective?"

"Yes."

"I poked my head out of the Social and saw you. And when the LAMBS showed up for a drink late last night, I told them something."

For once, Angela goes silent. It's so out of character it qualifies as a minor miracle. "What did you tell them?" I ask.

"I kinda said that you're doing a job in the hotel . . . incognito . . . as a maid. I kinda maybe suggested you've been working undercover as extra protection for Mr. Grimthorpe. I may have also said you work with Detective Stark and that you're actually a detective. An undercover one."

"You didn't say that. Please tell me you didn't."

"I did," Angela replies, her mouth turning upward into a smile so incongruous with the situation that it makes me want to scream.

"You lied. About me!" I say.

"For your own good, Molly. This way, we can team up."

"I'm not up for this particular partnership," I say.

"Why not? We need to find the real murderer before Stark pins this death on one of us workers. You of all people know how inept the cops are," she pleads. "They say they want justice, but do they really? They jump to the wrong conclusion and blame people like us all the time."

"This is ridiculous, a harebrained scheme that will undo us both," I say.

"Molly," Angela replies as she wags a finger in my face. "I may be an amateur, but make no mistake: I'm a kick-ass sleuth. I've always been good at putting two and two together when others can't. If we work together, we'll outdetect that stuck-up Stark and her squadron of goons. Also, now that the LAMBS know you're working undercover, they'll tell you everything. Just trust me, okay?"

Before I can respond, something at the other end of the lobby catches Angela's eye. "Uh-oh," she says. "They're early."

Coming the other way are two familiar-looking ladies led by the tall, curly-haired, flag-carrying leader of the LAMBS. The trio is heading straight for the Social.

"Yoo-hoo!" we hear before I can say another word. The president of the LAMBS is waving her red flag at us. "Detective, please join us for breakfast."

I want to correct her, to tell her exactly what I am and what I'm not, but Angela's nails are digging so deep into my arm that I cannot form words.

"How sweet of you to invite Molly to join you," Angela says as they approach. "We'll walk over with you."

"Oh, we're happy to cooperate," says the flag-bearing leader. "It's our solemn duty to J.D. We want to help you and . . . the detective," she whispers while pointing at me.

"I'm just a maid," I say. "That's all I am."

"Of course," says the president, her gray curls bouncing up and down as she nods.

"Absolutely," says another one of the LAMBS, the tiniest of the three, the one with the bright fuchsia highlights. "You're doing a marvelous job of keeping a low profile. I saw you cleaning my hotel room just the other day. I'm amazed at the lengths to which you detectives will go just to stay undercover. It's really impressive."

"I agree," says the third gray-haired lady, who—much to my horror—is wearing the same lumpy brown sweater she wore yesterday, still covered in cat hair.

And so it is that despite repeated protests and further attempts to clarify who I am, I find myself sitting down for breakfast at the Social with a gaggle of LAMBS, who believe me to be something I most definitely am not.

"You four can take that table right there," Angela says once we enter the restaurant. She points to a free table closest to the bar. "This way, I can look after you myself." She grabs some menus from the bar top and plops them on our table.

"Allow me," the woman in the brown sweater says as she pulls out my chair and beckons me to sit. "I'm Beulah, by the way," she announces as she takes a seat beside me. "Beulah Barnes, J. D. Grimthorpe's biographer."

"*Unauthorized* biographer," the flag-bearing leader of the LAMBS corrects as she settles into a chair across from me. "And I'm Gladys, Chief Literary Officer and President of the LAMBS. The little flaming-pink-haired one here is Birdy, Official Treasurer. The rest of the LAMBS are right over there—they're the early risers." Across the restaurant, numerous pairs of eyes size me up from afar.

"I'll grab you all coffees," Angela says.

"Tea for me," I say.

"Back in a jiffy," Angela replies. Then to me she only whispers,

"While I'm gone, Molly, *ask questions*. Lots of them. Remember, that's why you're here."

She winks, then rushes off. The three women are staring at me, leaving me at a complete loss about what to say. A question pops into my head. "I guess I'm wondering why it is you're still here," I say. "In the hotel, I mean. It's not as though there will be book events, not after what happened yesterday."

"When there's joy, we celebrate together. When there's grief, we grieve together," says the president of the LAMBS.

All three nod in unison.

"Also," says Beulah, "we crave answers about J.D. as much as you do. It will be a ghastly biographical footnote if it turns out to be . . ."

"Murder," Birdy squeaks, finishing Beulah's sentence. This is the only word the tiny woman has spoken since we sat down.

Angela appears with three coffees and my tea. She places them down on the table. "Ready to order?" she asks.

The LAMBS order identically—Le Grand Oeuf, the biggest breakfast on the menu.

"What will you have, Molly?" Angela asks.

"Nothing," I reply.

"She's on the job," Angela explains.

"Very professional," says Gladys the president. "We do have a question for you, Molly. Have you figured out what Mr. Grimthorpe was going to announce yesterday during his big event?"

"We have not," Angela replies. "I mean, *the authorities* haven't," she says as she points at me. "But we'd love to hear your theories."

"Oh no, here we go," says Beulah.

"You've stumbled upon a matter of great contention," Gladys says as she stirs a heaping spoonful of sugar into her coffee.

"We don't always agree," Beulah adds as she picks cat hair off her sizable bosom, sending it flying into the air above our table.

"My theory," Gladys offers, "is that J.D. was going to announce a sequel to his biggest bestseller."

"*The Maid in the Mansion*, 2.0," Birdy chimes in. "Do you know that as of yesterday, the auction price for a first edition of that book has soared to a whopping five figures?"

"Collectors," Beulah huffs through a halo of fur. "Such morbid vultures."

"Aren't you all collectors?" Angela asks.

"We are much more than that. To be clear," Gladys says, "we are researchers who take pride in what we study. We have not now, nor have we *ever*, sought to profit from J. D. Grimthorpe."

"That's right," Beulah adds. "Our mandate has always been to promote his *oeuvre*."

"I'll go place your orders now," Angela says. She turns and heads to the bar, leaving me dreadfully alone.

Diminutive Birdy leans in to speak. She is so small her head looks like a pink grapefruit hovering above the edge of the table. "We were wondering if you've considered that J.D.'s novels might contain clues. His biggest bestseller is about a novelist who is holed up in his mansion completing his greatest book ever. But someone—I won't reveal who—is out to kill."

"It was the maid," Beulah says. "She was the killer, working right in that mansion all along, and yet she seemed so innocent."

"For the love of good writing, there she goes again! Spoiler alert," Birdy says.

Gladys's gray curls shake in frustration. "How many times have we told you, Beulah? You know our policy."

Birdy raises a finger in the air as though conducting an orchestra. "The LAMBS shalt not spoil the ending of a whodunit for any mystery reader," she says. "It's our cardinal rule."

Beulah sighs, then fixes me with her apathetic gaze. "There are two twists in that book. I just gave away one. I swear, some readers read only for the twists. But there's more than that to J.D.'s novels. Any fool would be able to see as much," she says, practically spitting the words at her fellow LAMBS. Then she turns her attention to me. "I don't suppose you've read *The Maid in the Mansion*, have you?"

My words catch in my mouth. I feel like a fish out of water, gasping for oxygen.

"Molly?" Gladys asks. "Are you all right?"

"I . . . I have not read the novel," I say. "I do know its plot, though. I know it too well." A writer in a hollow, lifeless mansion kills his wife. He thinks he's found a way to get away with it, but he's wrong. The maid saw everything, and she exacts her revenge, killing him the same way he killed his wife, and then making his body disappear.

"Gladys is certain that J.D. arranged yesterday's event to announce a sequel to that book," Birdy offers.

"And Birdy is convinced that J.D.'s wife was the reason he was such a recluse," Gladys says. "Mrs. Grimthorpe died a few years ago, and Birdy believes yesterday's announcement was going to be about his new love interest."

"Mrs. Grimthorpe is dead?" I ask.

"Yes," says Birdy. "Which means there was nothing stopping the man from pursuing new love," she adds with a faraway look in her eyes.

"Stupidest theory I've ever heard," Beulah says. "You couldn't be more off base if you tried."

Gladys shakes her curly head. "Beulah doesn't like that theory because she's harbored a crush on J.D. for ages."

"Ridiculous," Beulah huffs. "If anyone's in love with him, it's Birdy. And neither of you knows the first thing about scholarship, about the fine art of uncovering clues," Beulah adds. "As J.D.'s biographer, I know more about him than you two ever will."

"Beulah claims to have uncovered hidden truths about J.D., but she refuses to enlighten us with proof or details, which is a source of—"

"Tension," Birdy offers as she smooths her fuchsia hair.

"Frustration," Gladys adds, punctuating this with a wave of her red flag.

"All will be revealed when I publish my official biography," Beulah says.

"*Unofficial*," Gladys corrects.

"You don't need permission from the dead," Beulah replies.

"But you have no one to corroborate your findings, which is your professional duty," Birdy notes. "She'd been petitioning J.D. ceaselessly to hire her officially. This has been her life's work for almost two decades."

"J.D. is—was—reticent to reveal certain sensitive details about himself," Beulah says. "That's understandable. We've had exchanges over the years, you know."

"Have you?" Birdy asks. "Have you really?"

"One day, the truth will come out," Beulah replies.

"Why not today?" I ask. Three dagger-eyed gazes turn my way. "In my experience," I say, "secrets have a way of punishing those who keep them."

"It's irresponsible to posit theories without absolute proof," Beulah replies.

"Your breakfasts." Angela arrives at our table with plates balanced precariously on both arms. She puts down the plates. Beulah and Gladys dig into their meals immediately. Birdy takes dainty bites as she stares off into space. I have to wonder, are all three of these women smitten with the famous writer? How that's possible is beyond me, but Gran always said, *When love is blind, frogs resemble princes.* Still, whatever tension existed amongst the trio moments ago has dissipated with the arrival of food.

I take this moment of calm to stir some milk into my cooling tea. I focus on the dull clank of the stainless-steel spoon against the ordinary ceramic cup. Only at the Social do we use such mundane cutlery, which lacks the pleasing tinkle of Regency Grand silver against proper porcelain.

Angela stands beside me with her hands on her hips, looking from one lady to the next as they eat their breakfasts without so much as a word.

Angela leans in to whisper in my ear. "Do you hear that?" she asks.

"Hear what?" I whisper back.

"The silence," she says. "The Silence of the LAMBS."

CHAPTER 11

Before

I'm swinging my legs back and forth under our worn-out breakfast table as I chew each bite of my breakfast twenty times because (a) it aids with digestion, (b) it's delicious, and (c) there are children in the world who don't eat every day, so best be thankful for every single bite.

It's now been a week since Mr. Grimthorpe's tirade, and from time to time I've heard his telltale footfalls beyond the fourth wall, but I haven't seen him in the flesh. I can't stop thinking about him, though. Why does a man who has so much seem so unhappy? And what did I do to anger him so? Will I ever see him again?

The great physicists are right—the universe *is* expanding, or at least mine is. The proof is in the number of new questions I have for Gran every single day. Last night, I lay awake in my bed searching for answers yet again. It wasn't like this before, when I was going to school every day. Then, my mind was imprisoned, a caged tiger, stunted and pacing restlessly behind bars. I couldn't think at all, much less question things. But since visiting the Grimthorpe mansion, my imagination is unfettered, my curiosity insatiable.

Sitting at our table, legs dangling, I come to an important realization—that education is not something that happens exclusively in classrooms, that education is a state of mind. I launch into my new set of queries with a dogged enthusiasm that must have exhausted my gran, not that she ever showed so much as an iota of frustration. She always treated me like an adult and spoke to me as though I were one. Did she know that one day I would remember our conversations, that I would replay them over and over in my mind, uncovering layer after layer of her wisdom?

"Gran, is it possible to be rich and poor at the same time?" I ask as I glug milky tea and prepare for a new bite.

"It most certainly is," she replies. "One can be rich in love and poor in worldly goods."

"Or one can be poor in health and rich in wealth," I add.

"Touché." She butters her crumpet with artful precision until her knife is wiped clean.

"Gran, how did the Grimthorpes get so rich?"

"When Mr. Grimthorpe became a bestselling writer, he earned a small fortune," she replies. She raises her crumpet but pauses before taking a bite. "However, he was rich even before his books hit it big. His grandfather was a wealthy investor and so was his father."

In my mind's eye, I try to picture Mr. Grimthorpe's father, but all I can conjure is the mustachioed banker from my Monopoly game board.

"Do you think his family was kind to him?" I ask.

"I don't know, Molly, but somehow I doubt it. What I do know is that Mr. Grimthorpe was an only child and that both his parents considered him a failure."

"Did he fail at school like I did?"

"He was brilliant at school. And for the record, Molly, you've never failed in my eyes. But as for Mr. Grimthorpe, all he ever wanted was to write rather than run the family investment business. And a creative temperament was considered a curse to his family in those days. Mr. Grimthorpe inherited this mansion, alongside considerable wealth, when his parents died. But he also inherited a great deal of baggage, Molly, the emotional kind, which he carries to this very day. He may be Old Money, but that hasn't brought him much happiness."

A thought occurs to me. "Gran, if the Grimthorpes are Old Money, does that make us New Money?" I ask.

She laughs out loud, but I know she's laughing with me, not at me. "My dear, we are No Money."

Of course, I know that. I know it from the way we cut coupons and darn our socks. I know it from the rarity of clotted cream, from having a landlord who demands the rent, a public library we have to walk to rather than a private one in our home, and from the mismatched cutlery we buy from thrift stores rather than have handed down to us through generations.

It's time to ask the question I most want to ask, the one that's been burning a hole in my brain for days. "Gran, if Mr. Grimthorpe is such a genius, why does he hide himself away in the mansion?"

She cocks her head and looks at me in a funny way that I don't quite understand. "Never judge a man until you've walked a mile in his shoes," she says. "Have you heard that one before?"

"I have," I say, "but I don't see how it applies. Mr. Grimthorpe wears slippers, not shoes."

"It applies to him nonetheless. And to you, my dear," she says, as she grazes my cheek with her palm. "It means you can't really know someone without experiencing all the things they have lived through. Make no mistake, Mr. Grimthorpe has reckoned with demons. He's recovered now, but the darkness took over during his illness."

"He was ill?"

"He was," she replies. "Terribly so. And his affliction turned him into a monster for a time. But we survived all that. We made it through. Mrs. Grimthorpe and I helped him at the mansion, and he improved. He got clean, Molly, do you understand what I mean by that?"

I imagine sharp-winged gargoyles surrounding Mr. Grimthorpe as Gran and Mrs. Grimthorpe fend them off. "How did you shoo the demons away?" I ask.

"With patience and persistence," Gran replies. "Mrs. Grimthorpe asked me to sit for hours by her husband's bedside and read to him, which I did. It distracted him from the worst of his symptoms. I also served him tea, Molly, which was certainly not his beverage of choice at the time," she says. "Tea is an amazing drink. I tell you, it can cure almost anything."

"But what if Mr. Grimthorpe gets sick again?" I ask. "What if his illness returns?"

"There's no need to worry. He's recovered. And Mrs. Grimthorpe and I have forgiven him for any past mistakes made under the influence. But as a result of those dark times, he keeps to himself. Shame is the scar the demons leave behind. You remember that, Molly," Gran says.

I look down at my half-eaten crumpet on the table. A moment ago, it looked so appealing, but it now appears congealed and grotesque on my plate.

"Are you finished with your breakfast?" Gran asks.

I nod.

"Good. It's time," Gran says as she puts a warm hand over mine. "To the mansion we go."

* * *

All morning long, I work in the silver pantry while Gran cooks and cleans in the kitchen. She sings like a sparrow just outside the pantry door. Mrs. Grimthorpe is elsewhere, at least for now, which is probably why Gran is singing.

With each passing day, I'm becoming more skilled at using the lye solution and much less elbow grease to remove the tarnish on the silver. Today, I have elected to clean silver in the morning and read in the afternoon. I have completed buffing a full tea service, several serving trays, and an entire set of cutlery, right down to the final silver spoon, which I'm holding in front of my face. I study my image in the bowl, contorted and reversed, a warped world turned on its head like everything in the Grimthorpe mansion.

Someone appears upside down behind me in the bowl of the silver spoon—it's Mrs. Grimthorpe, her frown turned into an incongruous smile. I face her as she surveys the newly polished wares on the table.

She tips her chin in begrudging approval. "You're dismissed," she says. "You may read your book in the library."

I curtsy and leave the room, joining Gran in the kitchen, where she's removing freshly baked scones from the oven.

"You're doing a fine job," Gran whispers. "Even Her Ladyship can't deny it. Go on up, then. I'll call you down later for tea."

I head to the front of the mansion and creep up the main stairs. I pause at the landing on the second floor, looking down the long damask corridor to the library at the end. Mr. Grimthorpe is not a troll—I know this now—and yet when I met him face-to-face a week ago, he raged and roared at the end of our encounter. He called me a terrible name and ordered me away. I still don't know what I did wrong, but then again, I never do until it's too late. I'm reminded of that time at school when I corrected a word Ms. Cripps misspelled on her blackboard, for which I was ordered to stand in the corner of the classroom, remaining there for so long that shame found its exit, streaming hotly down my legs.

Now, I tiptoe my way to the threshold of the library and pause. I don't enter, not yet. Instead, I look at the forbidden wall of books and the crack by the floor—dark, no signs of life on the other side.

I walk over to the shelf and remove *Great Expectations*, returning to my spot on the chaise longue to crack open the book. Over the last while, I've made good progress, and although I don't know that I fully understand everything about Pip, I'm fascinated by Miss Havisham, the old and withered bride with a singular mission in life—to torment a boy with a good heart. Somehow this is more frightening than anything I've ever read, so why is it that I keep turning the pages?

Click. A tiny sound, but it echoes in the vaulted silence of the high-ceilinged library.

Light through the crack in the wall spills onto the library floor.

Footfalls, the swish of slippers.

For the first time in days, there are signs of life beyond the forbidden fourth wall.

My eye is on the Oxford dictionary, which juts out past the other spines. And just like that, the wall of books opens to reveal Mr. Grimthorpe standing in the doorway looking rumpled and slack, his shoulders slumped. I clutch my book to my chest.

Then the strangest thing happens.

"I am sorry," Mr. Grimthorpe says.

I can hardly believe my ears. Is that an apology from the mouth of an adult man? The concept is so foreign that he might as well be speaking in tongues. I have to shake my head back and forth just to be certain I'm hearing correctly.

"My behavior the other day was inexcusable," he says. "I raged like an idiot. I called you a name that in retrospect refers more to myself than it does to you, for I am the true imbecile, the vain king with a title to nothing. The only explanation I can offer for my irrational lunacy is my personal ailment, one of its lingering symptoms being an unhealthy penchant for lashing out against the innocent. Please accept my apology."

I don't quite follow what he's saying, but his face is lined with pain. I make an important discovery in that moment: it doesn't matter if you understand another person's pain because their injury is real nonetheless.

"I forgive you, Mr. Grimthorpe," I say. "But do you know what 'sorry' means?"

"Enlighten me," he replies.

"It means you promise never to make the same mistake again."

He sighs and walks over to his desk, plopping himself down in his chair. "I'll never make that error again, though I can't be certain I won't make others. The truth is, Pip, I have lost all my mirth, if indeed I ever had any."

"Mirth?" I ask as I hang back in the doorway.

"Meaning: joy, contentment, happiness," he offers. "I used to find it at the bottom of a bottle, but I've given that up. And a few other things besides. Where mirth lives now, I do not know. Sometimes I'm convinced I'll find it when I reach the end of my next novel, but I'm contending with a new and even more severe affliction."

"Meaning: illness?"

"Yes. An affliction peculiar to writers known as writer's block. I find myself unable to complete my current work. It eludes me in every way, and yet if I knew how to finish it, I'm certain it would get me what I want."

"Which is?"

"Further infamy. Notoriety. A place on bookshelves for centuries to come. An end to my restlessness, a return of my mirth."

I carefully step forward into his study, pausing a safe arm's length away from his desk and from the teetering piles of mono-grammed black Moleskines.

"May I ask what your book is about?"

He leans forward. "It's a mystery. A writer is being held captive in his home by his wife. He has two choices: kill her or kill himself."

"Which does he choose?" I ask.

"He kills his wife. But then he has a new problem."

"Which is?"

"He must make her body disappear or face murder charges and a new form of imprisonment, this time in a jail rather than in the relative comfort of his own home."

I observe the spindly man sitting in front of me, with his errant hair and the eyes of a wild stallion. What if this isn't make-believe? The thought makes my stomach curdle and churn.

"Are you planning to kill Mrs. Grimthorpe?" I ask.

He throws his head back and laughs uproariously at my question.

"Why are you laughing?" I ask.

"Because it's absurd. I have no intentions of killing my wife. There'd be no point. She's been as good as dead for at least twenty years, and it's my fault. That long-suffering woman has spent her entire adult life protecting my reputation and seeing to my health and well-being. I assure you, I've not made any of it easy. Let's just say there are more faithful husbands in the world, but there are few wives quite as loyal as she."

"I don't understand," I say.

"Never mind. The point is I need a resolution to my novel. A dénouement. A twist. Maybe two. And I need to make that imagi-nary body disappear."

"Lye," I say.

"Lie about what?" he asks.

"Not that kind of lie," I say. "Lye as in the chemical. It burns. Use enough of it, and I suppose you could make an entire body disappear."

He stands and paces. He stops in his tracks, his icy blue eyes drilling into mine. "How do you know this?" he asks.

"There once was a maid," I say. "She was so unhappy with her master that she dissolved his hands in lye."

His eyes go wide. "Who told you this?"

"I made it up, kind of. Gran told me a true story, but then I changed it just now. What do you call it when there's truth in a story but it's not a fact?" I ask.

His face morphs. All the hard lines soften. All the pain dissolves. For the first time ever, he looks giddy and happy and light.

"A novel," he replies. "You call it a novel."

CHAPTER 12

I've excused myself from my breakfast with the LAMBS and am leaving the Social when Angela stops me at the front of the restaurant.

"Molly, you were amazing!" she says. "Those ladies totally believed you were a detective, bought it hook, line, and sinker!"

"That was humiliating and deceitful," I say. "And I'm not sure I uncovered anything of value."

"Sometimes what sounds like nothing at first becomes the key to unlocking the mystery. You just have to know how to piece things together."

"I'm not interested in piecing things together, Angela. I'm interested in doing my job—my job as a maid," I say.

"Okay," Angela replies. "Don't bust a gasket. Go be a maid. Ignore the shite-fest going on all around you. But, Molls, be careful, okay? And if you hear or see anything suspicious, will you let me know?"

"Yes," I say. "May I go now?"

I don't wait for a response. I simply march my way out of the restaurant and head for the lobby, where Mr. Snow spots me and beckons me to the reception desk. "Where are you going, Molly?"

"Angela's done with me," I say. "And vice versa. I'm going back to my real job now if that's all right with you."

"Very well," says Mr. Snow. "The maids upstairs will be happy to see you."

I make my way to the back staircase and head to the fourth floor. My stomach is turned inside out. I know exactly why I'm so distressed. During breakfast with the LAMBS, I pretended to be something I'm not, and even though Gran has no eyes to see it, I know my behavior would not make her proud. I'm a fraud and a hypocrite, two things she never taught me to be. Why didn't I just speak up and tell the truth? Why didn't I insist to the LAMBS that I'm just an ordinary maid?

As I reach the fourth floor, I find Sunshine in the hallway with her trolley and an overflowing bag of laundry.

"Oh, Molly," she says the moment she lays eyes on me. "Please tell me you're back to work with us. We can't keep up. New Boss Lady is in the staff lounge 'taking a load off,' and Lily—well, let's just say I don't know what's going on with her today. We're exhausted. Look at Sunitha."

Sunitha appears from the guest room next door, dragging a laundry bag full of soiled sheets behind her. She's glazed over like a frosted tea cake melting in the sun.

"The dream of clean works best as a team," I say. "Remember?"

"The team is nonexistent right now. Molly, something's up with Lily. I know yesterday was a shock, but she's acting stranger than usual and won't say what's wrong. Plus, she keeps disappearing. When we were cleaning a room earlier, I turned around to ask for paper towels, and poof! She was gone. Just like that."

"Where is she now?" I ask.

"Down there," Sunshine says with a nod down the hallway.

"Thank you," I say as I walk to the end of the corridor and find a door propped open with a trolley. Lily's inside, standing stock-still by the window with a bottle of cleaning spray in one hand and a cloth in the other.

"Lily?" I say, and she jumps halfway out of her skin. "Are you all right?"

She stares at me in a way that does not match any expression I have ever collected in my mental catalogue of human behaviors. "Who's the boss?" she asks, her voice a shaky whisper.

"What do you mean?" I reply.

"Is it Cheryl or you?"

"Today, Cheryl is Head Maid. Tomorrow things will return to normal. Is that acceptable?"

She shrugs.

"Lily, if ever you have a problem, you can come to me."

"Can I?" she asks. "Is that how it works?"

"Of course that's how it works," I say.

"But loose lips sink ships. You said so yourself when you hired me. 'Discretion is paramount at the Regency Grand.'"

"Lily, you're the last person I would ever accuse of indiscretion," I say. "It's taken me weeks to get you to speak at all. Please don't go mute on me now."

"I'm trying. But . . . it's not easy. I'm counting on this job, Molly. I got fired once before, and I can't have it happen again."

This is the first time she's mentioned a previous job loss, and the news comes as quite a shock. I swallow my surprise and gently ask, "What happened?"

"I was a cashier in a grocery store before this," Lily says.

"I remember," I say. "You had that on your résumé."

"But what I didn't tell you is that when I reported a theft by another cashier, it was blamed on me, and I was fired. I figured if I told you, you'd never hire me. And now, I'm scared to say anything at all. Molly, who should I trust?"

"Me," I say. "You're supposed to trust me." As I look at Lily, it's like seeing my old self in a mirror. When I started at the hotel, I trusted no one, and there are times to this day when that unsettling feeling returns.

"Molly, one day you're my boss, and the next day you're not," Lily explains. "And a man I served tea died in the tearoom." She turns away from me to obliterate some smudgy fingerprints on the window.

"Lily," I say. "If you're worried about a murderer in this hotel, I can tell you with complete sincerity there's no reason to believe there is one." My stomach does a flip-flop, because what I'm saying is not an irrefutable fact.

Lily turns and stares at me, her eyes expressionless and dull. "The maid is always to blame," she says, then returns to cleaning without another word.

I can't help it. I'm feeling quite exasperated by this conversation, and I sigh out loud. Honest to goodness, I am trying my best, but I don't know how to help this girl. It occurs to me that perhaps the best way is without words, by working with her side by side.

I tackle the bed in silence, removing the dirty sheets and putting on new ones. *A tidy bed calms the head,* I think to myself. But it's not working. My head is nowhere near calm, and it's clear that Lily is in her own state of dishevelment.

I take the soiled sheets over to her trolley and am about to bag them when I notice something in her recycling bin—a folded banker's box with the name *Serena* written clearly in black marker on the lid. It's the box that disappeared during the fire alarm yesterday.

"Lily," I say.

She turns to face me.

"Did you put this box in your trolley?" I ask.

She shakes her head.

"Do you know who did?"

She shakes her head again, then stares at me with those dark, glassy eyes.

"Tell me, Lily. I implore you."

She has only one thing to say: "Loose lips sink ships."

My nerves are frayed. As I help Lily clean Room 429, I feel desperately unsettled. I know the true source of my malaise. It is not really Lily, though of course I'm concerned about her. It's not even Mr. Grimthorpe's death or the strange occurrences in the hotel. It's the fact that I've become embroiled in a lie, and the very notion shakes me to the core of my being.

Tell a lie once and your truth becomes questionable. Gran's voice keeps echoing in my head, and I can't make it stop.

"Lily," I say. "It's lunch hour. Time for a break."

She nods, puts down her spray bottle, and quickly leaves the room.

I suddenly know what I have to do, and there's not a moment to lose.

I leave the room in a state of imperfection and hurry down to the lobby. I exit the hotel, making my way to the bottom of the plush, red-carpeted stairs. Mr. Preston spots me and stops me.

"Molly," he says. "Where are you off to in such a rush?"

"An errand," I explain. "I'll be back later."

"I've got one to run myself," he says. "Now, Molly, about that dinner we were going to have this Sunday, I was thinking—"

"Mr. Preston," I say, interrupting. "Can our dinner please wait until Juan Manuel returns? I'm barely managing as it is, and I just don't think I can handle anything more right now."

Mr. Preston's face falls like a cake taken out of the oven too soon, but before he can say anything else, some businessmen with luggage in tow wave him down. He jumps to their service while I make my hasty retreat.

I head toward the next street over. I walk briskly, turning left, then right, then left again. I arrive at the police station in exactly fifteen minutes. I take a moment to survey the building from across the street—a gray, brutalist block with tinted windows.

I cross the busy street and enter through the main doors into the police reception area.

A blond woman with long purple nails greets me. "Yes?" she says.

"I'm here to see a detective," I explain, trying to keep my voice steady.

"Complaint? Tip-off? Or are you turning yourself in?" the woman asks.

"The latter," I say.

She pauses. "You know 'the latter' means the last thing I said, right?"

"Yes," I reply. "I have a flair for vocabulary."

She of the Purple Talons stares at me with strange, unreadable eyes.

"It's Detective Stark I must speak with," I say. "She knows me. I'm a maid at the hotel where Mr. Grimthorpe dropped dead."

The woman stands then, very slowly. Still facing me, she opens a door behind her and yells down the corridor in a tremulous voice, "Detective Stark! Come quickly! Please?!"

She doesn't go back to her desk as I expect her to do. Rather, she just stands there, pressed up against the wall, eyeing me like I might steal something or pull a gun.

Heavy boots trudge down the hall, and then Stark, wearing all black as usual, is standing in the doorway. "Molly?" she says. "What the hell are you doing here?"

"She's turning herself in," Ms. Purple Talons whispers.

Detective Stark's eyebrows jolt up. "Come with me," she says.

I thank Ms. Talons, then follow the detective down a corridor to a room I've visited once before under circumstances I don't care to think about. The room is exactly as I remember it—with offensively bright fluorescent lights and covered in a layer of criminal filth and grime.

"Have a seat," Stark says, pointing to a dirty black chair in front of a smudged white table. I sit in the revolting chair. The detective takes a seat across from me.

I'm not exactly sure how to begin, since I've never confessed to a crime before, so I wait silently for some sort of cue. A red light flashes in the corner of the window behind the detective.

"Did you want a coffee?" Stark asks. "Would that make this easier?"

"It would not," I reply. Last time I was here, she brought me water, not tea, as I'd requested, and she delivered it to me in a squeaky, ear-offending Styrofoam cup. If that happens again, I don't think I'll be able to get my words out.

The detective stares at me. "Well," she says, "you said why you're here, so you might as well have out with it. You'll feel better after, I promise."

I take a deep breath, then exhale. "I couldn't live with the deception," I say. "I feel sick. It's eating me alive. I've been thinking about my gran and how disappointed she'd be if she knew what I'd done. Which she doesn't know. Because she's dead."

"You're doing the right thing now, Molly. And I'm ready for your confession," Stark replies.

"I've committed a crime," I say.

"Yes. I know. But you need to be more specific. You need to say out loud that you killed Mr. Grimthorpe, that you poisoned him."

"*What?*" I exclaim. I cannot believe my ears. "I did no such thing! What do you take me for, a murderer?"

"You said you're here to confess."

"To fraud, not murder!" I reply. "I impersonated an officer of the law, and I'm deeply remorseful. I tried to tell the truth about who I am, but the LAMBS wouldn't listen. Don't you see?"

"No, I don't, Molly," Stark says. "Because as usual you're not making sense. I don't know why that even surprises me anymore."

I take a moment to collect myself, then start from the beginning, explaining to Stark in minute detail how the LAMBS mistook me for a detective working incognito at the hotel and how despite my protests, they refused to believe the truth—that I'm really just a maid.

"So you see," I say as I come to my conclusion, "I committed identity fraud. And perhaps obstruction of justice, too. You can charge me now. I deserve it."

"Charge you?" the detective says. "Because a bunch of middle-aged book freaks mistook you for a detective?"

It's only then that what Detective Stark said earlier sinks in. "Wait," I say. "Was Mr. Grimthorpe poisoned?"

Detective Stark sighs. "We got the autopsy and the toxicology report. Ethylene glycol. In his tea. This isn't public knowledge yet, but you'd have found out soon enough since we're holding a press conference in an hour. Any idea how ethylene glycol got in his teacup, Molly?" Stark asks as she leans forward in a way that most certainly feels like a space invasion.

"How would I know how antifreeze got in his tea?" I reply.

Stark puts her elbows on the table in front of me. "I never said anything about antifreeze," she says.

"That's what ethylene glycol is," I explain. "Frankly, I'm shocked that an officer of your stature does not know this."

"God help me," says Stark as she brings her hands to her forehead. "Molly, I never told you ethylene glycol is antifreeze! And that's not exactly common knowledge, now, is it? Can you see how that makes me think you're Grimthorpe's killer?" She's squinting at me now in a manner that is most unbecoming.

"Do you take me for an imbecile?" I ask. "I'll have you know I'm quite knowledgeable about chemicals and poisons, and not just from *Columbo*. Angela once told me a true story about a woman who killed her first and then her second husband by baking common antifreeze into their scones. There was a made-for-TV movie about it—*Black Widows*, I think it was called. It's one of her favorites."

"Angela? Who's Angela?" Stark asks.

"The bartender at the Social," I reply. "The movie title is apropos, don't you think?"

Detective Stark crosses her arms. "What I think is that if you know so much about poisons, you know exactly why antifreeze was used to murder Mr. Grimthorpe."

"Indeed I do," I say. "Because it tastes sweet. Very sweet. You can hide it in almost anything."

"Exactly," Detective Stark replies. "And how did Mr. Grimthorpe take his tea, Molly?"

"With honey," I reply. "Lots of it."

"That's right!" says Stark in a gratingly singsong voice. "And who put the honey pot on his tea cart, Molly?"

"Me," I say with grave authority. I realize only after the word leaves my mouth that this could be misconstrued. "But I didn't poison Mr. Grimthorpe," I clarify. "I had no motive to do so."

"We found your prints all over his tea cart," Stark replies.

"Of course you did. And I'm sure you found Lily's, too."

Detective Stark sniffs but doesn't respond.

"I came here to confess to a crime you won't arrest me for only to discover you once again want to peg me for a murder I know nothing about. Detective Stark, if you're going to arrest me, then you better well have evidence that links me—without a shadow of a doubt—to the crime. You can't detain me without a motive, some evidence, and a weapon. And so far as I can tell, all you've got at the moment is the crime."

"So where is it, Molly?" Detective Stark asks. "Where's the goddamn honey pot? Did you keep it as some sort of sick trophy? Or did you throw it in a dumpster?"

"Why not check the hotel?" I ask. "If I'm daft enough to poison a famous man, leaving my fingerprints all over the tea cart, it stands to reason I left the honey pot right in my locker, too."

Stark guffaws. "Snow let me check your locker last night. Didn't find much."

I gasp out loud. "You went in my locker without my permission?"

"Are you serious?" the detective replies.

"Coming here was a terrible mistake," I say. "You'll never see me for what I am, no matter how hard I try. Are we done, Detective? May I go now?" I ask.

"I can't very well stop you, can I?" Detective Stark replies. "But I'll be watching your every move, Molly. I've got eyes in the hotel. I've got eyes everywhere."

Unless she's a dragonfly or a spider, this is patently ridiculous, but since it's clear the detective is more than a little enervated, I decide not to question her ocular exaggeration.

Instead, I say, "Goodbye, Detective." Then I curtsy deeply and leave.

* * *

It is only once I'm out of the station and back on the other side of the street that I start to breathe again, and as soon as I do, the gravity of the situation sinks in. Mr. Grimthorpe did not die of natural causes. He was murdered in cold blood. Someone poisoned him, and whoever did it is probably still in the hotel. I have to get back and tell Mr. Snow before the news becomes public.

I pick up my pace, rushing back as fast as my feet will carry me. I'm only a few blocks away when something across the street makes me stop in my tracks. I'm kitty-corner to the local pawnshop, the one with the big glass window display and the neon sign that blazes 24/7.

Mr. Preston is standing outside the shop. He's studying something in the display window. He saunters into the store, and I hear the chime of the doorbells as he disappears inside. This in itself is not remarkable—Mr. Preston, my friend, the hotel doorman, browsing the neighborhood pawnshop. That is not concerning at all.

The problem is what he held in his hands when he entered. That dark, wooden door and the single eye peeking through the keyhole—even from a distance, I could make out the cover design quite clearly.

It was a rare first-edition copy of *The Maid in the Mansion*, by J. D. Grimthorpe.

CHAPTER 13

Before

It has always been like this for me, me with my eye for details. I see one thing, but I miss another. I watch with care yet am somehow unaware of what others notice with relative ease.

In my mind's eye, I'm a child again, holding a report card that rates my social behaviors as EXTREMELY POOR and that officially declares me a FAILURE, and orders me to repeat my grade next year. I've been working alongside my gran at the mansion for nearly two weeks, and with each day that passes, I gain confidence in my abilities. But now, as I hold that report in my hands, my self-esteem evaporates in an instant.

I can't even look at Gran. My cheeks burn red from shame. I want to rip the paper in a million pieces, light it on fire, and reduce it to ash. But a part of me is curious, too—curious about how I'm different from my peers.

"Gran, what's it like to understand all social behaviors?" I ask.

She laughs. "Oh, Molly. No one, least of all me, understands *all* of them. Social interactions are complex. The more practice you get relating to others, the more you'll see how everything fits to-gether."

"Explain," I say.

Gran pauses to consider. "Sometimes it's what you can't see that gives something its shape and meaning," she says. "You'll suddenly be aware of what's never said out loud, and yet you'll know it's an essential part of the equation—the missing x—even if it's invisible, even if it's not actually there."

I try with all my might to make sense of what she's saying, but I can't. If something is missing, it's not there. If it's not there, there's nothing to see. I decide in that moment that it's hopeless, that *I'm* hopeless. I will never learn.

Gran crouches to meet me at eye level. "Don't take this report card to heart, Molly. You're not a failure. If anything is a failure, it's the system. This is just a silly piece of paper that refuses to quantify your strengths."

"Strengths?" I repeat.

"Yes. Strengths. You have plenty of them. You may miss certain niceties from time to time, but your heart and soul are in the right place."

My heart is on my left side. I know it because I can feel it when I place my hand on my chest, and according to my research at the library, I am anatomically correct. As for my soul, I don't know where it is. Maybe it's like the mysterious x in Gran's equation, something with a shape that's only revealed by what's around it.

"Since you've brought up social abilities," Gran says, "I keep meaning to mention that you don't need to say 'Yes, madam' quite so much in Mrs. Grimthorpe's presence, or in anyone's presence for that matter. It's fine to show respect, but when you overdo it, people might think you're obsequious."

"O-B-S-E-Q-U-I-O-U-S. Meaning: overly obedient."

"Yes, and servile. Someone lacking self-respect. And while

you're at it, when you want to know the meaning of words, you don't have to spell them out. I love your spelling bees, but not everyone does. Maybe that's something you can also do more sparingly?"

Gran approaches me then, and folds me into a hug, kissing the top of my head. "And Molly, just remember: no matter what, I'll always be proud of you. You have just as much right as anyone to carry your head high."

"Chin up, Buttercup," I say as I look up at Gran.

"That's my girl," she replies. "Molly, I'm going to run downstairs to collect the laundry. I'll fold it up and be back before you can say Jiminy Cricket."

She has three loads to fold today, and even if she had only one, for the time it would take her to fold everything, I could probably say Jiminy Cricket a thousand times. But I know Gran is using an expression. She doesn't intend it literally—meaning: precisely, strictly, exactly.

She opens the front door to leave, but then turns back. "If Mr. Rosso drops by, please give him the envelope I left on the kitchen table. And ask for the receipt, mind you. It's that time of the month again," she says with a weary look.

I know exactly what she means by "that time of the month." It means the first day of the month, which is when our rent is due. Mr. Rosso, with his big, bulbous nose and his matching belly, will be here any minute, pounding on the door, demanding what's his.

"Why is he called a landlord?" I ask my gran. "He does not behave like a lord."

"Doesn't he?" Gran replies. "He demands money for shoddy accommodations, expects deference for a lack of services, and covets property as if the entire world belongs to him. But give him the rent anyhow. After all, we want the lights to stay on. So be polite."

"I always am."

"Yes, you are," Gran says. She smiles and walks out the door, locking it behind her. I can hear her humming down the hallway all the way to the stairs.

Once she's gone, I crumple my report card into a satisfying ball and throw it in the kitchen garbage can.

It isn't long before I hear a knock on our door. "Coming!" I say as I grab a kitchen chair and make my way to the entrance. Gran always makes me look through the fish-eye peephole before I open sesame, so I position the chair, climb up, and peer out.

It's not Mr. Rosso. It's a young lady I don't recognize with jet-black hair and skittish eyes.

"Good day!" I call through the door. "Might I ask—who are you?"

"I'll tell you my name if you tell me yours," the young lady says from the other side of the door.

I pause to think about this, never taking my eye from the peephole.

"Gran says I'm not to tell my name to strangers. I'm also not supposed to open the door to them."

The woman shifts her weight from foot to foot as though she urgently needs the washroom. "I'm not a stranger," she says. "Your gran knows me well. And I know you. Her name is Flora, and your name is Molly. I've been here before, you know. You just don't remember because you were knee-high to a grasshopper, as your gran used to say."

This sounds reassuring, but I've read Ali Baba, so I know better than to open doors before sesame is said. "Prove that you've been here before," I demand.

She scratches her head. "Um, okay . . . Your grandmother's favorite teacup is the one with the cottage scene on it. She keeps it on the shelf by the stove in the kitchen."

She is absolutely, 100 percent right. And this is a detail only someone who has been in our apartment could know.

Still, I decide to exact another proof of truth. "How do you know my gran?" I ask.

"Oh," she says as she tries to look through the peephole. "Um, we used to work together?"

"Where?"

"At . . . um . . . that mansion. The Grimthorpe mansion."

"What did you do there?"

"What do you think? I was . . . a maid."

That settles it. I jump off the chair, turn the lock, and open sesame.

The young woman stands in front of me, staring down at me with wide eyes. Her face looks sunken and wan. She could use a bit more sunshine, and she's shaking as if she's cold, though it's not a cold day at all. I notice red marks up her arms. I know how she got them. We had bedbugs once, too. My legs were raw like that, a constellation of itchy connect-the-dots.

The young woman stares at me wordlessly.

"You're a friend of Gran's, you said?"

"Yeah." She nods vigorously.

She does not look like any friend of Gran's I've seen before. Gran's friends tend to have gray hair and glasses, just like Gran. They arrive with wool picked up from garage sales or freshly baked cookies they made themselves. But when I open the closet and take out the shoe cloth to clean the young lady's footwear, she takes it from my hand and knows just what to do. It's more proof that she's telling the truth—she most certainly has been here before.

She wipes the bottoms of her dirty, old sneakers and takes them off, placing them neatly on the mat inside. Her eyes take in the apartment.

"Wow. Time warp. Hasn't changed a bit." She notices the chair at the entrance. Resting proudly on it is Gran's recently completely embroidered pillow.

"She still does crafts," she says, picking up the pillow and reading out loud. "*God grant me the serenity to accept the things I cannot change, the courage to change the things I can, and the wisdom to know the difference.* Whoa," she says. "Sounds like my old sponsor."

"Sponsor," I say. "Meaning: to promote, to support."

"Something like that, yeah."

I realize then that I'm being impolite. It's not often that I'm in charge of guests. In fact, it's never happened before. "Would you like to come in?" I ask, thinking how proud Gran would be of my manners.

"Where is she?" the young lady asks. "Where's your gran?"

"Folding laundry downstairs," I explain. "She's got three loads today. We saved up lots of quarters in the Special Jar. Come," I say as I lead my guest into the kitchen. She stands in front of the table, extends a hand to touch it, gently, as if she were petting a friendly cat rather than a worn piece of furniture.

"Would you care for a cup of tea?" I ask.

"No," she replies. "That's okay."

"Please have a seat." I gesture to Gran's usual spot at the table.

"Thanks," she says as she pulls out the chair and cautiously sits. "You're really . . . polite. You're totally different from what I imagined. Come here, let me get a good look at you."

I stand in front of her and she grabs my hands in hers. She leans forward, her face close to mine. And just like that, she begins to sob.

"I'm terribly sorry," I say. "I recently learned I'm a social failure and that I'm not at the level of my peers, so whatever I did to upset you, I assure you, I didn't do it on purpose."

She lets go of my hands and wipes at her eyes. "You didn't do anything wrong," she says.

"Maybe you don't like me," I say. "Not many people do."

"No, I *do* like you. You have no idea. It's just . . . it's like looking in a mirror."

And then it comes to me. I know just what to do. I take a tissue from the box on the kitchen table. "Tissue for your issue?" I say.

She takes the tissue from my hand. "Thanks," she replies. "Molly, the last time I saw you, you didn't speak at all. Your gran was worried. She was worried that maybe you'd turn out . . ." She pauses like she can't find the word.

"Different?" I offer.

"Yeah. That."

"I *am* different," I say. "But I can speak just fine. In fact, it's hard for me to follow the rule of 'children should be seen and not heard.' Or 'not seen and not heard.' Or whatever the rule is. I enjoy words. Do you? I like the word 'loquacious.' What word do you like?"

She blows her nose into the tissue. "I like simpler words. Right now, I like the word 'home.'" She starts to cry again, but then her eyes spy the envelope on the table. Her tears turn off instantly, the same way the washroom tap does when I twist the knob right after rinsing my hands.

"Jesus. First of the month," she says shaking her head. "That same slumlord still own this place? What was his name . . ."

"Mr. Rosso," I say. "He's still the landlord. I expected him at the door, not you."

She starts to breathe in and out really fast. She scratches her head hard, so hard it makes me nervous.

"Molly," she says. "Do you have any Band-Aids?"

"Oh," I say. "You don't have to be ashamed of your arms. Bedbugs aren't your fault. Gran says they spread from apartment to apartment because landlords don't spend enough on sanitation. It doesn't mean you're not clean."

"I'm not clean, Molly," she says. "That's exactly my problem."

I go down the hall to the washroom and open the cupboard under the sink. At the back is our first-aid kit. I remove it and take out three of the biggest Band-Aids to offer Gran's friend. When I leave the washroom, she's standing by the front door putting on her dirty, old shoes. She's wiping at her eyes with the crumpled tissue in her hand.

"Are you leaving already?" I ask.

"I gotta run," she says.

"Aren't you going to wait for Gran? I'm sure she'll be glad to see you."

"No. This was a mistake. I don't want her to see me like this."

"Here are your Band-Aids."

"Keep 'em," she says. "Who am I kidding? Can't hide what I am."

She turns the knob and opens the door.

"Hold on!" I say. "What should I tell Gran?"

She stops for a moment. "Tell her . . . tell her she's taking really good care of you. And that I miss her." She starts to cry again, and I feel a hurt in my belly and my heart, a heavy pain I don't understand.

"Wait!" I say. "I don't even know your name."

"My name?" she says, pausing for a moment to look at me. "It's Maggie."

"It was nice to meet you, Maggie," I say. I reach out a hand, but instead of shaking it, she squeezes it in hers and kisses it before letting go.

"Come back for a visit anytime," I say.

She puts a hand on my hair, then takes it away. "Goodbye, Molly."

She turns away from me and pulls the door closed behind her.

I bolt it immediately. *Lock the door tight, in the day and in the night.*

I lean against the door for a moment. I feel off-kilter, dizzy but excited, too. I feel like a bona fide grown-up. I've hosted a visitor, my very own, all by myself! If this is what grown-up socializing is, maybe I can do it. It's not like this with kids, who are horrible and mean, rude and insulting. And even though Gran's friend was sad, I figured that out right away. And I knew how to make her feel better, too.

I head to the washroom to return the Band-Aids to the first-aid kit. As I'm putting them away, I hear the key turn in the lock. I exit the washroom as Gran enters with a heaping hamper full of neatly folded laundry, which she puts down with a big huff. "My heavens, Molly, it's hot as Hades in that laundry room," she says as she closes and locks the door. She removes her shoes, wipes them, then goes straight to the kitchen for a tall glass of water. I follow her in.

"Gran, we had a visitor," I say. "But don't worry. I knew she wasn't a stranger because I asked her questions, and she answered them all correctly. I knew she knew you, and she knew me, too, back from when I was only as tall as a grasshopper's knees. She's a maid, Gran. You worked together. It was nice to meet another maid, even if she has bedbugs. It's just like you said. You can't blame people for their circumstances. Oh, and she says you're taking good care of me and that she misses you. I'm supposed to tell you that."

Gran puts down her water glass with an audible *thunk*. Her mouth is wide open, so open that if we still had bedbugs, they could climb right in. Her gaze turns to the kitchen table.

"Molly," she says. "Did Mr. Rosso come by? Please tell me he picked up the envelope."

I look down at the kitchen table.

That's when I understand it, what Gran was saying earlier about invisible things.

Two variables come together in my mind: our recent guest and the envelope containing our rent money. I see the equation forming, but it's too late.

Both are gone.

Chapter 14

I did not sleep well. I tossed and turned all night. I reached out for Juan Manuel, found him absent, missing, only an empty space left behind on the mattress. I thought of calling him in the middle of the night, telling him everything that's happened over the last couple of days, but at such a distance, he can't do a thing to help me. And what was I supposed to say to him? *Juan, I failed to inform you that a man dropped dead in the hotel tearoom two days ago. His death has since been deemed a murder, and it's entirely possible the killer is on the loose in our hotel. Oh, and one more thing—our very good friend, Mr. Preston? He's a thief. And now I'm starting to wonder if he might be something worse than that.*

No wonder I didn't sleep a wink.

I cannot erase the unthinkable thoughts from my mind. What if Mr. Preston, my dear friend and colleague, a man whom I've considered the purest personification of a good egg, is a thief? And if he's capable of stealing, what else could he do?

It's ridiculous. Absurd. I hear Gran admonish me in my head—*Only fools jump to conclusions.*

She's right. And yet there's no refuting what I saw at that pawn-shop—Mr. Preston, selling a rare first-edition copy of J. D. Grimthorpe's *The Maid in the Mansion* the day after the author died and the value of said book skyrocketed. Is it possible that Mr. Grimthorpe was murdered out of pure and simple greed? And is it possible that Mr. Preston could have something to do with it? That's the improbable, inconceivable notion that has me turned inside out.

I tear the blankets off me, jab my hot feet into my slippers, and stomp into the kitchen. It's five in the morning, far too early to get up, but I can't lie awake any longer. I grab a bucket from under the sink and fill it with water. I root around in the drawer for a reliable cleaning cloth, then I march into the living room and set my supplies down beside Gran's curio cabinet.

I turn the TV on as a distraction, but sure enough, the news channel is replaying yesterday's press conference in which Detective Stark declared Mr. Grimthorpe's death a murder. I watch as reporters pelt Stark with questions.

"Detective, do you have any leads?"

"We're following every lead we have," Stark replies.

"Detective, is the murderer a guest or a hotel employee?"

"If I knew that, would I be here?" she replies.

"Detective, you said his tea was poisoned with antifreeze. Do you know how that could have happened?"

"We're working on that," she says. "We're tracking an important piece of evidence."

"Detective, do you have a message for the killer?"

Stark pauses. It's as though she's looking right through the TV at me. "You can hide the truth for a while, but it won't stay buried

The Mystery Guest

forever. Just remember that," she says, before walking away from the scrum.

I turn off the TV.

I pick up my cloth and carefully open the glass doors of Gran's curio cabinet. *Deep cleaning gives life meaning. Just grab a duster, Buster.*

Yes, Gran, I think to myself as I remove her precious treasures—a secondhand menagerie of Swarovski crystal animals, her pride and joy, and her souvenir spoons from far-flung places she never got to see with her own eyes.

I furiously polish each trinket, then turn to the framed photos on top of the cabinet. There's a new photo of me and my dear Juan Manuel with matching ice cream mustaches. There are older photos, too, of Gran and me. But it's the photo of my mother when she was young that I study with care. Dark hair like mine and a porcelain complexion, bright apple cheeks, not wan and hollowed out like that strange young woman who stole the rent on the first day of the month so long ago. As a child, I had no idea who she was. I realized only when I was much older that Maggie—the stranger at the door that day—was my mother, and that one of the reasons she'd come was to see me. How I failed to put two and two together at the time, I do not know. Why is it always like that? Why do I understand everything too late?

Now, I put all of Gran's treasures back in the cabinet. I shower, then scrub the washroom until my fingers pucker into dried prunes. I eat a crumpet at the worn kitchen table, chewing every bite exactly twenty times. Then I leave the apartment and head to work, anxiety powering me like a jet engine.

Now that everyone knows Mr. Grimthorpe was poisoned, this workday at the Regency Grand will be the furthest thing from normal. I have no idea what to expect.

When I arrive, Mr. Preston is standing at the doorman's podium,

153

directing the throngs of guests on the plush red landing. I elbow my way through the crowd until I'm standing right in front of him.

"Molly," he says. "Have you heard? About how Mr. Grimthorpe died?"

"Yes," I say. "And I'm most distressed. Who do you suppose might be capable of such a thing?"

"A lot of people. That man wasn't what he seemed."

I search Mr. Preston's face, which is grim and tense, his lips concealed in his mouth. "What about you, Mr. Preston? Are *you* what you seem?"

"Molly, are you all right?" he asks as he places a hand on my arm. "Are you feeling faint?"

I pull away. "We need to talk," I say. "But not here. Not now."

"My dear, I've been saying so for some time."

"Olive Garden. Five-fifteen P.M.," I say. "I expect you to arrive on time."

"Naturally. Molly, are you sure you're well?"

I can't believe he's asking this again. "You should ask yourself that question, not me," I reply.

Mr. Preston stares at me as though trying to place someone wholly unfamiliar.

"Good day," I say, and then I stomp up the red stairs and push through the revolving doors of the elegant Regency Grand.

The lobby is even busier than it was yesterday, filled with wide-eyed guests and onlookers whispering to one another in little cliques, but given the number of people about, it's far too quiet, a funereal hush in the air. And no wonder.

I spot Mr. Snow at the reception desk. He's murmuring instructions to a concierge who looks piqued and jittery and strained. I walk over to Mr. Snow as he finishes his conversation. The concierge hurries away. Mr. Snow turns his owl eyes to me. "Molly, I can't believe it," he says. "A man was poisoned. Here. In our hotel. How is this even possible?"

"I don't know, Mr. Snow," I reply. "We've spent the last few years buffing our tarnished reputation, but we're now besmirched in a new and most grievous manner. I wonder—will the stain ever come out?"

"It doesn't bear thinking about, Molly. The police are pointing fingers, asking questions."

I look around the lobby and spot several men in black clothes standing by themselves, earpieces in their ears. "Who are they?" I ask. "They don't look like guests."

"They're undercover officers," Mr. Snow replies. "And they're everywhere, watching our every move. Rather than close the hotel, Detective Stark demanded we remain operational and attempt to 'act normal.' She and her special agents are convinced this is the best way to flush out the killer."

"Wouldn't the killer have fled by now?"

"Apparently, the manner of death suggests the murderer might stick around. Detective Stark mentioned something about trophies and 'the pathology of the poisoned cup.' It seems for some killers, hiding in plain sight is part of the thrill."

A tremor runs through me, and as I glance about the lobby, I see everything and everyone veiled in suspicion.

Mr. Snow gazes past the lobby, through the glass revolving doors where Mr. Preston directs foot traffic from his podium on the stairs. "Hard to imagine," Mr. Snow says, "but the detectives are convinced the killer is . . ." He pauses.

"Spit it out, Mr. Snow. A worker? One of us?" I ask.

Mr. Snow nods gravely.

An invisible vise clenches around my heart, and for a moment I wonder how I'm supposed to carry on. *Chin up, Buttercup.*

"I'd better go," I say. "This hotel isn't going to clean itself." What I don't say is that a criminal layer of grime lurks in every hidden nook and cranny of this hotel, but we cannot clean what we cannot see.

"Be vigilant, Molly," Mr. Snow says.

"I always am," I reply.

I leave him and am heading toward the elevators when I hear a familiar "Yoo-hoo!" at my back. I turn to see two LAMBS sitting on an emerald settee by the grand staircase. Gladys, the curly-haired president, is waving her little red flag at me while Beulah intently picks cat hair off that same awful sweater of hers. They're the last people I wish to talk to right now, but as Mr. Snow often reminds staff members, "You're at the behest of every guest."

"Ladies," I say as I approach. "I hope you're well."

"Well?" says Gladys. "How could we possibly be well? J. D. Grimthorpe has been murdered in cold blood."

"We're in deep mourning," Beulah adds as she wraps her arms around herself.

"Do you know if the Social will open at the regular time for breakfast today?" Gladys asks.

"It will," I reply. "At the Regency Grand, we pride ourselves on predictability and timely service."

"Good," says Beulah. "I could use something in my stomach to settle it."

While I don't always have the most reliable read on human emotions, I can't help but notice the incongruity here. Both women appear more afraid of missing breakfast than they are of a potential murderer on the loose. And why have they stuck around when there's quite literally a zero percent chance of them meeting the very man they came here to see? It suddenly strikes me that the third member of their usual trio, the little one with the pink highlights, is separated from the flock.

"Where's the other number-one fan you two are always with?" I ask. "Ms. Birdy. Has she flown home?"

"Home? Are you kidding? And miss the action?" Beulah says. "She's wandering the hotel, collecting clues. She's pitching theories and motives to your people."

"My people?" I say.

"Yes. The secret agents, the men in black who're all over the hotel today. We know they're working with you," Gladys says. She points to one of the men with earpieces littering the lobby at intervals.

"They are *not* working with me," I reply. "I am just a maid. That's it. That's all."

"Of course. We understand," Gladys says. "Nod, nod. Wink, wink. We won't say a word. But we do have something important to tell you—as a maid, of course."

"If it's truly as a maid, then I will listen. What is it?" I ask.

"It's about Birdy," Gladys says.

Beulah scratches at her fur-covered sweater, then says, "As you probably noticed, Birdy and I don't always get along. We share a love for all things Grimthorpe, but let's just say the love ends there. For many years, there's been a professional rivalry between us."

"A professional jealousy is what I'd call it," says Gladys.

"You see, I'm something that Birdy is not—only I am Mr. Grimthorpe's biographer."

"*Unofficial* biographer," Gladys adds.

"One thing I've learned over the years is never to underestimate a tiny woman. Birdy may be small, but she's strong, wily, and . . ."

"She has a history with poison," Gladys says.

The two women exchange a look.

"What are you talking about?" I ask.

"Two years ago, during our biannual symposium on The Genius of J. D. Grimthorpe, an esteemed academic from a local university was in attendance. After Birdy's rather long-winded lecture about crime and punishment in J.D.'s mysteries, this academic raised her hand and said she'd never understood why his work was so popular. She called his writing rigid."

"'Constipated' was the exact word she used," Beulah says. "Birdy was apoplectic."

"On the second day of the symposium, when the academic returned for our Crime & Crumpets Salon, Birdy served her a special brownie she'd baked herself," Gladys says.

"Brown as my favorite sweater, and laced with laxatives," Beulah adds. "Let's just say that academic never attended one of our symposiums ever again."

"Typical Birdy," says Gladys, shaking her curly head. "The punishment befits the crime."

The two ladies nod in unison.

"When that detective on the news said Mr. Grimthorpe was poisoned, we both had the same thought: Birdy," Beulah says.

Gladys leans toward me. "If Birdy could poison a brownie, what else might she be capable of?"

"But why would she poison her idol?" I ask.

"Because she's angry," Beulah offers. "With him and with me. Killing J.D. punishes us both." Beulah leans into me conspiratorially, lowering her voice. "Lately, I'd been getting closer to Mr. Grimthorpe, uncovering research Birdy knows nothing about. He and I had discussed me becoming his official biographer. She was not happy about that. She's always wanted to be more than his number-one fan. Let's just say she was green with envy when I told her I beat her to the punch."

"And as mentioned," Gladys adds, "Birdy has always had a penchant for *Poison & Punishment*—the novel, I mean."

"It's her favorite book by J. D. Grimthorpe because the villain gets what's coming to him via a tainted drink. I doubt that's a coincidence," says Beulah.

"Beulah and I discussed all of this last night," Gladys adds, "and while it's hard to imagine Birdy stooping to such a low, we decided it would be prudent to mention her backstory to someone official. You know, just in case."

"I'm not official," I say. "Unless you mean in my capacity as Head Maid."

"Of course," Gladys says loudly. "We understand."

Beulah grabs my arm. "You'll investigate this, right?" she whispers.

"I'll do no such thing," I say. "Speak to the authorities. Now if you'll excuse me, I must be off. Hotel rooms don't clean themselves."

"Especially Beulah's," Gladys says. "Her hotel room looks like a pack rat moved in."

"It's not that bad," Beulah replies as she brushes the shoulders of her sweater, sending a raft of fresh cat fur into the air.

I turn on my heel and leave without so much as another word. It must be said: I'm relieved the moment I'm out of their sight. Everything about these women sets my teeth on edge.

I rush downstairs to the housekeeping quarters, where I change into my uniform, placing my Head Maid pin in its proper position, right above my heart. Lily has already arrived. Her shoes are lined up neatly in front of her locker.

Once uniformed, I check myself one last time in the mirror, then head to the second floor. The elevator doors open, and I spot Lily's trolley at the end of the hall, but when I look the other way, Cheryl is exiting a room, her fleshy hand full of small bills.

No. Not again. It's the second time in less than twenty-four hours that I've caught a thief red-handed, in flagrante delicto.

Cheryl is up to her old tricks. She's filching tips from rooms she doesn't even clean, tips meant for Lily and me.

"Cheryl!" I say, or rather shout, because I'm hot as a steaming kettle. I march down the hallway and stop in front of her. "How dare you?" I say. "Stealing tips from other maids. You'll recall that it's expressly forbidden to interfere with remuneration intended for other staff members. Do you realize that's cause for dismissal?"

"Whoa, Molly!" Cheryl says, her hands raised. "No need to get so worked up. As I told Lily earlier, I thought it would be a good idea for all of us maids to pool our tips and then divide them evenly. You know, like you always say—'fair and square, the maids all share'?"

"That statement refers to the workload," I say. "You have misconstrued my meaning."

Lily's head pops out of a room. The dark circles under her eyes are so pronounced she resembles a raccoon.

"You tell her, Lily," Cheryl says. "We agreed to pool tips, right?"

Lily is about to say something, but the words catch in her mouth. "I . . . guess?" she manages, then she shakes her head and goes quiet.

This does a grand total of nothing to placate me. Rather, it makes me want to submerge Cheryl's greedy paws in a bucketful of concentrated lye, but instead I force a smile and say, "I am Head Maid. It is up to *me* to decide how tips are doled out amongst maids. And for the record, I've had enough of dirty thieves for one day."

"Dirty thieves?" Cheryl repeats, punctuating this with a snort. "That's a very nasty name you just called me. Who's breaking her own rule book now? I wonder what Mr. Snow would have to say if I decided to report you, Molly? I've gotta go," Cheryl says. "Be sure to shout out if either of you see an axe-wielding murderer behind a hotel room door. Or better yet, don't shout. Just. Stay. Quiet," she says as she eyes Lily. Then she clomps off down the hallway.

Once she's gone, Lily emerges from the room she was cleaning and stands in front me, her eyes downturned and watery.

"Did you really agree to pool tips with her?" I ask.

Lily's not talking. She's not even moving.

"Will there ever be an end to this silent treatment?" I ask. "I know this place is upside down right now and it's quite frightening, but everything will right itself. Things will be okay in the end."

Lily's face remains impassive—a mask of worry and concern. "This hotel?" she whispers. "It's dirtier than I ever realized. I don't know what to do."

"There's only one thing to do in the presence of dirt, Lily. And that's clean it."

Lily stares at me for a moment, then she slips behind her trolley and disappears down the hall.

CHAPTER 15

Before

I'm standing in the kitchen with Gran. She's asking a question, but the floor under my feet is warping, and while she's right in front of me, hands on my shoulders, it's as though she's speaking from inside a corked bottle bobbing at sea.

"Please tell me Mr. Rosso picked up the envelope," she repeats. "Molly?"

"He didn't come," I say. "Mr. Rosso didn't stop by." My eyes are on the kitchen table. I'm willing the envelope with the rent to reappear, but it doesn't. And I know it won't.

"That lady knew you. She said her name was Maggie."

Gran's hands slide off my shoulders and she covers her face with them. A sound escapes her, a strange one that I've heard only once before, in a nature documentary—the sound a mother sheep made after a lion snatched her lamb and ran away with it.

"Gran, who is she? Maybe it's not too late."

Tears stream down Gran's face. "Oh, my dear girl," she says. "It's years too late."

"But who is she?" I ask.

Gran is silent. A deep furrow settles into her brow. "You don't know? You really don't know?"

I shake my head.

"Why would you," she says. "After all, she's a stranger to you."

"She's a thief," I say. "We should call the police. They can catch her and get our rent money back."

"It's no use, Molly. She's long gone, and the money's gone with her."

Gran crumples onto the kitchen floor. I sit cross-legged in front of her. I feel my ribs tighten around my heart, the gravity of our predicament sinking in.

"Gran, please don't cry. I'm so sorry."

Just then, there's a pounding at the door. We both jump. It's her, I think to myself. It's Maggie. She's had a change of heart and is returning our money. She's a good egg after all!

I hop to my feet and help Gran to stand. I pull a tissue from the box on the kitchen table, passing it to her. Then I grab a kitchen chair and rush to the front door. I stand on it, looking through the fish-eye peephole.

I'm instantly deflated by what I see. "It's Mr. Rosso," I say.

"Leave him to me," Gran replies, as she sniffs and blows her nose. Then she comes to the door as I move my kitchen chair away.

She opens the door to our landlord, with his bulbous nose and his arms crossed against his round belly.

"Good day, Mr. Rosso," Gran says. "I trust you're having a pleasant one." Her singsong voice catches in her throat.

"Rent day's only pleasant when everyone pays," he replies.

Gran presses her hands together, then rubs them against her thighs. "Mr. Rosso," she says. "I'm afraid we've encountered an unforeseen situation that has led to a delay in our rent payment."

"Now say that again in plain English," Mr. Rosso replies.

"We don't have the rent money. But I'll pay you soon."

Mr. Rosso's face goes from regular red to a shade somewhere between flaming beet and blood-red rose. "This building is crawling with good-for-nothing bums, but I thought you were better than them, Flora. I really did."

"I'm terribly sorry to disappoint," she replies. "There's that saying about lemons and lemonade, but in this instance, I don't even have lemons, so there's not much I can do. Sometimes, Mr. Rosso, life interferes with a person's best intentions."

"Not without consequence," Mr. Rosso replies, his nostrils flaring. "It's the only way people like you ever learn." He turns and shuffles down the hall.

"I'm sorry?" Gran calls after him. "Might you explain what you mean by people like us?"

Gran and I stick our heads out the door in anticipation of a response, but Mr. Rosso never offers one. He doesn't so much as glance back our way.

We step into our apartment, and Gran gently clicks the door closed and locks it.

"What did he mean, Gran?" I ask. "What's going to happen?"

"Idle threats, dear. Nothing to worry about." She takes in a deep breath, exhales, and then claps her hands together. "Why don't we do what we do best? Why don't we deep-clean the apartment?"

"Deep cleaning to give life meaning," I chime.

"Tidy up to cheer us up," Gran answers.

"What are you waiting for? Grab a duster, Buster!" I say, as I race to the kitchen to prepare a bucket and rags for our Deep Cleaning Adventure.

We spend the entire afternoon scrubbing and dusting, polishing and wiping. Though Gran looks tired and doesn't hum the way she usually does, I feel glorious, invigorated by the scent of zesty lemon that billows in the air, the comforting smell of home.

As dusk settles in and the day fades to black, everything in our modest apartment, from the kitchen to the washroom, from the front entrance to both of our bedrooms, is spotlessly, immaculately, perfectly clean.

Gran and I always save the best for last. We're in the living room, clearing out her curio cabinet. We sit on the floor surrounded by Swarovski crystal animals, souvenir spoons, and framed photos. Gran holds the photo of my mother in her hands. A deep furrow reappears on her forehead as she rubs the gold frame, trying to make it shine.

There's a strange sound—an electric sizzle. Then suddenly, the lights go out.

Silence.

"Gran?" I call out.

I can't see anything. It's pitch-black in the living room, where I'm sitting on the floor, but I discover my ears work even better in the dark.

What I hear next is a plaintive, distinctive sound—a mother sheep calling out to a lamb she will never see again.

Chapter 16

I work side by side with Lily for the rest of the day in the hope that my presence might help her open up to me, but alas, my efforts fail to yield results. She utters a grand total of two sentences through the remainder of the day: "Pass me a fresh towel, please?" and "May I take a washroom break?" Whatever is bothering Lily, I know better than to pry it out of her—*Good things come to those who wait.*

The only spot of good news is that together, in near silence, we managed to clean more than our allotted roster of guest rooms, leaving them immaculate and pristine, as though life had never sullied them, as though all manner of filth and grime never existed. If only that were true, though. We both know it's not. Because as much as we clean these rooms, we don't know the guests inhabiting them, and one of those guests might be Mr. Grimthorpe's murderer. And if the culprit wasn't a guest, then who was it?

It is now precisely 5:00 P.M., and our shift is over. "The day is done," I tell Lily. "Thank you for your diligent, if silent, work," I say.

She does not respond, does not even look me in the eye. She gets behind her trolley and pushes toward the elevator, heading down to the housekeeping quarters, where she will change out of her maid's uniform and become a civilian until tomorrow.

It's nearly time to meet Mr. Preston at the Olive Garden, and truth be told, I've been thinking about him all day—Mr. Preston, who for years has been a trusted friend. Mr. Preston, who comes for regular Sunday dinners with Juan and me. Mr. Preston, who I've long considered family. Mr. Preston, who pawned a stolen book. Mr. Preston, who appears to be—at best—a thief, and at worst . . .

Rats and scoundrels, fly-by-nights, and wolves in sheep's clothing. How could Mr. Preston have any association with that lot? And yet I saw with my own eyes how he pawned that first-edition book. He walked right into the shop with it under his arm.

In the housekeeping quarters, I peel off my uniform and change into my plain clothes. Lily is already gone, and so are the other maids. I'm all by myself yet again. I look at my face in the mirror. I'm carrying luggage on it—matching black bags under my eyes. If Juan Manuel were around, he'd write something on a pad like he did the last time I worked myself to a state of exhaustion.

"What's this?" I asked when he handed me the paper.

"A prescription," he replied.

"R & R, once daily for Molly Gray," I read. "To be administered by J. M., via a bubble bath, a foot massage, and spaghetti and meatballs for dinner—no cleanup by Ms. Molly allowed." There was a heart after my name.

I miss him so much. If he were here, he'd know just what to do. In his absence, who can I turn to?

Just then, Angela appears in the doorway of the change room, making me jump.

"You scared me half to death!" I say. "What are you doing down here? You should be upstairs at the Social."

"Yeah, I get that," Angela says. "But I'm doing a little private investigating. I talked with the kitchen staff to see if the police had tested all the liquids in the pantry for poisons."

Here she goes again, I think to myself. "Angela, why are you getting involved? Just stay out of it," I say.

"And miss my big chance to solve a crime? No way. Anyhow, just so you know, the police tested everything in the kitchen. They didn't find a thing out of place. But I did my own tests anyway."

"You did what?" I ask.

"I taste-tested a drop of every liquid in the kitchen to see if it would made me sick."

"And what did you discover?"

"That orange juice and vinegar followed by soy sauce and honey causes serious indigestion. The good news? I haven't dropped dead yet," Angela says.

"I can't believe you did that, Angela. You're taking this too far."

"I'm not," she replies. She pops out of the doorway, looks both ways down the empty hallway, then tiptoes back into the change room. "Look, Molly. Things are getting really weird in this hotel. The undercover agents are closing in on a suspect. I heard them say so. There are things you need to know."

"There are things *you* need to know, Angela," I say. "And the first is that I'm not an investigator, nor do I want to be mistaken for one. I told Detective Stark that I'd made a terrible mistake and had impersonated an officer of the law. I turned myself in for fraud. I did not, however, tell her whose terrible idea that was in the first place."

Angela stares at me in disbelief, one hand on her hip. "That's officially the dumbest thing I've ever heard," she says.

"You sound like Detective Stark," I reply as I open my locker and fish out my purse. "I keep trying to tell the LAMBS I'm just an ordinary maid, but they won't listen. Because of your deceptions, they keep feeding me leads."

"Good. That will come in handy."

I find myself growing enervated and annoyed. I do like Angela, but sometimes, she's the most stubborn person alive. I close my locker with a clank and head for the door.

"Wait! Molly, we have to talk," she says. "Are you on your way home?"

"No. I'm meeting Mr. Preston." I turn to face her. "Angela, I'm telling you this in confidence, and I don't want you sharing it with anyone until I speak to him first, but yesterday, I caught Mr. Preston selling the rare first edition that disappeared from the box in the lobby. He was pawning it at a shop a few blocks from here. I saw him with my very own eyes."

"Molly, who cares?" Angela replies. "It was just a book."

"But what if it's all related?" I ask. "What if Grimthorpe was killed to raise the price of his rare editions?"

Angela pauses. She's fiddling with the tie on her apron as she considers the possibility. "Nah. Impossible. Mr. Preston wouldn't hurt a fly. You shouldn't jump to conclusions."

"You sound like my gran. Listen, I have to go. Goodbye, Angela," I say.

I turn and head up the stairs to the lobby without another word. Feeling shaky and unsettled, I push through the revolving doors, rush down the stairs, and head to the Olive Garden, which is less than a block away.

Once I'm there, a familiar waiter greets me with a smile, leads me to a booth, drops two menus on the table, then walks off.

Just then I spot Mr. Preston at the entrance and wave him over. I pull out my phone from my purse—5:14 P.M. At least tardiness is one thing I won't need to berate him about.

"Molly," he says as he slides into the banquette across from me. He's dressed rather formally, wearing a navy pullover with a crisp shirt underneath and a tie, something he rarely wears, not even for our Sunday dinners.

"How wonderful to see you outside the confines of work," he says once seated. "I've been wanting to speak to you privately for some time." He smiles, crow's-feet nestling into the corners of his eyes.

Even this I cannot trust—his familiar face lined with what I once thought was pure kindness. "Mr. Preston," I say. "I've called you here today because you are a liar."

His eyes grow wide in an instant. "Excuse me?" he replies.

"A liar. A dissimulator. A thief," I say. "You've always told me that appearances can't be trusted, that not all frogs turn out to be princes. Mr. Preston, it is with a heavy heart that I tell you I've seen you for what you are—warts and all."

"My dear girl, I don't know what you're talking about. There must be some mistake."

"There is not," I say. "Yesterday, on my way back from the police station, I spotted you outside the pawnshop with a particular tome in your hot little hands. You sold it, the first edition of *The Maid in the Mansion*."

Mr. Preston shrugs. "I don't deny it. The price has gone up substantially, and while I can see that you may interpret that as profiteering from the writer's death, the truth is, Molly, I'm in need of a bit of extra money. I'm getting old. That's one of the things I've been wanting to talk to you about, but I was worried you'd be upset. Hauling suitcases is a young man's job, and I'm not sure how much longer I can do it. I'm thinking about retiring. And I need a financial cushion, a little nest egg to make things work."

"Stealing is no way to amass a Fabergé!" The words roar out of me, something I realize only after the heads of several diners pivot my way.

"Stealing?" whispers Mr. Preston as he leans across the table. "I haven't stolen anything in my life, least of all a Fabergé."

I study his face, looking for telltale shiftiness, which so often betrays a lie, but I find nothing.

I try a new tactic. "Once upon a time, there was a box," I say. "Inside was a rare first-edition copy of *The Maid in the Mansion*, belonging to Ms. Serena Sharpe. One second it was on the reception desk. The fire alarm was pulled and—*poof*—the box disappeared. The next time I saw that book, it was in your hands."

"Oh, Molly," Mr. Preston says as he puts his elbows on the table and hides his face in his palms.

"Elbows are not meant for the table, not now, not ever," I remind him.

Mr. Preston sighs. He does, however, remove his offending appendages from the tabletop.

The waiter saunters over. "Hey there. Are you two ready to order?" he asks.

"Chardonnay, two glasses," Mr. Preston says.

"I will *not* be drinking wine," I say. "Water for me. This is hardly a celebration."

The waiter looks from me to Mr. Preston, expecting further explanation. When he doesn't receive it, he slinks away.

"Molly," Mr. Preston says. "I have a confession to make."

Here it is, the moment when all my fears congeal into ugly reality, when all my trust in a man who has been like family to me is destroyed in an instant. But I will beat him to the punch. "So you admit it: you poisoned Mr. Grimthorpe."

"What?! I did no such thing!" Mr. Preston replies. "How can that even cross your mind?"

I look at him carefully, studying his face. He is on the verge of tears.

"Molly, the only thing I'm guilty of is a little white lie," he says.

He grabs a napkin from the holder on the table, then dabs his fore-head before continuing. "A few days ago, when you asked me about Mr. Grimthorpe, I suggested I did not know him, but I do. Or rather I did, a long time ago." He pauses, staring at me as though waiting for me to figure something out.

"Go on," I say.

"That book I pawned is one Grimthorpe gave me himself, years ago when I was under his employ and you . . . well, you were knee-high to a grasshopper."

Nothing makes any sense. This sounds like fancy footwork to distract me from the terrible truth. "The Grimthorpes never had a doorman," I say, crossing my arms. "I know this for a fact."

"Correct," Mr. Preston replies. "But they did have a gatekeeper."

My head starts to swirl. The banquette under me tilts and whirls. Memories and feelings collide as though a tornado is sweeping through me.

"Molly? I'm not a murderer. I'm not even a thief. That you could think I'd stoop that low, well . . . that breaks my heart." Mr. Preston reaches across the table for my hand. "The only thing I'm guilty of is not confessing to you earlier that I knew Mr. Grimthorpe. And the day after he died, I walked past the pawnshop on my way home from work and saw a first-edition copy in the display window. It was listed at an astronomical price. That gave me the idea to sell my own copy. Plus, I've always despised Mr. Grimthorpe, so why keep his book? Your gran used to preach patience, but she put up with too much working in that coldhearted place, especially when Grimthorpe was drunk. She thought if he could just get sober, everything would change, but she was mistaken. Mrs. Grimthorpe trusted almost no one near her husband, just your gran and his personal secretary. She said they were the only women besides herself strong enough to deal with his antics. For a long time, your gran stood by the Grimthorpes. But even she saw the truth in the end. Grimthorpe was a vile and odious man, not worthy of her loyalty. And Mrs. Grimthorpe let your gran down, too. They both betrayed her in different ways."

"Gran never told me any of this," I say.

"No. She wouldn't have. She was ashamed, humiliated. She wanted to put it all behind her, make a fresh start."

"Why are you telling me this?"

"Because it relates to what I've been trying to tell you for some time."

"That you knew me. Before. When I was a child at the Grimthorpe mansion. I get it," I say.

"That's only part of it. I remember you, the brave little girl who held her grandmother's hand and walked up the path of roses. That same little girl made the reverse trip one day to stand in front of the cameras at the gate and deliver a gift to the gatekeeper. Do you remember?"

Of course I remembered. How could I ever forget the kindness of that stranger? But I didn't know who I was speaking to. I had no idea at the time.

My stomach churns and agitates. "Mr. Preston," I say. "I've made a terrible mistake." Shame burns in my throat, and I struggle for a moment to find the words. "I've made an A-S-S, not out of U, but out of myself. I don't know who stole that book from the reception desk, but I see now that it wasn't you. And I see so much more than that. I'm terribly sorry. Will you ever forgive me?"

"Forgive you? Molly, that's a given. Now and always."

I breathe a sigh of relief. "There was something else you were going to tell me," I say.

Mr. Preston pats my hand. "I've just told you a lot," he replies. "Maybe it's best we leave the rest for another time."

"You won't forget?"

He stares at me with his warm, watery eyes. "I could never forget, Molly. Never."

CHAPTER 17

Before

I'm a little girl sitting in the darkness, frightened as her gran sobs unseen on the living room floor. It wasn't Gran's tears that frightened me. And it wasn't the dark either. I was afraid of myself, of my infinite capacity for understanding things too late.

The sobbing stops. I can't see Gran, but I hear her shuffling about. Then footsteps, the familiar creak of the vanity in the wash-room, the sound of rummaging.

"Gran?" I call out.

"I'll be right there," she answers. "Stay where you are."

More shuffling and footsteps. A raspy swish.

"Let there be light," Gran says as she places a lit candle on a side table and begins to light the others at her feet, placing them at in-tervals throughout the room. The effect is wondrous, the entire room cast in an enchanting glow.

"Where there's a will, there's a way. I lost my will for a moment, Molly, but it's back. Tea?" she asks.

"The power is cut. The kettle won't work."

"We still have ice in the freezer, at least for a while. I can make the cold kind."

She grabs a candle and heads for the kitchen. She rummages about as I sit motionless on the floor, listening to her humming as though all is right with the world. She emerges a few minutes later with a candle, two tall glasses, a pitcher, and some biscuits on a silver tray.

"Tea for two?" She places the tray on the living room table, sits on the sofa, and pats it.

I take my place beside her.

For the rest of the evening, we drink iced tea and eat biscuits. We cannot watch David Attenborough or *Columbo*, so Gran regales me with stories of fairies and princesses, lords and ladies, maids and servants who work downstairs. At some point, I feel my eyes closing. A hand wraps around mine and guides me to bed.

My gran. She was always like that. She always found a way to ignite hope. And what is hope if not the decision to shine light into the dark?

The next morning, the sun is up and candles aren't needed even though the electricity is still cut, no hot water in our apartment either. I wash up with cold water, a cat bath, as Gran calls it, even though there are no felines in our apartment.

On the way to the Grimthorpe mansion, I interrogate Gran. "What are we going to do about the rent? What if Mr. Rosso never turns the electricity back on? What if we have to live in darkness for the rest of our days?"

"Not to worry, Molly. Your gran has a plan."

When we arrive at the mansion, we stop at the gate as usual.

She presses the intercom, but instead of saying hello and requesting entrance, she says, "I'm coming to the watchtower." This is highly unusual. She's never gone to the watchtower before, that impenetrable fortress that stands guard over the Grimthorpe mansion just a stone's throw away from the gate.

There's a buzzing sound, and the gate opens.

"You wait here a moment," Gran tells me.

I nod, confused, but trusting that Gran knows best. She walks along the wrought-iron fence to the watchtower, then enters through a door I never even knew was on the far side. What for? Why is she going in? What is she doing?

I bide my time by the gate counting the pointy spears on top of the fence line. Just when vertigo begins to ripple the ground at my feet, Gran exits the tower and starts walking back my way.

She pauses when she reaches me. "I've received an IOU," she says in her singsong voice. "I'll have the rent money later today. Which means power will be restored. Let there be light." She lays a gentle hand on my back, then guides me up the path of roses toward the mansion.

As we walk, I try to process the news, but I'm having trouble putting the pieces together. "So, who gave you the rent money, Gran?" I ask.

"The gatekeeper," she replies.

The invisible one, the man of mystery in the tower? "Why would the gatekeeper lend us money?"

"Because there are still some good eggs left in this world, Molly. There's one in that tower. He's been watching over us this whole time."

I glance behind me at the three-story pillar of cold, gray stone with the tinted windows from which anyone can look out but no one can look in. I decide then and there what I must do.

* * *

I spend the morning polishing silver in the pantry. Mrs. Grim-thorpe enters at around eleven-thirty to survey my work.

"That will do," she says. "You may go upstairs and read quietly."

I leave her, then go up to the library, where I grab *Great Expectations* and arrange myself on the chaise longue. No sooner am I seated than I hear a click and see light flow onto the floor through the crack in the wall. The shuffle of slippers, the Oxford dictionary moves, and a moment later, the wall of books opens, and Mr. Grimthorpe stands in the threshold, grinning from ear to ear.

"Pip," he says. "Where have you been? I haven't seen you up here in days. I've been hoping you'd appear. You really are the child prophet, the young soothsayer, she-who-knows-all."

"I know nothing," I reply. "With each passing day, I know less than before."

"But you gave me the answer," he says. "I've been struggling for ages, and you offered the solution—the lye solution. The end is nigh, Pip. I've almost finished my latest novel."

I stare at the rickety man before me. His face is glowing like the Fabergé on the mantel downstairs.

"Really?" I ask. "You're done writing your book?"

"Almost," he replies. "The lye and the maid. Both of them were your ideas. You figured it out—how a body can be there one moment and be gone the next. Dissolved. Disintegrated. Disappeared. Invisibility and absence, the impact left behind. It will take me a few more days to scribble the last words, but I'm nearly there. And I think I've done it. I think I've earned a new place on the literary shelf—*in perpetuum*."

He begins to pace the room. He picks up a black monogrammed Moleskine and his fountain pen, scrawling something in it with big, loopy strokes. His angular body is different today, transformed. His knotted asymmetry, his sharp angularity—everything about him is intensified, sleek, and purposeful, like a panther on the hunt.

Rat-a-tat-tat-tat.

There it is again. The typing, clear and resonant. The lady in blue must be in her office, and wherever that is, she's busy now, typing up the ending to the great writer's new work.

Since Mr. Grimthorpe is in such a buoyant mood, I decide to take my chances. "Mr. Grimthorpe," I say. "Where is your secretary's office? I see her enter through the side door every day, and I hear her typing away, but never once have I seen where she works."

"Not looking too closely, then," says Mr. Grimthorpe. He claps his Moleskine closed and flashes me a lopsided grin.

"She never walks around the mansion," I say. "Sometimes I wonder if she's real."

Mr. Grimthorpe chortles out loud. "Oh, she's real. She's definitely real."

I have no idea what's funny, but I'm grateful his humor is holding. He strides over to where I stand in the threshold of the library. "Nothing can touch me today, Pip," he says. "I could walk on water. I feel the way I used to before I quit drinking, back when my first book hit the bestseller list and I was on top of the world. Today, I'm capable of anything."

Just then, I hear Gran calling up the main staircase: "Ten minutes to tea!"

Mr. Grimthorpe hears her, too. "She used to come up here and sit with me every day. Did you know that? She'd listen if I felt like talking. Through the worst of it—the shaking and the sweats— she'd regale me with stories. She'd distract me during the darkest days. Now she barely comes up here at all." Mr. Grimthorpe licks his lips, his tongue darting across the ivory of his teeth before disappearing into the cave of his mouth.

"If you need my gran, why don't you just go downstairs?" I ask.

He nods and smiles his beguiling grin. "Good idea, Pip. Maybe I will."

"I have to go now," I say.

"Ah yes, polish and shine. Restore everything to a state of perfection, my wife's futile endeavor to preserve the illusion of a perfect marriage and a perfect husband, the two things she's never had. I'll let you in on a secret, Pip: the bloom never lasts. Nothing gold can stay."

"I have to go now," I say. "There's something I need to do. Goodbye, Mr. Grimthorpe." I reach out and push the Oxford dictionary. The wall of books closes, and Mr. Grimthorpe disappears behind it.

I don't have much time. Gran will no doubt call for me yet again. I rush into the corridor and tiptoe down the front stairs. I grab my shoes from the vestibule, slip them on, then turn the front doorknob and sneak out the front door, closing it soundlessly behind me.

I skip down the path of roses, beyond their best bloom now, their necks heavy, petals dropping onto the cobblestones. As I walk, I search for a specimen that's not yet faded and spent. It takes some time, but eventually I spot a dark crimson flower hidden deep in a thicket, its petals unfurling into its zenith of splendor. I reach my arm into the prickly brambles, ignoring the sting of thorns until my fingers find the stem that feeds the last resplendent rose. I pinch the stem and crack it, then pull the flower from the dense brush. There are scratches up and down my arm, red pinprick tracks, but that doesn't matter, because what I hold in my hand is worth it—a fleeting treasure, the last specimen of this year's crop.

I walk the rest of the path with my rose carried gingerly in both hands. When I reach the wrought-iron gate, I press the intercom button just like Gran always does. I speak into the little slats.

"Can you hear me?" I ask. "Can you see me? I am Molly, Maid-in-Training. Over and out."

I wait for a response. Nothing. I look out at the watchtower, then push the button again.

"Whoever you are, I know you helped my gran and me. You lent us money for our rent. I think that's very generous. I just wanted to bring you a gift," I say. "And to tell you myself: thank you."

A click, the sound of static.

"My dear girl, you're most welcome," I hear.

I look again at the watchtower. The tinted windows reveal nothing, but that doesn't stop me from holding up my rose to the man in the tower before leaving it on the ledge by the intercom.

I bow deeply, executing my very best curtsy in his direction. Then I hurry up the path of roses and back to the mansion.

CHAPTER 18

Ever since I was a small child, I've been told—in direct and indirect ways—that I am a failure. Not good enough. Doesn't meet the bar. Fails to grasp what others understand with relative ease. Molly the Mutant. Roomba the Robot. Oddball Moll.

Before this very moment, I never fully believed any of these pronouncements. I railed against the assumption that my differences made me lesser than. I refused to accept it. But now, as my feet pound the sidewalk and I rush off to work, where I will have to face Mr. Preston for the first time since I mistook him for a murderer, I'm starting to believe that everything that's always been said about me might be true. Maybe I *am* lesser than. I most certainly am a fool, an A-S-S if ever there was one. How could I ever mistake Mr. Preston for a bad egg? How could I make such an awful blunder? And if I'm daft enough to do that, what other colossal errors am I capable of?

Juan Manuel called me this morning while I was finishing chew

#14 of a bite of English muffin. I swallowed, then asked him, "Am I a good person? Am I a good egg?"

He was silent for a moment on the other end of the line. "Mi amor, what are you talking about? You're more than a good egg. Molly, you're my Fabergé."

I gulped down my tea, then changed the subject entirely, asking Juan about his trip and his mother and his siblings, until he cheerily chirped away and forgot all about my strange questions.

Now, I arrive at the front entrance of the Regency Grand, with its elegant façade. Valets bustle about, helping guests with their luggage. Mr. Preston, in his doorman's coat and cap, stands at his podium on the landing, a portrait of dignity and grace. He sees me pause at the bottom of the stairs. My legs won't move. I don't deserve the red carpet. I never have.

He rushes down the stairs and grabs my arm. "Molly, are you all right?"

"I am not all right. I have never been all right."

"There, there," he says, guiding me up the staircase. "One foot in front of the other. It's the only way to get anywhere in this life."

"Gran used to say that," I tell him as I steady myself on his arm.

"I know," he replies.

We stop at the landing in front of the revolving doors. "I accused you of a terrible thing. You shouldn't forgive me, Mr. Preston. I don't deserve your kindness."

"We all make mistakes. It's what we do after that matters."

"Gran used to say that, too."

He smiles and squeezes my arm. I never fully appreciated until now just how old he's become in a short time, how gray his hair is, no longer tinged with black but fully sterling. Even this I have not seen clearly until now. Mr. Preston is going to retire at some point soon, which means I won't see him every day. The very thought makes my heart heavy.

"Molly," Mr. Preston says, "I spoke with Angela last night. She wants to talk to us. Right away."

"You spoke with Angela?" I repeat dumbly as I wonder why on earth Mr. Preston would be in touch with her after hours.

"When you and I talked yesterday, it got me thinking. I called her because I wanted her thoughts on that missing box that was in the lobby and that rare first edition of Grimthorpe's novel I saw in the pawnshop window. You were right about one thing, Molly—there's something fishy about all of it. Angela didn't have much light to shed last night, but this morning, she has a bee in her bonnet. She wants to see us in the restaurant."

"Very well," I say. "I have a few minutes before my shift."

Mr. Preston tells the valets he's taking a break, then points the way through the revolving front doors of the hotel, following close behind me.

We find Angela behind the bar at the Social, her brazen hair in disarray, her expression pinched in concentration as she stares at the screen of her laptop, which is open on the bar in front of her. She's so entranced by whatever she's looking at, she doesn't even glance at us. At last, she notices our presence and waves us over. Mr. Preston and I sit side by side on barstools in front of her.

"Will this be quick?" I ask. "I really should get to work."

"Molly, you're always half an hour early for your shift," Angela says. "And believe me, when you see what I'm about to show you, you're going to lose your mind. You, too, Mr. Preston," she adds. "Best settle in."

Mr. Preston takes off his cap and places it on the bar.

With a flourish, Angela turns her laptop to face us. On-screen is a website called KultureVulture.com. Its logo is an ominous bird of prey with an old book in its talons.

"What is this?" Mr. Preston asks.

"An online shopping site for memorabilia," Angela replies.

"People auction off used books, autographs of famous people, collector's items, and anything else they think they can sell. There's even a listing for a rock star's dirty underwear. And the worst part? They sold. Look at this page," Angela says as she clicks into another tab. "This vendor calls themself 'The Grim Reaper.' "

Mr. Preston reads out the vendor's description. "Selling original goods owned by the rich, dead, and infamous. One hundred percent bona fide! Anonymous inside source!"

"Now check this out," Angela says as she scrolls down the screen to reveal various items labeled as sold.

I can't believe my eyes. I gasp out loud.

"Are all of these items related to Mr. Grimthorpe?" Mr. Preston asks before I can even get words out.

"Most," says Angela. "There's one item that isn't." She scrolls to a photo of empty minibar bottles of scotch. The description underneath reads: "The Last Liquid Supper of Mr. Charles Black—*the* Mr. Black—from the day he dropped dead at the Regency Grand Hotel!"

My head is spinning. My heart starts to race.

"Check this out," Angela says. She hovers over a sold listing for a fountain pen and a note card. "This twofer could be yours!" the caption reads. "J. D. Grimthorpe's fountain pen and a scandalous love letter he wrote to his personal secretary!"

"Goodness gracious," Mr. Preston says. "Click on it."

Angela clicks to enlarge the photo.

I study the black-and-gold fountain pen with its elegant tapered nib. "That's Mr. Grimthorpe's pen," I say. "It was in the box that disappeared."

"Is it my old eyes or is that love note illegible?" Mr. Preston asks.

"The vendor blurs things on purpose," Angela explains. "Only the buyer gets 'the inside scoop.' "

"That's Regency Grand stationery," Mr. Preston says, noting the familiar logo even though it's fuzzy.

"Well, I'll be dipped in shite. You're right," says Angela.

"But they're wrong about the note," I say. "Mr. Grimthorpe didn't write it. Mr. Snow did. He admitted as much."

"Figures," says Angela. "As the name implies, these online vendors really are vultures. They'll lie about anything just to make a buck."

"And this pen and note sold for how much?" Mr. Preston asks.

"Five hundred dollars," says Angela. "Plus express shipping and handling."

"Who would spend money on such rubbish?" he asks.

"Lots of people," Angela says. "And not just collectors either. Podcasters and reporters, too. Look at this." She clicks on a photo of a black Moleskine notebook with the monogram JDG, followed by a shot of the same notebook spread open, the pages filled with unintelligible scribbles and doodles. "It says it belonged to J. D. Grimthorpe, but I doubt it's real," Angela says.

"Oh, it's real," I reply. "It's most definitely real." Another listing catches my eye. "Scroll up, please," I say.

Angela clicks into a sold item advertising "J. D. Grimthorpe's last words! Be the first to read the speech he never gave!"

My heart beats faster as recognition dawns. "Those are the cue cards that disappeared from the podium," I say. "They're blurred out, but those are the cards!"

"That confirms it. An inside job for sure," Mr. Preston says. "This vendor either works here or is in cahoots with someone who does."

Angela nods, her mouth a tight grimace. "Are you getting the picture, Molly?" she asks.

Our worst fears have just been confirmed. "There's a thief who works here," I say. "And they might also be . . ." I pause. I don't want to say it out loud.

"A coldhearted killer," Angela replies. "There's one more thing. And I have to warn you, Molly. This part will come as a shock."

I ball my hands into fists on the bar top. I don't know how much more I can take. The barstool I'm seated on is swaying from side to side.

Angela scrolls to the final listing, the only Grimthorpe-related item that hasn't yet sold. It advertises his most recent book, "one of the last he ever signed!" selling for the "low, low price of $100!"

"Get ready," Angela says. She clicks on the photo to reveal the book opened to the title page, where J. D. Grimthorpe personalized it:

Dearest Lily,
In return for your sweetness, my thanks for reading.

This message is followed by his signature, the very same one in the book he signed for me and in every signed edition I've ever seen, the letters rickety and ramshackle, as wildly unpredictable as the man himself—an unmistakable, authentic Grimthorpe autograph.

Angela isn't looking at the screen anymore. She's looking at me with an expression I recognize from my mental catalogue of human behaviors. Mr. Preston's expression is a Xerox copy of hers. I used to confuse this look with anguish, but now I know the name for this acutely painful embarrassment, one that's felt not for yourself but for someone else: it's called pity.

"Please," I say. "Please tell me Lily is not the Grim Reaper. I can't believe it. It can't be!"

"Molly, let's not jump to conclusions," Mr. Preston says. "There may be a rational explanation."

"He's right," Angela adds. "Innocent until proven guilty and all that. We don't know anything for sure. Not yet."

"Plus, Lily didn't work here during all that funny business with Mr. Black," says Mr. Preston. "She couldn't possibly know that scotch was the last thing that man drank before he died."

"She knew," I say. "Because I told her. When I trained her, we spent hours together cleaning rooms. I told her about the day Mr. Black drank all the scotch from his minibar, leaving a mess of empties behind. I told her how I thought he'd passed out in his bed when in fact he was dead. I told her how all fingers after that pointed my way. You can never be too careful as a maid, I said. It was a cautionary tale."

Angela and Mr. Preston exchange a concerned look. It does nothing to make me feel better.

I don't tell them what I'm hearing over and over in a loop in my head, Lily's quiet whisper of a voice, repeating what I already know: "The maid is always to blame."

CHAPTER 19

Before

There. I've done it. I've left a little gift for the mysterious man in the watchtower to thank him for helping me and my gran. It feels good to have done so, even though something in me longs to know more about what makes this man so generous. Maybe I'll ask Gran tomorrow at breakfast, find out what else she knows about him.

I've made my way back to the entrance of the mansion, where I open the heavy front door and slip through it, closing it quietly behind me. I've managed to sneak in and out so stealthily that neither Gran nor Mrs. Grimthorpe will have noticed I left.

I wipe the bottoms of my shoes and slip them back into the vestibule. I hear voices coming from the parlor. For a moment, I think I'm hearing things because one of the voices is a man's.

In my stockinged feet, I tiptoe down the corridor to the parlor entrance with its open French doors. Inside, Gran is standing behind the tea cart she's prepared for me. Standing on the other side of the cart is Mr. Grimthorpe. It's the first time I've seen him out of his study, and that in itself is a shock, never mind that he's on the main floor, talking to Gran in the parlor, addressing her in low tones. It seems he's taken my advice after all and has come to seek her out for himself. But there's something strange about what I see before me. I decide to watch for a moment, silent and out of sight.

I press myself to the wall in the shadowy corridor. I study Gran more closely. The way she's standing is peculiar, rigid behind the tea cart, her hands gripping the handle, her face and knuckles white.

"You abandoned me in my time of need. What kind of a nasty woman would do a thing like that?" Mr. Grimthorpe asks. His voice is even and measured, but there's something about it that makes my stomach churn.

"Mr. Grimthorpe, I did nothing of the sort," Gran says. "My job was to see you through the worst of your withdrawal. But when you . . . when you . . ."

"When I *what?*" Mr. Grimthorpe asks, the last word coming out louder than the rest.

"I'm very busy today, sir. I have a lot of work to do for Mrs. Grimthorpe. I really need to go."

"Because you serve my wife, not me? Is that it? Did my wife order you to stay away from me? Did you complain to her about me?"

"Sir, your wife and I agreed that since your recovery, my job here is to clean the mansion. And to cook. Nothing more."

"Your job is to do as you're told. That's what I pay you for," Mr. Grimthorpe says, taking a step toward the tea cart.

"You were getting better," Gran says. "You were through the worst of it. That's why I stopped coming upstairs. And just so it's clear, I don't blame you for . . . for what you did before. You were ill. The demons had their grip on you. Let's just leave it at that."

"I'm a changed man, Flora," says Mr. Grimthorpe as his lips curl into a lopsided smile.

Gran relinquishes her viselike grip on the tea cart handle. "I'm truly delighted that you're clean."

"Clean. Meaning: sober, immaculate, pristine," Mr. Grimthorpe says. "Remind you of anyone?" he asks.

Gran's shoulders rise.

Mr. Grimthorpe slips around the cart with sudden stealth and grabs at Gran. It happens so quickly, I don't quite understand what I'm seeing. It's as though in an instant he's transformed from a man into a wolf. His hands grope at Gran's waist. His teeth flash white, and his mouth gloms onto her neck. What is he doing? Is he trying to eat her? Gran's hands flail as she struggles to push him away.

I step out of my hiding place and rush into the parlor. "Gran!" I yell.

Mr. Grimthorpe freezes. He releases her instantly. His hair is rumpled. One of his monogrammed slippers has slid off his foot. It points at me like a deadly arrow.

"Pip," Mr. Grimthorpe says. "I was just . . . inviting your gran to tea." Casually, he slips his foot back into his roving slipper.

Gran's mouth is tight. Tears pool in her eyes as she stares at me. She wants to speak, I can tell, but the words are caught in her throat.

"Tea is a fine drink, don't you agree?" Mr. Grimthorpe remarks. "It got me through the worst of the darkness. Sweet tea with honey. Isn't that right, Flora? A bitter man always craves sweetness. Care to join us for a cup, Pip?"

His eyes are steely blue, as they've always been, not bloodshot. He's tall, lean, and well dressed, not hunchbacked and hirsute. He's clean and looks respectable, not a wolf in sheep's clothing. There are no piles of bones in the corners of his study, nor does he live on a bridge, terrorizing whoever wishes to pass.

But I see it now. I see it clearly as I never have before—how a man can be a man and a monster at the very same time.

CHAPTER 20

"Molly? Molly?"

It's Mr. Preston, sitting beside me on a barstool, two hands supporting my back, keeping me upright.

Angela looks on, her face full of concern. She clicks her laptop closed.

"I'm all right," I say.

"No you're not," Angela says. "You fainted, Molly. If Mr. Preston didn't catch you just now, you would have fallen off your barstool and landed smack on the floor."

I feel light-headed and foggy. Pinpricks of light twinkle in my peripheral vision.

"There, there," says Mr. Preston. "Deep breaths, Molly."

I breathe as instructed.

"She's back in the land of the living," Mr. Preston tells Angela, releasing his supporting arms. "No need to panic."

"Look what a mess I've caused," I say. "I brought filth into this hotel. I hired a rat, a rat named Lily."

Mr. Preston swirls on his stool to face me. "Now you listen to me, young lady. Do not make the same mistake twice."

"What mistake?" I ask.

"Assuming," he replies. "You know exactly where that will lead. There's only one way around it."

"Which is?" I ask.

"Letting Lily speak for herself," Mr. Preston replies.

"But she can barely utter a full sentence," Angela says.

"She speaks," I say. "With me. When she's comfortable. It takes time."

It is decided then that we must at least try to get Lily to talk to us, to hear her defense in her own words. We enact a plan immediately.

"Are you well enough to bring her here?" Mr. Preston asks.

"Yes," I reply. I stand for a moment beside my barstool, testing my steadiness. "I'm feeling better now," I announce, and it's mostly true. The world has stopped spinning, at least.

"Off you go, Molly," Angela replies. "And keep breathing."

I nod at them both, then hurry out of the Social, heading downstairs, where I find Lily in the housekeeping change rooms putting on her uniform and getting ready for her day. Her entire face falls when instead of "Good morning," I say, "I have a matter of grave importance to discuss with you," and then order her to follow me upstairs to the Social.

When we arrive, Mr. Preston and Angela are exactly where I left them. Lily stops in her tracks the moment she lays eyes on them.

"What's going on?" she asks, her voice hardly above a whisper.

"That's precisely what we need to find out," I say.

Mr. Preston stands as Lily and I approach. "Please, have a seat, Lily," he says, offering her his stool. She sits stiffly, avoiding eye contact.

"Lily," I say. "You may be in some trouble, but we aren't sure yet.

We want to give you a chance to explain yourself. Let me make one thing clear: we are not assuming that you are a thief or a scoundrel or a murderer. That would be foolhardy and preemptive."

"What Molly's trying to say," Mr. Preston adds, "is that we're offering you the benefit of the doubt."

Angela places her laptop on the bar and opens it in front of Lily. "We wanted to show you this," she says as she points to the KultureVulture homepage on the screen. Next, Angela walks Lily through every posting from the Grim Reaper and ends with the autographed copy of Mr. Grimthorpe's book, inscribed to *Dearest Lily*.

Lily barely moves through the entire demonstration. It's as though she's turned to stone. Even when prompted to speak, Lily says nothing. Nothing at all.

"Surely you can see how this is concerning, how all fingers point to *you* stealing from the hotel, to *you* being this Grim Reaper," Mr. Preston says.

Lily nods.

"Don't you have anything to say for yourself? An explanation, perhaps?" I ask.

Lily looks me right in the eye. "The maid is always to blame," she says.

"So you're admitting it," Angela replies. "You stole those goods and posted them for sale on this crappy website."

"No," Lily answers. Her voice is so quiet we have to huddle close to hear her. "I didn't say that. I didn't mean me."

"If you're not to blame, then who is?" Mr. Preston asks.

"Loose lips sink ships," she says, her eyes two glassy pools.

"Lily," I say, "you've been repeating that for days, but I don't know what you mean by it."

"One day, you're the boss, Molly, the next day you're not," she replies. "I do her job and my own. She forces me to do her bidding, says I'm a goner if I don't, but I don't want to protect her anymore. She made me pull the alarm so she could take that box in the lobby. She steals tips from all the rooms. And if I don't keep quiet, I'll lose my job again and never get another. 'Keep your mouth shut. Loose lips sink ships.' That's what she says."

Mr. Preston's mouth falls open. Angela slaps a hand over her own slack jaw.

"Who says all of this, Lily?" Mr. Preston demands. "We need to hear her name."

He may need to hear it, but I do not. Her name hangs like a pestilent odor in the air.

Funny, it's just as Gran always said: sometimes everything falls into place, making something absent feel as though it's been there all along.

"Cheryl," Lily says with finality. "She's your rat."

It feels like déjà vu. We've finished speaking with Lily, and now I'm rushing through the lobby and down the stairs to the housekeeping quarters to find a maid but a different one this time. I'm late for my shift, which concerns me deeply, but not as much as Lily's recent revelation does.

I find her by her locker, fully dressed and about to fasten a Head Maid pin on her left side, right above her heart. How dare she. It's all I can do not to rip it from her hand and stab her with it.

Anger solves nothing. Good things come to those who wait.

"Cheryl," I say, forcing an ersatz smile to my lips. "How lovely to see you this morning, and only fifteen minutes late, too. I've come to tell you there's free orange juice and muffins upstairs at the bar."

Her floppy feet shuffle my way until she's standing right in front of me.

"Angela said you love freebies," I add.

She puts a hand on her hip. "Did she?" she says.

"Yes," I reply. It actually happened like this: when I asked Mr. Preston and Angela how on earth I was supposed to convince slovenly, ornery, petty-thieving, good-for-nothing Cheryl to join us upstairs at the Social, Angela contrived the trap. "Just tell her there's food. She'll take the bait."

Now, Cheryl eyes me, then shrugs. "Muffins sound good. Anything to get out of work."

And just like that, I'm walking up the stairs and through the lobby making small talk about the weather with my archnemesis and chief rival. I smile and smile and smile as I lead her through the glorious front lobby to the bar at the Social, where Mr. Preston is midway through a chocolate chip muffin that he's lifted from the heaping plate Angela has placed on the bar. Lily sits stock-still on her stool.

"Oh, hello, Cheryl," Mr. Preston says as he offers her his seat. "We're thrilled you're joining us. Do me the honor?"

Cheryl plops herself down. "Thanks," she says as she helps herself to a muffin and snaps her fingers at Lily for a glass of orange juice, which Lily pours and hands to her without a word.

"Uff, nice to take a load off," Cheryl says.

"Working hard this morning, though you've just arrived for your shift?" I say, which is when Angela shoves the plate of muffins at me and kindly suggests I stuff one in my mouth.

"Hey, if Snow wanders in and sees us all shirking, this was your idea, not mine," Cheryl says.

"Of course!" Angela replies. "We wouldn't want *you* taking the blame for something *we* did. What kind of people do you take us for?"

Cheryl rips into a muffin and starts chewing a hunk of it. Her beady eyes search our faces, but she doesn't find what she's looking for. "All right, this is too weird," she says. "What do you all want? What's really going on here?"

Mr. Preston clears his throat. "Since you mentioned it," he says, "we have something we wanted to raise with you."

Angela doesn't waste a moment. She whips out her laptop, open to KultureVulture.com. "Such a nice day," Angela says. "And yet a Grim one, too, isn't it, Cheryl?"

Cheryl takes in the screen. "This has nothing to do with me. Nothing."

"They know the truth, Cheryl," Lily whispers. "I just told them."

Cheryl swivels to face Lily. "You little snitchy bitch. The pawnshop just gave me thirty thousand dollars for that rare first edition. I would have given you a cut, Lily. How could you be so stupid?"

"I told you before," Lily says, her voice a quiet knife. "I don't want your dirty money. I just want my job."

Cheryl's beady eyes shift from Lily to Angela to Mr. Preston, then finally land on me. "Wait," she says. "We can make a deal here, can't we? Split the proceeds of my sales four ways as long as you all keep quiet? We'll be a hell of a lot richer if you can just hold your tongues."

If I were to hold any tongue right now, it would be Cheryl's—for the express purpose of ripping it from her mouth.

"I think I've heard enough," Mr. Preston says. "Do we agree?"

Angela nods and so do I.

"I've definitely heard enough," says Lily, her voice no longer a whisper. The clarion sound fills me with overweening pride.

"Molly, would you mind fetching Mr. Snow?" Mr. Preston says.

"Would I mind?" I reply. "On the contrary, it would be my pleasure."

I curtsy to Cheryl, bowing more deeply than I've ever bowed to anyone in my life, because it's the last courtesy she'll receive from any of us for a very long time.

CHAPTER 21

Before

There are moments in life that are so seismically altering they divide everything, cutting a clear rift in time between Before and After. I experienced this powerfully the day my gran died. But that was not the first time in my life I felt it.

The first time was the day I saw what Mr. Grimthorpe did to Gran in the parlor at the mansion. Though I did not understand it entirely until much later, witnessing that moment turned me from a child to an adult in an instant.

I suppose I should have known all along that Mr. Grimthorpe was a monster. My instincts told me so even before I met him. But as with many things, I couldn't quite believe what was right there in front of my face. I couldn't piece together the clues the way I can in retrospect.

Now I know why some days were so hard for Gran, why she'd open my curtains but forget to say "Rise and shine." How she'd prepare breakfast in silence rather than humming her cheery little tune because she dreaded going to work and was so fearful that

Mr. Grimthorpe would force himself upon her. I recall how some nights at dinner she'd sit across from me, her eyes dull, moving her food around her plate but barely eating anything, her mind clearly elsewhere.

She rallied—my gran always rallied—searching for the bright side, focusing on the positive, convincing herself that Grimthorpe was a changed man, that once he was sober, he would never attack her again. That was my gran. She had an infinite capacity to light hope in the dark. And for the most part, she was successful. She certainly convinced me that all was well in our cloistered little world, that our future was impossibly bright. Everything she did was so I would not just survive but thrive. Only now do I know just how much she suffered in the dark, how she carried her burden alone.

In my mind's eye, I'm a child again. Gran and I are sitting at our old kitchen table having breakfast the day after Mr. Grimthorpe transformed from a man into a ravenous wolf right before my eyes. I'm swinging my legs back and forth under my country-kitchen chair as I always do, but nothing will ever be the same again. At least that much I understand. Usually, in the mornings, I hurl a barrage of childlike questions at Gran, my existential quandaries and would-you-rather quizzes. But not that day.

I push my oatmeal down my throat, but when Gran tells me it's time to go to the Grimthorpe mansion, I don't move. I can't.

"It's not right," I say. It's the first mention I've made of what I saw in that parlor. I pause. "Gran, you can't go back there." I don't know how to say what I want to say, because I don't have words for what I saw.

"Molly, today is a brand-new day." Gran jumps up from her chair so quickly it screeches against the floor. "The sun is shining. The birds are chirping." She takes our barely touched bowls to the sink, turning away from me. Her hands clutch the edge of the counter. "Let's go now," she announces. "It's time."

When she turns to face me, she's smiling, and I swear to you that smile is genuine. She has willed it from some wellspring deep within, and now she offers it like a bouquet of fresh roses. She dons her bravest face because what other choice does she have?

That rhetorical question had kept me up the night before. I lay awake in bed with Gran's lone-star quilt pulled up to my neck. I stared into the darkness and contemplated our options. A plan emerged in my mind. Suddenly, I saw it clearly. I knew what I had to do.

Gran once told me that sometimes in this life, you have to do something wrong to make something right. I've never forgotten that. It has become a motto to live by.

As I swing my legs under the table, I've already decided.

It is a brand-new day. The sun is shining. The birds are chirping. I have a plan, and there's nothing that will stop me from seeing it through. Nothing.

We arrive at the mansion right on time. The invisible gatekeeper has buzzed us through the gate. Now, Gran and I are standing on the path. Suddenly, I'm filled with doubt. What if I can't do it? What if it's the wrong thing to do? What if I'm making a terrible mistake? No. I won't listen to doubt. We must escape the monster. We must run from the wolf.

I haven't mentioned a thing to Gran, and I won't, but my feet are tethered to the ground before we've even reached the front door. Gran puts a warm hand on my arm. My feet loosen and release. Together, we walk up the rest of the path toward the Grimthorpe mansion.

The roses flanking us are all expired now, every last one, their blooms spent, their heads bowed and withered. Jenkins is up the path, sweeping crispy fallen petals into a pile that he rakes into his wheelbarrow. There's a new smell in the air, the sweet scent of expiration.

"Good morning, Flora," Jenkins says as we pass. "How are you and the little mite on this fine day?"

"Well enough, Jenkins, I suppose," Gran replies.

"Rose season is over," he replies, "but there's always next year."

"Something to look forward to," Gran replies.

"We all need that, don't we?"

Gran nods. "Indeed we do."

We continue up the path until we reach the front door. I grab the lion's brass mandible and knock three times. The massive door swings open, and Mrs. Grimthorpe lets us in. Gran and I take off our shoes, wiping them down as usual and slipping them into the space at the back of the vestibule, in the dark corner reserved for the help.

Mrs. Grimthorpe starts in without delay. "Today is wash-and-dry day. Flora, go upstairs and collect all the laundry. Be quick about it. Lots to do."

Gran flinches ever so slightly. It's something I wouldn't have noticed before, but on that day I do.

"Once you've got all the dirty laundry, bring it downstairs to the cellar. Stay down there and monitor the machines. The washer has been acting up again. And do be careful with the bleach. Last time, you used so much on the whites, you burnt a hole into one of Mr. Grimthorpe's shirts."

"There was a stain, madam," Gran says. "I was trying to remove the blot."

"Is burning it to oblivion the only way?" Mrs. Grimthorpe asks. "Surely any half-decent maid knows better."

"Yes, ma'am," Gran replies.

"Child, you may read upstairs in the library," Mrs. Grimthorpe says. "You can polish silver in the afternoon."

"Would it be all right if I read in the parlor?" I ask. "Just for today?"

Mrs. Grimthorpe's forehead scrunches up, then she says, "I suppose, provided you sit in one chair only and touch a grand total of nothing. Do not clean or polish anything, you understand? Keep your paws off Mr. Grimthorpe's treasures."

"Yes, ma'am," I say.

"Off you go, then."

Gran gives my arm a squeeze, then follows Mrs. Grimthorpe through the main corridor toward the back of the mansion. I hold on to the banister for a moment, steadying myself before I head up the main staircase to retrieve my book.

The creaks and groans of the floorboards sound different today, like a warning. *Don't do it. Don't go upstairs.* I make my way to the first landing and look out the window. There she is, Mr. Grimthorpe's personal secretary, wearing her blue kerchief and blue gloves, entering through the side door of the mansion as usual. It makes me wonder: has she had to fend off the monster, too?

I start up the next flight of stairs, then turn down the damask corridor, forcing my feet forward to the library. I pause at the threshold, looking in. Light is shining through the crack under the hidden bookcase door. It's spilling onto the floor. I hear the shuffle of Mr. Grimthorpe's slippers on the other side.

I tiptoe into the library, grab *Great Expectations*, and leave as quietly as I came.

I head down the main stairs and through the French doors of the parlor, taking a seat on a royal-blue high-back chair, where I begin to read quietly.

Rat-a-tat-tat-tat.

The sound starts up just as I finish a chapter, the familiar rhythm, the background drone of Mr. Grimthorpe's secretary typing in her secret lair somewhere deep inside the mansion's walls.

I wait, pretending to read my book until I see Gran walk by the open French doors. She smiles at me, then continues on her way. I listen as she climbs the creaky main staircase. A few minutes later, she comes back down with two large bags of laundry on her back. She stops for a moment in the doorway.

"All's well?" she asks.

"All's well," I reply. "And you?"

"Perfectly fine," she answers. "Today's a brand-new day."

She lugs her heavy burden down the hallway toward the kitchen. I listen as Mrs. Grimthorpe barks out orders at Gran, cutting her down with her razor-sharp tongue.

I hear the cellar door open, and the *thump, thump, thump* as Gran pushes the heavy laundry bags down the stairs.

"For the love of God, can you not do a single thing the proper way?" Mrs. Grimthorpe scolds. "Why wouldn't you carry the bags down?" Her rebuke reverberates through the entire house. Gran's response is the same as always: "Yes, ma'am. Yes, ma'am."

A few moments later, Mrs. Grimthorpe clicks down the corridor toward the parlor. She appears between the open French doors, eyeing me with her familiar look of disdain.

"I'm going out front to instruct Jenkins on the proper disposal of dead roses. When they have blight and you mix them into the compost, the disease infects the entire garden, not that he'd know that. The help these days don't seem to know anything at all."

"Yes, ma'am," I say.

"I won't be gone long. And remember," she says, pointing a bony finger at me, "you are not to touch a thing."

I nod. She turns on her kitten heels and makes her way to the front door.

I stay put until I hear the front door close behind her. Then I snap my book shut and place it on the side table.

It's time.

I walk to the mantel and stand in front of it, taking in the glowing Fabergé. It's just as beautiful as the first day I laid eyes on it, delicate and enchanting, encrusted with rows of precious, sparkling jewels and resting on an ornate pedestal of the finest, purest gold.

I know that after I do this, there will be a new rift in time, a new Before and After. But that doesn't stop me. Nothing will.

I reach out and grab the Fabergé. The weight of it is satisfying and substantive in my hands. I rush back to my seat and open *Great Expectations*, concealing the treasure on my lap behind my book just as I hear Mrs. Grimthorpe coming back through the front door.

"Flora!" Mrs. Grimthorpe shrieks in that ear-piercing way of hers.

It's now been hours since I executed the first step of the plan. I'm in the cellar of the Grimthorpe mansion. I have gone downstairs to use the washroom because for once Gran is there, and I don't have to brave the spiders alone.

"Flora!" Mrs. Grimthorpe shrieks again, more shrilly the second time.

This can mean only one thing: she found it.

I dry my hands quickly, then exit the scary washroom.

Gran is folding one of Mr. Grimthorpe's crisp white shirts. She freezes the moment she hears the second shriek from the banshee upstairs.

"Flora Gray! Do you hear me? Come up to the kitchen this minute! And bring that wretched grandchild of yours as well!"

Gran looks at me and shrugs.

I shrug back, not saying a word.

Gran leads the way up the damp cellar stairs. I follow behind her, exiting into the kitchen, where Mrs. Grimthorpe stands, huffing and puffing, her face raging red, her pupils two pinholes of fury.

"Come," she says, not an invitation but an order as she marches us to the silver pantry. We follow her in.

I've left all the polished wares from the day before neatly organized on the table. It's filled with silver, ready for an elegant banquet that will never happen. I've worked days and days now so that every shelf behind Mrs. Grimthorpe glimmers and shines, each silver platter, cutlery set, and tray polished to a high sheen. There's only one shelf of tarnished silver left for me to clean. It's a pity I won't be able to see the job through to completion. But so be it. It doesn't matter. Not anymore.

"Flora," Mrs. Grimthorpe says. "I was in the parlor just now checking that this little varmint of yours didn't touch anything. Everything looked just fine, until I noticed a bare spot on the mantel. That's when I realized the Fabergé egg was gone. I searched for it everywhere. Then it occurred to me to check the silver pantry. And guess what I found."

Mrs. Grimthorpe lurches forward and opens the cupboard where I store my rubber gloves, my cleaning basin, my tattered apron, and the jug of lye solution.

"Look!" Mrs. Grimthorpe says. "Just look at what's wrapped up in her apron."

Gran picks up my apron and pulls the Fabergé egg out of the threadbare front pocket. She turns to me, her eyes wide, her mouth open, puzzlement and shock writ large in every line on her face.

"She was going to steal it, Flora! She was about to sneak it out of the mansion, the greedy little devil," says Mrs. Grimthorpe. "You can't trust anyone in your home these days. No loyalty. No boundaries. No morals."

"But, ma'am, she's just a child," Gran says. "I'm sure there's an explanation."

"She's just a thief is what she is. You should be instructing her, showing her right from wrong. If I've learned anything in my years, it's that the apple never falls far from the tree. If she's a thief, guess what that tells me about you."

"No. You're wrong about that last part," I say, facing Mrs. Grimthorpe squarely. "But you're right about the rest. I meant to steal the Fabergé. I took it and was going to bring it home with me. But it was all my idea. Gran had nothing to do with it. She would never do such a thing."

"Molly, how could you?" Gran says. "You know better."

"I do know better," I say. "But I did it anyway."

"You see?" Mrs. Grimthorpe says, the words spitting from her mouth. "No moral compass. No understanding of right and wrong. It's bred in the bone with you lot. If you're not thieves, you're liars, like all those others before you. Get out, both of you. Now!"

"Please, don't do this," Gran says. "You know how hard it is to find reliable help these days."

"Out!" Mrs. Grimthorpe shrieks, a sound that makes Gran flinch. She grabs my hand and rushes us out of the room.

Mrs. Grimthorpe follows us through the kitchen, down the corridor past the bourgeois blobs and the "gold de toilette," until we reach the front entrance. Mrs. Grimthorpe opens the vestibule and watches, fuming, as Gran fumbles to find her shoes and I do the same.

Once our shoes are on, Mrs. Grimthorpe opens the door wide, then grabs me by the collar and tosses me out, with Gran following close behind. "You're a disgrace. You're never to come back here—never—do you understand?"

She turns her back on us and goes inside, slamming the heavy door behind her.

Gran and I stand outside for a moment, too stunned to move. Jenkins is just up the path, frozen beside his wheelbarrow, watching helplessly.

Gran takes me by the arm and we leave together, walking for what I think is the last time down the path of roses toward the Grimthorpe gates.

"I can't believe it," Gran says when we're halfway up the path. "Molly, why on earth would you do such a thing? Why would you want to steal the Fabergé?"

I don't answer because it doesn't matter now.

All that matters is that Mr. Grimthorpe will never lay a hand on my gran ever again.

Chapter 22

I find Mr. Snow in his office doing paperwork. I march right in and say, "Mr. Snow, your presence is required at the Social posthaste. While this is not a life-or-death emergency, it is, nonetheless, a situation requiring your immediate attention."

"What kind of a situation?" he asks.

It takes a moment to find the words, but then I say, "Pest control. There's a rat in our hotel. And not your garden variety either."

This gets his attention. He closes the file folder he's working on, stands, and readjusts his glasses, which have, as per usual, gone off-kilter on his face. I lead the way out of his office, and he follows at a clipped pace as we make our way through the labyrinthine corridors to the Social.

He spots the anomaly as soon as he walks in. Cheryl is sitting on a barstool flanked by Mr. Preston on one side and Lily on the other. Angela is behind the bar.

"Doesn't anyone in this hotel actually work anymore?" Mr. Snow asks. "This better be good."

"I realize we look like the beginning of a bad joke," Angela replies. "A doorman and two maids walk into a bar."

Mr. Snow sighs. "Molly said something about vermin. What exactly are we dealing with this time?" he asks.

"Her," I say, pointing a finger at Cheryl, etiquette be damned.

Mr. Snow's brow wrinkles in confusion.

Angela opens her laptop and proceeds to walk him through each of Cheryl's items on KultureVulture.com. As Mr. Snow's eyes grow wider and wider behind his tortoiseshell glasses, Cheryl remains as impassive as a lump in a gravy boat, her arms crossed against her chest, her mouth a defiant pout.

When Angela's show-and-tell is done, Mr. Snow turns to Cheryl. "You had Lily pull the fire alarm? And you took the items in that banker's box meant for Serena? Are you really this"—he waves a hand at the laptop screen—"this Grim Reaper?"

She shrugs. "I see myself as more of a recycling entrepreneur. By the way, what you pay maids sucks. You know that, right? And when you demoted me from Head Maid, my pay got worse. What did you expect?"

"What I expect," says Mr. Snow, "is that you do not cheat, pillage, or steal, especially from your own colleagues."

"You forced Lily to aid and abet you," I say. "How could you do such a thing?"

"Oh, that's rich," says Cheryl. "How many times have I seen you stealing tiny jam jars off discarded guest trays in the corridors? Or pocketing turn-down chocolates guests leave behind in their rooms?"

"That's not theft," I say. "Those items were destined for the trash bin, and I merely liberated them from waste. There's a provision for this in *A Maid's Guide & Handbook*," I say.

"You and your goddamn handbook. Admit it. You're as much of a trash panda as I am."

212

My backbone goes rigid. My blood pulses in my temples. I've been called many things over my life span, but never before has a name felt more offensive than this.

"Why do you call yourself the Grim Reaper?" Angela asks Cheryl. "Why that name in particular?"

"Because it sounds good. It's called marketing."

"Perhaps it's more suggestive than you ever intended," Mr. Preston says.

"Suggestive of what?" Cheryl asks.

"Of murder," Lily says, her voice strong and clear, the furthest thing from a whisper.

Cheryl guffaws and slaps her thighs. "Those cleaning chemicals you two love so much must be frying your brains. I may take the odd thing here and there, but I'm no killer."

"Glad to hear it," says Mr. Snow. "Please, enjoy another muffin, Cheryl, courtesy of the Regency Grand." He stands abruptly, removes his cellphone from his pocket, and dials a contact. "You can explain everything yourself," he says.

"Explain? What do you mean? I just did," Cheryl says.

"I'm phoning the lead investigator. I'm calling in Detective Stark."

Twenty minutes later, a detective walks into a bar. She heads straight for the source of commotion, where three maids, a bartender, a doorman, and a hotel manager are arguing about a first-edition book put up for sale in a local pawnshop.

"I sold my very own property, but *you* sold ill-gotten goods! Can you not see the difference?" Mr. Preston asks Cheryl.

"If the book in that box was so valuable, it should have been locked in a safe," Cheryl replies. "You can't be too careful these days."

"Holy forking shirtballs, Cheryl. Are you for real?" Angela says.

Some familiar-looking special agents enter the Social behind Detective Stark. They stand at the entrance, guarding it, while Stark stops in front of all of us gathered at the bar. Lily, Mr. Snow, and Mr. Preston stand up from their barstools immediately.

"Thank you for coming so quickly, Detective," Mr. Snow says.

"Is this really necessary?" Cheryl asks. "Shouldn't I get back to work?"

"You're not going anywhere," Mr. Preston replies.

"Does someone here care to explain what the hell is going on?" Stark asks.

Angela wastes no time. She places her laptop in front of the detective and guides her through the evidence as Cheryl sneers on the stool right beside her, her arms crossed against her chest.

"All of the items on the site are related to Grimthorpe, minus one," Angela notes. "The minibar bottles of scotch. Cheryl admits she's the Grim Reaper. She sold nearly the whole lot of stolen Grimthorpe goods to a single vendor."

Stark turns to Cheryl, staring at her for a moment. "Exactly how long have you been selling items on this website?" she asks.

"For as long as she's worked here," Angela answers. "Or so it seems."

"The minibar bottles of scotch," Stark says. "You say they're the last thing Mr. Black drank before he died."

"They were," Cheryl replies. "I liberated them from Molly's maid trolley. But that was years ago."

"Who else are you working with in the hotel? The kitchen staff? Or maybe some other maids?" Stark looks at me and Lily, and though I want to scream, I have, for once, the good sense to keep quiet.

"Are you kidding me?" Cheryl says as she points to me and Lily. "This lot wouldn't know a gold nugget if it hit them on the forehead."

"She forced Lily to be an accessory to her crimes," I say.

"I didn't want to help her, Detective," Lily says. "But . . . but . . ." The words catch in her throat.

"Go on," I say. "Speak up."

"It's just that I need this job so badly," Lily continues. "And I didn't think anyone would believe me over her."

Cheryl is about to say something but then thinks better of it. Her lips are so pursed they call to mind the puckered orifice of a cat's hind end.

"Those blurry cue cards," Stark says. "What was written on them, Cheryl?"

"How should I know? I never read them closely. Looked boring," she replies.

"Who bought them?" Stark demands.

"No idea," Cheryl says. "I couriered everything to some PO box right here in this city. My customers demand anonymity. I don't even know their real names."

"Don't you keep the buyers' addresses?"

"Yeah, but they're useless. Can't sell them."

"Lower than a squirrel's behind," Mr. Preston mutters under his breath.

"Cheryl, you'll get me the details of that PO box," Stark demands. "I'll run the address at the station."

Cheryl shrugs. "Sure," she says.

"What about this love note?" Detective Stark asks. "It's blurred out, too. I suppose you didn't read it either?"

"Actually, that one was juicier, so I did read it," Cheryl admits. "But it was sentimental hogwash. Sounded like a Hallmark card from the nineteen hundreds. It was signed *Your Chiefest Admirer.* Old Man Grimthorpe was obviously getting it on with his personal secretary. Same old story. Ancient geezer, young mistress. Kinda like the Blacks."

"She's wrong," I say. "That note was not written by Mr. Grimthorpe." I watch as Mr. Snow's face turns crimson.

"It was written by me," Mr. Snow confirms. "I've held a certain . . . affection for Ms. Sharpe—for Serena—ever since she approached us several weeks ago about holding a press conference in our tearoom. That note, the one I put in the banker's box . . . well . . . I admit it was a declaration of my romantic intentions."

"You left a love note in her room as well, didn't you, Mr. Snow?" I say.

"Along with twelve long-stem roses," Detective Stark adds.

"I did," Mr. Snow replies. He removes his pocket square from his breast pocket and wipes the dewy beads that have proliferated on his forehead. "Serena's an enchanting young woman—intelligent, enterprising, and elegant. How you could ever think she'd be Mr. Grimthorpe's mistress is beyond me, Cheryl. She's a paragon of beauty."

"Oh dear," Mr. Preston says. "Love is blind."

"Were you romantically involved with Ms. Sharpe?" Detective Stark asks.

"Goodness, no!" Mr. Snow replies.

"Not for want of trying," Angela adds under her breath.

Stark turns to Lily. "Did you give Cheryl your signed copy of Mr. Grimthorpe's latest book?"

"Give?" Lily says with her chin held high. "She took it. She said I could have it back when I proved myself to be a good maid by cleaning all her rooms and mine in a single shift."

"That's impossible," I say. "No maid could ever do that."

"Exactly," says Mr. Preston.

"The first edition that was in the banker's box. Why isn't it listed on your site? And where is it now, Cheryl?" Stark asks.

"Sold," she says. "I pawned it to the guy in the shop down the street. He gets top dollar for old books, even better than on the website."

A thought occurs to me then. I suddenly see it with clarity. Cheryl took everything she could get her grubby hands on. She even took the cue cards off the podium. So, what if she took other items, too? "The honey pot and spoon," I say. "The ones that were on Mr. Grimthorpe's tea cart the day he died. Did you take them, Cheryl? That spoon was the last thing to touch Mr. Grimthorpe's lips."

"A honey pot and spoon?" Cheryl asks. "I don't know anything about that."

"Lying will get you into even more trouble than the considerable amount you're already in," Stark warns. "Admit it. You took them."

"I didn't," Cheryl replies. "But that spoon is really good thinking—'the last thing to touch the lips of the famous writer!' The copy writes itself. The Vultures love that crap. 'Unique ephemera,' they call it."

"The Moleskine notebook," Stark continues. "You blurred out photos of many of the other written items. Why didn't you blur out that one as well?"

"Because there was nothing to see," Cheryl replies. "It was filled with doodles and gobbledygook. For a big-time writer, it's kinda weird there wasn't even a single legible word on the pages."

During this entire exchange, I've remained steady and calm, but now, a hairline crack threatens my composure. How is it possible I never realized before? Deep in my being, a fracture splits and vertigo sets in. The revelation I experience is so seismic it takes effort to remain upright.

I feel a hand on my arm—not Mr. Preston's, not Mr. Snow's. Lily is holding me steady, pulling me close to her side.

"Molly!" I hear Mr. Preston shout.

"What the hell is wrong with her?" Detective Stark asks.

The x in the equation, the missing key—it's been there all along, right in front of my eyes!

"Detective Stark," I say. "I have a confession to make. There's something you need to know. I knew Mr. Grimthorpe when I was a child."

The detective shakes her head. "So? What does that have to do with anything?"

All eyes are on me. Cheryl's face is filled with predatory glee.

"Mr. Grimthorpe suffered from writer's block," I explain. "The evidence is right there in that black Moleskine notebook. He was perfectly literate, but he couldn't write a single word. I remember it so clearly—on his desk at the mansion were stacks of Moleskines he claimed were his first drafts. They were just like the one Cheryl stole from that box—monogrammed and filled with doodles and indecipherable scrawls. When I was a child, I thought it was code or a secret language. But it wasn't. I see that now."

"As usual, Molly, you're making no sense," Stark says.

"Can't you see? The black Moleskine is proof of a motive," I say. "There was a good reason why someone wanted Mr. Grimthorpe dead."

"Even I don't know what you're getting at," Angela says.

"Nor do I," Mr. Preston adds.

"For god's sake, Molly," Stark says. "Spell it out for us, will you?"

"Motive," I say. "M-O-T-I-V-E. Meaning: a reason to kill. Mr. Grimthorpe didn't write his books, not a single one of them. Someone else did."

CHAPTER 23

I used to think it only happened in movies, the classic black-and-white kind that Gran and I used to watch together on Movie Nights in our apartment, snuggled side by side on our threadbare sofa. But now I know it can happen in reality, too—that a segment of your past can play out like a movie montage, that life can flash before your very eyes, reminding you of everything you've lived through that has brought you to the present moment, that has made you who you are.

That's what I've been experiencing as I reveal the truth to Detective Stark about that fateful couple of weeks I spent working alongside Gran in the Grimthorpe mansion, polishing silver, reading in the library, and befriending a troubled man, an author to whom I fed ideas I had no clue would lead him to write an international blockbuster. I have relived all of this in Technicolor. I have seen it again through fresh eyes.

Mr. Snow suggested that Detective Stark and I retire to his office to speak privately, and for the last hour, that's where we've been.

I'm sitting in a chair across from an imposing detective who has always intimidated me. And I'm telling her my life story.

I'll grant her this: for the first time ever, Stark is listening intently, patiently. For once, she realizes I'm ahead of her, that I know things she doesn't. I can see her struggling to piece things together, to connect the past with what has happened recently—the unsolved mystery of a poisoned author in the Regency Grand Hotel.

Gran used to say, *Stories are a way to walk a mile in someone else's shoes.*

She was right. Every fairy tale teaches a lesson.

The monster is always real, just not the way you thought.

No secret stays buried forever.

The maid shalt be redeemed in the end.

"Rat-a-tat-tat-tat," I say to Detective Stark. "That sound was always in the background, the sound of his personal secretary typing. Mr. Grimthorpe wrote longhand, yet never once did I see him doing anything but doodling in those monogrammed black Moleskines. As a child, I was told his personal secretary typed up what he wrote, and I believed it. But now, I don't think that was true."

"You said just now that you gave him the idea for the end of his most popular novel," Detective Stark says. "The lye solution."

"Yes. That was my idea, but what if someone else gave him the rest of the story, the rest of all his stories? Maybe that secretary was more than a typist. Maybe she was . . ."

"A ghostwriter?" Stark offers.

"Yes," I reply.

"A ghostwriter working in secrecy while the fraudulent front man took all the credit and fame," Stark says.

"And reaped the staggering monetary rewards," I add. "Would that not breed discontent? Would that not be a motive for revenge?"

Detective Stark stands suddenly. She paces the perimeter of the room. The reverberation of her footsteps travels right up my spine.

"I've met some writers in my time," she says. "The ones who write police procedurals sometimes consult with me. They want to know if they got their details right. Let's just say, those writers know a hell of a lot about how to murder someone without leaving a trace. The question is: Could a writer—or a ghostwriter—apply their knowledge to a real murder? And if so, could they get away with it?" The detective pauses in her tracks. "Molly," she says. "I think I've underestimated you."

"What do you mean?" I ask.

"I don't always know what you're going on about. But you just put together a whole series of clues I didn't even realize *were* clues. I need your help."

"My help?" I say. "With what?"

"We're going on a road trip."

The thought of going anywhere with Detective Stark is the most terrifying thing I can imagine right about now. "Where are we going?" I ask.

"To the Grimthorpe mansion, of course."

Now, I find myself on the outskirts of the city in a police cruiser chauffeured by Detective Stark. It gives me only an iota of solace that I'm seated in the passenger seat rather than beyond the bulletproof barrier in the back. I'm feeling very much like a little girl as I head to a place I never thought I'd see again, this time not with my beloved gran but with the imposing detective at the wheel beside me. My hands tremble. I grip the door handle just as I did all those years ago in a taxi on my very first visit to the mansion.

Before embarking on this trip, Stark made a call and spoke to a judge. She explained everything and argued for a search warrant, the corner of which is sticking out from the hidden interior pocket of her black coat.

"Is it far from here?" Stark asks as she surveys the road ahead.

"No," I reply. "Just five minutes away."

Stark nods, then surveys the various grand mansions punctuating the dense, forested suburb. "Bloody posh neck of the woods," she says.

"Beyond my wildest dreams," I say.

We round the last bend in the road, and the Grimthorpe mansion comes into view. "That's the one. Up there."

The monolithic, three-story mansion is just as imposing as it was when I was a child, with black-framed windows set in three rows—the terrifying face of an eight-eyed spider.

The detective drives right up to the wrought-iron gate. The black paint is peeling, rust setting in. The watchtower is a stone's throw away, its tinted windows obscuring whoever is inside.

Detective Stark stops the car. We both get out and approach the gate.

The buttons of the hidden intercom are faded and cracked with age. "You have to buzz the gatekeeper," I say. "He's in that watchtower."

Stark puts a hand on the gate and pushes it. It creaks open with ease.

"Oh," I say. "Things have changed."

I pass through the gate, following the detective.

We walk down the familiar path of blood-red roses flanking the driveway. The buds are beginning to open. They emit an ambrosial fragrance, hypnotic and treacly sweet.

"This place has seen better days," Stark says. "Looks like Fawlty Towers."

The mansion is in a state of disrepair—the façade faded and cracked. The roses are the only things that look tended at all.

We arrive at the imposing front door with the lion knocker, the brass blackened and weathered. The last time I was here, my tiny hand was tucked into Gran's as we made our way to this landing. The memory hits my heart with a wallop.

"You knock, I'll do the talking," Detective Stark says.

I grab the mandible and pound three times.

Clomping footsteps, some shuffling, then the turn of the knob as the enormous door swings open. Standing in the threshold is a gray-haired man with protruding eyes and a leather tool belt around his waist containing an array of trowels, secateurs, scissors, and clippers. He is rounded with age, his body no longer an exclamation point but shaped more like a question mark. Regardless, when I look into those eyes, I recognize the man who stands before me.

"Jenkins? Is it you?"

"Molly? Molly Gray?"

"You remember me."

"Of course I do," he replies. "My Little Mite. The silver girl, polishing everything to perfection. Oh, that was such a long time ago. It was a dark place in those days. But you made everything shine."

"You were kind to me," I say, "though I was a bit afraid of you. I was too young to tell the good eggs from the bad."

"You were a lovely little thing, filled with youthful energy. I used to listen in on the fanciful stories you told. Hard worker, too. Your grandmother was so proud of you. How's she doing? Flora?"

"She died," I report matter-of-factly.

"Oh, I'm so sorry. She was a good woman."

"The very best," I say.

"So much for me doing the talking," Detective Stark says with a sigh.

Jenkins turns his attention to the imposing figure on the landing. "And you are?"

"Detective Stark," she replies. "I'm in charge of investigating the death of the owner of this estate. I was wondering who was in the mansion these days. Thought I'd pay a visit."

"I'm afraid there's no one else here but me at the moment," Jenkins replies. "We're waiting for the will to be read. I figure the property will go up for sale sometime soon. I'm sure Mrs. Grimthorpe is rolling over in her grave."

"Jenkins, may I ask how she died?" I say.

"A stroke, five years ago," Jenkins replies, "right after plucking a rose from her very own garden. As you know, Molly, Mr. Grimthorpe was always strange, but he got even stranger after that. More paranoid. Said without his wife his secrets would never be safe. He never did go back to the bottle, though. He made a promise to Mrs. Grimthorpe, and he kept it. I suspect that's the only way he was ever loyal to her." Jenkins pauses and looks down at a box by his feet. It's filled to the brim with tarnished silver, trinkets, and paintings. "I'm clearing house," he says. "I've received orders."

He eyes Stark from head to toe. "So . . . do you have a search warrant?" he asks.

"Yeah," says Stark. "I do." She produces it from her coat, and Jenkins eyes it for a moment before giving it back to her.

"Jenkins, would you mind terribly if I had a look around, too?" I ask. "It would mean so much to me. I have such fond memories of this place."

"You might be the only person who does," he says. Turning to Stark, he asks, "Have you figured it out yet—who poisoned Mr. Grimthorpe?"

"No," Stark replies. "But we will. It's only a matter of time."

Jenkins nods, the deep lines in his visage a map of untold secrets. "You can come in," he says. "I'll be in the parlor, cleaning it out. No love for old things nowadays. Change is nigh."

"Thank you, Jenkins," I say as he moves the box of discarded objects, allowing us to pass. Overhead the shards of the modernist chandelier are so covered in cobwebs the entire fixture looks more like driftwood than glass.

"This way," I say to Detective Stark, as I lead her up the main staircase. The steps are even creakier than they used to be, groaning and heaving under every footfall.

We reach the top of the stairs. "Follow me," I say as we walk down the hall, the lights turning on automatically—at least the ones with working bulbs. The damask wallpaper in the corridor is faded and dull. I once saw eyes in its pattern, but I can't see them anymore. Were they ever really there, or did they exist only in my imagination?

We pass bedroom after bedroom, the doors all open but the curtains drawn in every single one.

"It's filthy," Detective Stark says.

Every nook and cranny, every wall sconce is coated in a thick layer of grime and dust. "There has not been a maid in this mansion for a very long time," I say. I wonder to myself if Gran was the last. Maybe Mrs. Grimthorpe trusted no one after firing her.

We make it to the room at the very end of the hall. I walk over to the window, pull back the curtains, and let the light stream in from the floor-to-ceiling window.

This room is not what it used to be. The books are neglected, a layer of dust coating every leather-bound spine. Detective Stark takes it all in—the ladder on wheels, the dust-covered nymph holding up a grubby lampshade, the bookshelves lining all four walls. She spots the anomaly quickly, the one book that juts out awkwardly and that isn't covered in dust—the shiny Oxford dictionary on the fourth wall.

"This it?" she asks, pointing to it.

"Yes," I say. "The secret doorway, a portal to another dimension." I step forward and push it. The fourth wall springs open to reveal Mr. Grimthorpe's study.

"Get a load of that," Stark says, her face wide with surprise.

His desk is in the same spot it always was. On it are teetering stacks of black monogrammed Moleskines. They've multiplied considerably since the last time I was here. There are stacks on the desk like before, but now there are more on the floor, some of them piled waist high. The room is so filled with Moleskines that the only empty space is a narrow pathway to Mr. Grimthorpe's desk and another leading to his bookcase on the far wall.

"Whoa," says Stark. "This is bonkers. Was Grimthorpe a hoarder?"

"In a way," I say. "The lord of everything. And of nothing."

She picks up a Moleskine, opens it gingerly to a random page filled with scribbles and doodles and unintelligible scrawl. "Indecipherable. Just like the one Cheryl sold," she says.

Stark checks a few other Moleskines, and I do the same, though I'm loath to besmirch my hands with grime. The contents are exactly as I remember—scrawls and scratches, not handwriting or even code, and certainly not any novel written in long-form.

"There's nothing in here that anyone could have typed up," Stark says.

"Exactly," I reply. "And Mr. Grimthorpe never typed. It was always his secretary typing away, unseen, while these notebooks multiplied, untouched."

The detective spots something on Mr. Grimthorpe's bookcase on the far wall, another book that stands out, the only one on the shelf that is clean—a second Oxford dictionary. She walks over and presses on it. A wall springs open.

"What?" I exclaim. "I never even noticed that was there!"

"Glad I'm good for something," Stark replies. She walks through the narrow doorway into a modern office, spotlessly clean and gleaming white, the contrast extreme. I follow behind her. There's a spiral staircase in the corner that leads down to the mansion's side door. Modular Ikea shelves line one wall, and in each cubby are stacks of printed manuscripts, perfectly organized and bound with elastic bands. There's a cubby for each of Mr. Grimthorpe's past books, the titles printed neatly above each stack, all of them ordered by year of publication, from the most recent on crisp, white paper to his biggest bestseller, *The Maid in the Mansion*, the paper yellowed with age.

"Looks like his novels in manuscript form," Stark says as she crouches for a closer look.

She stands and walks over to a simple desk at one side of the room. There's a rose-gold Mac laptop on it, closed, and a printer to one side, nothing else.

Then I see it. In an arched niche behind the desk sits an old typewriter. On the wall above it is a single photo in a simple gilded frame. I approach for a closer look.

What I see is an utter surprise, but in some ways it all makes sense. There she is, the woman in the blue kerchief and gloves, standing with her arm around a young girl who looks her spitting image. "That's her," I say. "The lady in blue, his previous personal secretary. When I was a child, she came here every day through the side entrance. I could never figure out where her office was, but I heard her typing away."

Stark approaches and leans into the photo. "But who's that child beside her?" she asks.

Yet again, I know something before Detective Stark does. I put two and two together and come up with a sum that is more than I thought it could ever be. "You don't recognize her? Look closely."

Stark squints. "Jesus," she says. "Is that her?"

"Yes," I reply. "The resemblance is uncanny, isn't it? That little girl," I say, "is Ms. Serena Sharpe."

CHAPTER 24

"How very nice of you to trespass. Please make yourselves at home while you snoop around my office."

Detective Stark and I both jump and turn around. Standing in the doorway is Ms. Serena Sharpe, car keys clinking in one hand.

"The man downstairs let us in," Stark explains.

"So I hear. May I ask what the hell you're doing in my office?"

"I knew your mother," I blurt out. "Or rather, I didn't know her. But I saw her here when I was a child working alongside my gran. She was Mr. Grimthorpe's personal secretary. This photo—you're her daughter," I say as I point to the picture on the wall.

Ms. Sharpe sighs. "Yes. That's my mother. So what?"

"You never mentioned that before," Detective Stark says.

"And you also failed to mention that your mother is the real author of Mr. Grimthorpe's books," I add.

Ms. Sharpe affixes me with her sphinxlike gaze. Then she strides across the room to stand in front of the niche containing her mother's typewriter. She puts one finger on the letter *I*. "How did you figure that out?" she asks.

"The Moleskines," I say. "They're filled with nothing but doodles, and yet *rat-a-tat-tat-tat*. Your mother was always typing something. Every single day."

She nods slowly. "Mrs. Grimthorpe picked her for her discretion, amongst other things. My mother was good at keeping a low profile, brilliant at keeping secrets, too." Ms. Sharpe ponders the photo on the wall. "Grimthorpe was never a writer, not really. In the old days, before he got writer's block, he'd come up with outrageous plots and intrigues, which he'd deliver to my mother in long verbal rants. She'd coax his madness into something sane and novelistic, something that intrigued on the page. She was so good at it she turned him into a bestselling writer. But she was always the real magic behind his books."

"He kept her a secret," I say.

"Yes," Ms. Sharpe confirms. "Mrs. Grimthorpe knew the truth, but no one else."

"Why didn't you tell me any of this before?" Stark asks. "When you met me at the station, you said nothing about your mother and you refused to say a word about what Mr. Grimthorpe was announcing."

Ms. Sharpe crosses behind her desk and takes a seat in her pristine desk chair. "I couldn't tell you because I signed a contract," she says. She gestures to the two white chairs in front of her. "Please," she says. "Sit."

Detective Stark complies. I take a seat beside her.

Ms. Sharpe interlaces her hands and places them on her desk. "I've known for many years that my mother was his ghostwriter. I begged her to ask for proper compensation and a share of J.D.'s royalties, but she was a single mother terrified of her boss and of losing a stable job. She knew she deserved more, but she could never bring herself to confront him or his wife. She didn't want to face their wrath." Ms. Sharpe goes quiet as she stares through the open door into Mr. Grimthorpe's chaotic study. "Such a literate man, and yet he could never write a decent book. So damaged."

"Damaged and powerful," I say. "He had a way of making you feel special and yet small at the very same time."

Ms. Sharpe's eyes go wide. "That's exactly right. When my mother died last year without ever receiving proper compensation for her writing, my anger seethed. She'd scrimped all her life. She'd been paid a secretary's salary for decades. Fear kept her quiet, but that didn't work on me. I devised a plan."

Detective Stark and I exchange a look. "Go on," she says.

"I quit my MBA and took over as Mr. Grimthorpe's personal secretary. He was thrilled. He had continuity and secrecy, all in a younger, prettier model. He was foolish enough to think that I, too, could write, but I've never had my mother's gift for storytelling. When he figured that out and threatened to fire me, I threatened him right back."

"Threatened him how?" Detective Stark asks.

"I told him I was going to reveal him for the fraud he was, that I'd tell the entire world my mother was the real author of his books," she says as she gestures to the cubbyholes filled with manuscripts. "I threatened to sue him for every penny he ever made . . . unless he met my terms."

"Which were?" I ask.

"A lump-sum fee of five million dollars payable to me, and one hundred percent of his royalties going forward for every book my mother wrote."

"Meaning all of them," Stark says.

"Yes," Ms. Sharpe replies.

"How did he react?" I ask.

"With icy calm. I think he knew he had it coming." Ms. Sharpe lays her hands on the closed laptop in front of her. "He agreed to my terms. He didn't even try to convince me to stay quiet about my mother's contributions. But in return, he had a few requests of his own."

"Which were?" I ask.

"He insisted on publicizing the news himself. He wanted to control the message."

"Hence the press conference at the hotel," Stark notes.

"Yes. And he made me sign a contract that specified if I let anything leak before the big event, our entire deal would be null and void."

"Meaning no money for you," Stark says.

"Meaning no credit for my mother," Ms. Sharpe replies, her voice razor-sharp. "That's why I couldn't say anything when you asked about what Mr. Grimthorpe had planned to say at the press conference. I didn't want to nullify the contract."

Ms. Sharpe falls silent as she produces the contract from a file drawer and hands it to Stark, who peruses it somberly and then nods.

"What happens now?" I ask. "Since dead men tell no tales."

"I've consulted a lawyer. Seems I'm in a bit of a bind," Ms. Sharpe replies. "If I reveal the truth, no deal, even after death."

"So getting credit for your mother means forfeiting all financial gain?" I say.

"Correct," Ms. Sharpe replies with a smile that doesn't quite reach her feline eyes.

Detective Stark stands and paces in front of Ms. Sharpe's desk. "You must have hated him," she says suddenly.

"I still do," Ms. Sharpe replies.

"Then let me ask you this: did you hate him enough to poison him?"

Ms. Sharpe laughs, but the sound is tinny and thin. "Have you understood nothing? He's no good to me dead."

"He was no good to you alive either," I point out.

Stark looks at me, her lips curled into an almost imperceptible smile.

"Make no mistake," Ms. Sharpe says. "I hated that man with every fiber of my being. He took advantage of my mother in more ways than I can enumerate. He used her talents and palmed them off as his own. He did other things, too."

"Such as?" Stark asks.

"He made unwelcome advances on your mother and then used them against her," I say.

Ms. Sharpe eyes me with curiosity. "How did you know that?"

"My gran," I reply. "He did the same to her. I suspect he did the same to all his female staff, which is why Mrs. Grimthorpe insisted on having only the two women she trusted in the mansion. And by 'trusted,' I mean women forced to keep quiet."

"Your gran and my mother."

"Yes," I reply.

"He got away with this his whole life, even tried it on me," says Ms. Sharpe. "I swear, I pushed him off me so hard, I nearly killed him. Such a powerful man and yet so weak. I always figured he'd drop dead one day since he was so susceptible. I looked forward to it. I just didn't expect him to die on exactly the wrong day."

One word she said stands out from all the others. "Susceptible," I say. "Why would you describe Mr. Grimthorpe as susceptible?"

"His years of alcoholism had taken their toll. His liver and kidneys were shot," Ms. Sharpe says.

"Which explains why the antifreeze took him out so quickly," Detective Stark adds. "His organs couldn't process the poison at all."

Just then, Jenkins appears at the door of the office. He's carrying a tray with a steaming teapot and porcelain cups I recognize from long ago. "Ma'am?" he says. "Your tea. I wasn't sure if you wanted cups for your guests."

"My guests? You're the one who let them in, Jenkins," Ms. Sharpe replies.

"I didn't have much choice," he says, though he doesn't meet her eye. "Anyhow, I brought tea for three." He places the tray on her desk, smiles at me, then slinks out the door.

Ms. Sharpe picks up the pot and pours tea into three cups. "You might as well help yourselves," she says to Detective Stark and me.

"I take mine black," Stark says as she grabs a dainty cup that looks too small for her large hands. "Not much of a tea drinker. Coffee's more my thing."

I take a lovely porcelain cup from the tray. I add a drop of milk and stir with a tarnished silver spoon. It makes a delightful tinkling sound as it grazes the fine porcelain, the same sound that a Regency Grand spoon makes against a Regency Grand teacup.

I gasp out loud and nearly spill hot tea all over myself. I set the teacup and spoon down on Ms. Sharpe's desk.

My heart starts to pound. It comes together in an instant, every missing piece, every variable falling into perfect place. My breath catches in my throat. The room tilts to one side. "Detective Stark," I say. "We have to get to the hotel. Right away!"

"But we just got here," she replies. "And I have more questions for Ms. Sharpe."

"No! No more questions. We don't have time. We must go to the Regency Grand, posthaste!"

"What the hell is going on, Molly? Why are you suddenly in such a rush?" Stark asks.

"Because it's not Ms. Sharpe who killed Mr. Grimthorpe. And I know exactly who did."

Chapter 25

Long ago, my gran told me a true story about a maid, a rat, and a spoon. I have never forgotten it. A maid working in a castle is blamed for the disappearance of a silver spoon, but years later, that spoon is found in a nest beside the petrified skeleton of the rat who stole it.

That's what I'm thinking about as I sit beside Detective Stark in her parked police cruiser. We are just outside the gates of the Grimthorpe mansion, and there's a jewel-encrusted egg in my lap, a parting gift from Jenkins.

I have just finished explaining to the detective, in minute detail, why it is we must hurry to the Regency Grand. I've told her everything I know, everything I remember.

"I can't believe it," she says once I'm done talking. "Molly, how in hell did you piece all of that together?"

"Details," I say. "You've been told before that I'm very good at them, but you didn't believe it. I may miss what you think is obvious, but I've always been attuned to what others ignore. We're all the same in different ways, Detective Stark. My gran taught me that long ago."

"I . . . regret that I . . . underestimated you," Stark says. It's as though there's a frog caught in her throat, because it takes her a good long time to spit so few words out of her mouth.

"Most people underestimate me," I reply. "But that doesn't matter right now. We've got to hurry."

Detective Stark nods and starts the cruiser. My back is pushed into the seat as she picks up speed and races down the road.

"By the way," she says once we're sailing, "why did that strange man insist you take that silly old trinket?" She looks away from the road for a moment at the tarnished egg in my lap.

"The Fabergé?" I ask.

"You don't actually believe that's a Fabergé, do you, Molly? It's a dime-store knickknack."

"Beauty is in the eye of the beholder, Detective. This egg meant a lot to me when I was a child, and I shall treasure it. One must look beyond the surface to see true value in anything."

"Are you still talking about the egg?" Stark asks.

"What do you think I'm talking about?" I reply.

Detective Stark doesn't answer, but I feel the speed of the cruiser increase. She turns the lights and siren on as we barrel down the road toward the Regency Grand.

We arrive in record time, screeching to a halt in front of the red-carpeted steps.

"Molly, what's going on? Are you all right?" Mr. Preston asks as I jump out of the cruiser and rush past him.

"No time!" I call back to him.

"You can't just leave a flashing cruiser in the landing zone," a valet yells out to Detective Stark.

"Oh, yes I can!" she replies as we both hurry through the revolving doors.

We run to the reception desk, where Mr. Snow is assisting guests.

"Have the LAMBS checked out yet?" I ask him.

"Molly, you're interrupting," Mr. Snow says.

"My most sincere apologies for contravening guest protocol," I say, "but this happens to be an emergency."

"Did you hear her?" Stark says. "When do the goddamn kook-balls check out?"

"Tomorrow," Mr. Snow replies.

"We're going into one of their rooms. Immediately," Stark announces.

"You can't just enter a guest room without provocation," Mr. Snow says. "It's a violation of privacy."

"Your maid has just uncovered crucial information in this case. She's on to something big," says Stark.

Mr. Snow's eyebrows peak on his forehead. "In that case, follow me," he says.

The three of us head toward the elevator, where we get on and take a silent trip up to the fourth floor. The doors open and we enter the hallway. Sunshine and Lily are there with their trolleys. Sunshine's face falls the second she sees us. Lily stops cold in her tracks.

"Molly, what's going on?" Sunshine asks.

"No time!" I say, as I march behind Mr. Snow and Detective Stark toward Room 404.

The three of us pause outside the door. "You do the honors," Mr. Snow says.

"Molly, just act normal," Detective Stark advises.

"That's definitely not my strong suit," I reply. Regardless, I knock on the door three times. "Housekeeping!" I call out in a firm but authoritative voice.

We wait, leaning our ears toward the door.

Nothing. Not a sound.

"Unoccupied," Mr. Snow says as he takes out his universal key-card and opens the door.

We enter and look around.

"This is definitely the right room," I say.

It's been cleaned recently—the bed perfectly made, hospital corners crisp and tight—and yet every square inch beyond the bed is occupied with detritus of all kinds. Cardboard boxes filled with binders line the floor, each one labeled GRIMTHORPE, followed by a number. A suitcase lies open by the window, clothes heaped in haphazard disarray, every item covered in heaps of cat hair.

Mr. Snow covers his nose.

"This is disgusting," Stark says. "It looks like a rat moved in. Don't the maids clean this room every day?"

"We do," I say. "But we can't do a deep cleaning until a guest departs. Maids can clean only clear surfaces in a guest-occupied room."

I walk over to the minibar by the window. It's just as I remember it: on top of the bar fridge is a hoard of incongruous miniature Regency Grand shampoo bottles beside various snack food packages, all left open, their contents spilling onto the floor—half-eaten cereal, an open package of crackers, and a big jar of peanut butter.

Detective Stark approaches the desk opposite the bed. It's a cluttered mess of papers, file folders, notepads, books, and crumpled receipts. "Molly, check this out," Stark says.

I join her by the desk, where she's pointing at a black Moleskine notebook with the monogram JDG. Beside it is another black Moleskine, but with a different monogram: BB.

I'm used to touching people's personal items in their hotel room, but it feels strange when I pick up Beulah's Moleskine, not to tidy it but to look inside. The first page is titled "Close Encounters," and after that, point-form notes run page after page after page.

"It's a ledger," I tell Detective Stark as Mr. Snow looks on.

"So it is," Stark exclaims. "It's every attempt at an encounter with Mr. Grimthorpe."

I flip through the dated pages, which go back years. I read at random:

- mailed flyer to acquaint him with the LAMBS: NO RE-SPONSE.
- sent email to website declaring me his #1 fan: NO RE-SPONSE.
- located private phone number and home address. Left voicemail with contact info: NO RESPONSE.
- sent 5th request to be his Official Biographer by regis-tered mail: NO RESPONSE.

I flip to the most recent entries in the book:

- slipped note under hotel room door suggesting dinner date at the Social: NO RESPONSE.
- waited for J.D. outside his room at the Regency Grand: LOCATED!
- requested his denial of troubling new facts: DECLINED.
- requested permission to be Official Biographer: DENIED.
- requested permission to enter his room: DOOR SLAMMED IN FACE.

"What's the date on that last entry?" Stark asks.

"The day before the press conference," I reply.

The detective and I lock eyes.

"I don't see how this adds up to much," Mr. Snow says, shaking his head.

"I do," I say. "I need Lily."

I put down the Moleskine and rush into the hall. Her trolley is propping open a door at the other end of the corridor. I find her inside, vacuuming the carpet into Zen-garden lines.

"Lily!" I call out, but she can't hear me.

I turn off her vacuum. "Lily," I repeat.

She shrieks and jumps back into a shadowy corner by the bed.

"It's okay," I say. "You're not in any trouble. But I need you to come with me right now."

I don't waste a moment, I grab her by the hand and rush her out of the room, down the corridor, and back to Room 404, where Mr. Snow and Detective Stark are waiting.

Out of breath, I stand in front of the detective, with Lily by my side.

"Lily," I say. "Do you remember a few days ago, when we were cleaning this very room?"

She nods.

"And do you remember what a state this room was in?"

She nods again. "It's always a mess. Hard to clean around all the junk. It's been like this every day I've tried to clean it."

"Exactly," I reply. "And do you remember how we laughed about all the little shampoo bottles and how there was food everywhere just like now—half-eaten boxes of cereal and crackers, and that big jar of peanut butter right there?"

Lily nods. "Yes. It's the same now."

"Not quite," I say. "There was something different about the pea-nut butter jar that day."

"It was open, and there was a spoon in it," she says.

"Exactly! I took the spoon out and closed the lid, remarking about who would leave it open like that with a spoon sticking out. I washed that spoon, which is when I realized it wasn't a Regency Grand silver spoon but an ordinary stainless-steel one from the Social downstairs. Do you remember?"

Lily nods. "Yes, I do. I asked if I should return it to the restaurant, and you said no, if the guest was using it, it was fine to leave it in the room."

"Precisely! And I put that stainless-steel spoon on the minibar right beside the jar of peanut butter," I reply. "But it's not there now. It's gone. Lily, did you clean this room today?"

"As much as I could," she says. "It's never easy."

"And have you seen that spoon?" I ask.

Lily looks from me to Mr. Snow to Detective Stark. Then she nods.

"Where?"

She points to the bedside table, then walks over to it. "It's right there," she says. "By the lamp."

I hurry over. There it is—the same ordinary, stainless-steel spoon. "That's the one," I say.

The detective and Mr. Snow approach. Stark looks at it, then leans forward and pulls open the drawer of the bedside table. Inside, tucked into an open-faced, red-satin-lined box, is a silver Regency Grand honey pot.

"Oh no!" says Lily the moment she spots it. "I washed the bedside table. The whole thing was slick and sticky," she says. "I wiped it down thoroughly, just the way you taught me, Molly—deep cleaning to give meaning. I didn't know. I didn't know what was in that drawer!"

"Don't worry," I tell her. "You did everything as you were supposed to."

Detective Stark's face is drawn, her eyes wide. "So the killer kept the weapon. She put it in a satin-lined box. This is officially the strangest murder trophy I've ever seen," she says. She turns to me. "Molly, we always knew the crime. And the location."

"Murder. In the tearoom," I reply.

"Now we have a motive," Detective Stark adds.

"Revenge," I say. "Revenge for rejection."

"I'm afraid I'm not following," says Mr. Snow. "How on earth have you deduced that the occupant of this room is guilty of murder? All you've uncovered is a piece of silver a guest was trying to steal."

"That's where you're wrong, Mr. Snow," Detective Stark says. "We found the murder weapon. It's right here."

"But it's just a honey pot and an ordinary spoon," says Mr. Snow.

Detective Stark reaches forward and plucks the pocket square from Mr. Snow's breast pocket. "Do you mind?" she asks.

He shrugs and adjusts his glasses.

Detective Stark unfolds the pocket square, then gingerly removes the silver lid of the honey pot, all without ever touching it with her fingers. A sweet, burnt odor instantly fills the room.

"It smells strange. The honey is off," says Mr. Snow. "And it's not quite the right color."

"Because it's not plain honey," I say.

"Then what is it?" Mr. Snow asks as he looks back and forth between me and the detective.

"Honey mixed with another key ingredient," I offer.

"What?" he asks.

"Household antifreeze," says Detective Stark.

Chapter 26

When I was a child, Gran and I watched *Columbo* while curled up on the couch. Gran used to love it when the murderer began to lie.

"Don't you smell it, Molly?" she once said.

"I don't smell anything," I replied.

"I smell a rat," she chimed in her singsong voice.

"We must trap it, quickly!" I was deeply concerned that a new pestilence had invaded our apartment.

"I don't mean it literally, Molly. I mean the murderer on *Columbo*. Watch her behavior. Can you see how she's lying? How she's trying to cover everything up?"

The shifty eyes. The changing details. The desire for secrecy competing with the great need to have her criminal genius acknowledged. "Yes," I said. "I see it now."

"Watch what Columbo does next," Gran replied. "Watch the way he lures the rat from its nest."

"How?" I asked.

"With words. He baits the trap."

It's this memory that gives me the idea for what to do next.

The four of us are standing by the reception desk in the lobby—Mr. Snow, Lily, Detective Stark, and me. We have left Room 404. Detective Stark has just ordered three of her special agents to secure the evidence inside.

"Beulah's not in her room, but she's probably lurking nearby," I say.

"The important thing is to take her by surprise," Detective Stark advises.

"How?" Lily asks.

"We bait the trap," I suggest. "We make an announcement about a free seminar on Mr. Grimthorpe."

"Smart," says Detective Stark.

I can't quite believe she said that word, at least not in relation to me.

"We can plan that for tomorrow," Mr. Snow offers.

"No. We do it now," Stark says. "In fact, *you* do it, Mr. Snow. You make the announcement on the hotel's intercom, right away."

Beads of sweat collect at Mr. Snow's hairline. "We can't create a seminar out of thin air. Event planning takes time."

"I'm not asking for doilies and those damn finger sandwiches," Stark says. "Just make the announcement. And be quick about it."

Mr. Snow goes behind the reception desk, turns on the microphone, and speaks. "Calling all Regency Grand Hotel guests. This is a special announcement for J. D. Grimthorpe fans. There will be a free seminar on the life and times of the famous author to be held in the Grand Tearoom . . ." He pauses, covering the mic with his hand. "When?" he whispers to Stark.

"Now!" she mouths.

". . . in five minutes," he says into the mic. "Tea will be served.

And finger sandwiches. Also: the event will feature a live VIP guest."

He clicks the mic off and leaves the desk as the questioning eyes of the reception clerks follow his every move.

"VIP guest?" I ask when he returns to my side.

"I couldn't very well say 'detective,' could I?" he explains.

"You promised tea," Lily tells Mr. Snow.

"And finger sandwiches," I add.

"Oh dear. So I did. Lily, please alert the kitchen. And ask for Angela's help, too."

Lily runs toward the Social. I'm about to follow, but Detective Stark holds me back. "Molly, you stay with me. Watch and listen. If you see something I don't, you tell me, okay?"

"Very well," I reply.

She turns and strides out of the lobby, down the corridor toward the entrance of the Regency Grand Tearoom. Mr. Snow and I trail behind her.

We arrive not a minute too soon. Coming the other way is a familiar gaggle of ladies—about ten in total—led by a tall, curly-haired woman carrying her small red flag.

"We're here for the free seminar," Gladys, the leader of the LAMBS, announces. "Who's the special guest?" she asks Mr. Snow. "Is it Serena Sharpe?"

"There was a mistake in that announcement," Detective Stark says. "The VIP guest we're looking for is Mr. Grimthorpe's number-one fan. Do you know where she might be?"

An electric charge pulses through the LAMBS. Hands fly up and various members step forward.

"Me! I'm his number-one fan!"

"No, not her. Me!"

"Me! Here!"

"I'm over here!"

The LAMBS push closer. Mr. Snow extends his arms to keep them from charging the tearoom en masse.

"Please!" I call out in my most firm but authoritative maid's voice. "There can be only one number-one fan."

"You," Detective Stark says, pointing to the now familiar-looking woman wearing a lumpy brown sweater covered in cat hair. "We met right here a couple of days ago. You're Mr. Grimthorpe's official biographer, right?"

"Unofficial," Gladys corrects as she waves her flag.

"Not only are you his number-one fan," I say to Beulah, "but you're also the world's foremost expert on Mr. Grimthorpe, are you not?"

"There are many other LAMBS just as knowledgeable as Beulah," says Gladys with a huff.

"That's right!" I hear. It's a small voice from the middle of the gaggle. It's Birdy, her fuchsia hair distinguishing her from all the other LAMBS. She's standing on her tiptoes to be seen. "I'm his number-one fan. It's me you want to speak to," Birdy insists.

"I'm sure it's not," says Detective Stark. "Now if you'll excuse us, we're holding a private audience with J. D. Grimthorpe's biographer."

"Are you tracking a lead?" one of the LAMBS calls out. "Have you found J.D.'s murderer?"

"I'm afraid not," says Detective Stark. "We're stumped," she says. "Isn't that right, Detective?" Stark looks at me. "Detective?" she says again.

"I'm not a detective," I say.

"You're better than a lot I've worked with," Stark insists. She turns back to Beulah. "We could really use your help, ma'am, as a true Grimthorpe aficionado."

Beulah stands taller and adjusts her sweater.

"Thank you, everyone," I say. "We have the expert we need. Now move along." Mr. Snow politely directs the LAMBS toward the lobby as Detective Stark ushers Beulah into the Grand Tearoom. I enter as well and head for the white-linened table at center stage where they're seated. I pull out a chair and sit across from them.

I'm fully expecting Stark to launch into some version of *You are under arrest for the murder of J. D. Grimthorpe*, but she doesn't do that. She does something else entirely.

"What an honor to speak privately with an expert such as yourself," she says. "When Detective Gray and I met you the other day, we instantly realized we were in the presence of a truly great literary biographer."

Beulah begins to blush. "I rarely get the credit I deserve, not even from the LAMBS. How nice to be acknowledged," she says.

"Of course," Stark replies. "And I'm sorry we dragged you here on false pretenses, but we need your help. There appears to be an organized ring of corruption at the Regency Grand Hotel, and while we know you are not in any way involved, we have reason to believe that you, as Mr. Grimthorpe's number-one fan and biographer, can help us. Molly, tell her," Stark says.

"Tell her what?" I ask, utterly confused.

"About the website," Stark prompts.

"Right," I say. "Someone's selling stolen Grimthorpe collectibles on a popular website. Detective Stark has—I mean, *we* have—been called in to investigate that crime as well."

"Last I heard, buying off a website wasn't a crime," Beulah says.

"We're investigating the seller, not the buyer," says Stark. "Whoever that buyer is, they're really clever. Very enterprising."

Beulah holds up her hands. "You caught me! I'm the clever buyer. I bought the entire Grimthorpe collection as soon as the listings went up. I assumed the goods were bona fide, though, not ill-gotten gains. Naturally, I wanted to protect his legacy."

"Naturally," I say.

Detective Stark nudges me under the table.

"Tell me," Stark says. "Given your superior research skills, why aren't you Mr. Grimthorpe's *authorized* biographer?"

Beulah picks at the hairs on her sweater. "Beats me," she answers. "But it doesn't matter anymore. He's dead. I can write whatever I want about him. And I will."

"I, for one, look forward to reading your biography on Mr. Grimthorpe," I say. "It's sure to be most enlightening."

"Oh, it will be. Did you know that I've been researching him for about two decades? I've dedicated much of my life to that man, and my efforts were underappreciated. I always thought my biography would be flattering." She leans in close and lowers her voice. "But let's just say recent evidence suggests he was not what he seemed."

"Fascinating," says Stark.

"Do tell us more," I add.

Beulah puts her clasped hands on the table. "If I tell you, you must assure me that none of my research will be used in an unauthorized biography or publicly disseminated in any way. My book must be the first to market. It will cement my place as the foremost literary biographer of our times. My name will live on shelves *in perpetuum*."

"Remarkable," I say out loud. What I don't say is how her use of Latin mirrors Mr. Grimthorpe's so precisely.

"We won't steal your research," says Detective Stark. "And you know, I have a funny feeling you're right. Beulah Barnes *is* a name that will go down in history." Stark smiles a smile that doesn't quite reach her eyes. "Now about those Grimthorpe items," she says.

"Bought fair and square," Beulah replies. "And sorry, I don't know anything about the seller if that's what you're getting at. But I'm now the proud owner of an original monogrammed Grimthorpe Moleskine, amongst other valuable items. For years, the LAMBS were certain his notebooks meant he wrote his first drafts in longhand. Like with most things, they were wrong."

"Wrong?" Stark says.

"He only doodled in them," Beulah explains.

"That doesn't seem so damning," I say. "Why has your opinion of the man changed so much?"

"Because of other evidence. The love note, for instance."

"Love note?" I repeat.

"J.D. was having an affair with that pretty, young secretary of his, Serena Sharpe," Beulah says.

"He was not," I reply, but I feel another nudge under the table.

"Molly's right," Detective Stark adds. "Turns out that note was from someone else in this hotel."

"Look, not every KultureVulture item has a clear provenance, but let me assure you that J.D. was a fraud," Beulah says. "His cue cards from the day of the big event prove it."

"So you have his cue cards?"

"I do," Beulah says. "I bought them alongside everything else."

"You knew we were conducting a murder investigation, but you never thought to hand over those cards?" Stark says.

Beulah snorts. "Some investigation. You don't know a thing about the man. J. D. Grimthorpe had a closet full of secrets."

"Secrets?" Stark says. "Such as?"

"Did you know that at one point in his life, he was a raging alcoholic?" Beulah offers. "I tracked down employees who used to work for him—security guards, gardeners, and a maid. They were all fired. According to the maid, J.D.'s wife was a tyrant and he himself was *not* who he appeared to be. The maid accused him of getting handsy, then got fired for speaking up. He didn't dare lay a hand on me, though." Beulah picks more cat hair off her bosom and sends it flying.

"So you met him?" I ask. "You met J.D. in person?"

"Yes, I did. Right outside his hotel room. Lesson learned: beware of meeting your idols. They don't always live up to expectations."

"His books were powerful," Stark says, "and yet he was kind of weak, wasn't he?"

"He was," Beulah says. "Liver and kidney damage from years of alcohol abuse."

"So you were aware of that as well," Stark says.

"Of course. Like I said, J.D. was my life's work."

Just then, Lily and Angela appear at the entrance of the tearoom. They wheel a tea cart toward the table. Angela is wringing her hands on her apron, her eyes flitting about the room. Lily's shoulders are back, her head held higher than I've ever seen before. For once, she doesn't look skittish at all.

"My apologies for the interruption," Lily says, her voice resonant, a clarion bell.

We all turn her way.

"Angela and I were instructed to bring in this tea cart," she explains. "It's complimentary, for Mr. Grimthorpe's number-one fan." She pauses and executes the most perfect curtsy I have ever seen.

"That's very thoughtful," says Beulah.

"You're not wearing your pin," Angela notes, pointing to the spot on Beulah's sweater where her #1 FAN pin used to be.

"I lost it," Beulah explains.

"That's funny," says Angela. "I thought I saw you take it off the other day at the Social. You tossed it on the table and left it behind."

"Must've been someone else," Beulah insists. "No one can tell us LAMBS apart. It's rather insulting."

Lily picks up the teapot from the cart and pours steaming tea into a Regency Grand cup. She places it in front of Beulah. "How do you take your tea, Ms. Barnes?" she asks.

"Four lumps of sugar," Beulah replies. "Bit of a sweet tooth."

"Ah yes," says Lily. "You take your tea the same way Mr. Grimthorpe did."

"No," Beulah replies. "J.D. took his with honey, not sugar. Always honey. Loads of it."

And there it is—another telling detail, which Lily set her up to reveal. A Mona Lisa smile edges onto Lily's lips as she ladles four sugar cubes into Beulah's cup. She stirs the tea with a Regency Grand silver spoon, which makes a pleasing tinkling sound against the porcelain cup.

"Thank you," Beulah says when Lily passes her the cup.

Just then, three undercover officers appear in the doorway. One of them holds a plain banker's box.

Beulah is taking a sip of tea but stops mid-sip. "What are they doing here?" she asks.

"Extra security," Detective Stark replies. "We can't be too careful with delinquents running loose in the hotel. Please excuse me a moment," Detective Stark says as she walks over to the men. They exchange a few words and pass her the banker's box. Stark walks back to the table with it, putting it down in front of Beulah. She removes the cardboard lid. Inside is an ordinary stainless-steel spoon and beside it, a silver Regency Grand honey pot in a red satin case.

"Can you explain this, Beulah?" Stark asks as she looks from the objects in the box to Beulah's slack-jawed face.

"Were you in my room? Why were you touching my things?"

"Why were you keeping these items in your room?" Stark asks.

"For goodness' sake. Sometimes a cigar is just a cigar."

"But this spoon is no ordinary spoon, Beulah. It's a murder weapon. And so is that silver honey pot," Stark says. "You added a key ingredient to it before Mr. Grimthorpe's big announcement, didn't you? You contaminated it with antifreeze, and because you knew about Grimthorpe's sweet tooth, you realized he'd never detect the taste in his tea. You also knew it would kill him quickly, what with the liver and kidney damage he'd sustained as an alcoholic."

"This is preposterous. Why would I poison my idol?" Beulah asks.

"Because he rejected you," I say. "Which meant your life's work was for naught."

"You're accusing the wrong person. You should talk to her. She's the one who served him the tea!" Beulah says as she points a pudgy finger at Lily.

"Oh no," says Lily. "The maid is not to blame. Not this time."

"Unbelievable," says Angela. "How can you live with yourself, Beulah?"

"You took a plot point right from one of his books—killing a bitter villain with a cup of sweetness. Isn't that right, Beulah?" I say.

Beulah's fury is mounting, and she turns on me without warning. "You! You pretend to be an investigator, but I don't believe it. You're just a maid. You killed him. You and that quiet one are in cahoots! This place is teeming with lowlifes who'll stop at nothing for their personal gain, including selling a dead guest's trash just to make a buck!"

Detective Stark stands. "That's enough, Beulah Barnes. The game is up. You're under arrest," she says as the undercover officers rush forward to handcuff Beulah. "You have the right to remain silent. Anything you say can and will be used against you in a court of law. And bloody hell, silence really is your best option right now because you most certainly have said too much."

"Said too much? I haven't said nearly enough!" Beulah shouts as she struggles against the men holding her by her handcuffed wrists and escorting her to the exit. "And it's still your word against mine!"

"Your 'word' has been recorded, Beulah," Angela says as Lily picks up a napkin from the tea cart to reveal Angela's cellphone underneath, the live voice memo recording.

"You're not to go back in my hotel room!" Beulah shrieks. "That's an invasion of privacy! I'll sue the Regency Grand!"

"Stop talking," Stark says. "You're digging yourself deeper."

As Beulah disappears down the corridor, it occurs to me that her true nature has just been revealed—because digging deeper is exactly what rats do.

Chapter 27

We continue to hear Beulah's protests as Stark's men drag her toward the lobby.

Finally, the room is quiet.

We all turn to Lily, her Mona Lisa smile still blooming on her face.

"Was that your idea, to bring in the tea cart?" Detective Stark asks.

Lily nods.

"You made her admit to knowing how Grimthorpe took his tea," I say.

Lily nods again.

"Incredible," says Stark. "And Angela, well done with that recording."

"Thanks," Angela replies. "True crime podcasts. They taught me everything I know."

"Would you two mind standing guard for a minute at the entrance while I have a private word with Molly? I have a funny feeling the LAMBS might make a reappearance here sometime soon, and I'm in no mood to answer their questions."

"Of course," Angela says as Lily nods. The two of them make their way to the door.

Detective Stark and I remain where we are. We're both staring at the trophies in the banker's box on the table.

"Molly, there's one thing I still don't understand," Stark says. "How did you know that spoon was the key to everything?"

"The sound," I say. "When Jenkins brought in tea at the mansion, I remembered my childhood and the first time I heard the tinkling sound of a proper silver spoon against a fine porcelain teacup. I love that sound. Then I remembered that day at the podium when Mr. Grimthorpe was about to make his speech. He took the teacup from Lily, added honey with the spoon from the honey pot, and stirred."

"So?" says Detective Stark.

"I know the sound of a Regency Grand teaspoon against a Regency Grand teacup," I explain. "That high-pitched tinkle—music to my ears. But the sound that day was all wrong—a dull clank."

"Because the spoon Beulah used was not Regency Grand silver?" she asks.

"Exactly," I say. "It was a stainless-steel one from the Social, the same one I saw sticking out of her peanut butter jar days earlier."

Detective Stark shakes her head. "You really do have an eye for the strangest details. And an ear for them as well."

"Mostly, I notice the wrong things at the wrong times," I say. "That's been my downfall for as long as I remember."

"And you think that makes you different from anyone else?" Stark asks. "Molly, I was wrong about you. I read you the wrong way from the very beginning. "

"Never judge a book by its cover. My gran used to say that."

"Bit of an occupational hazard," says Stark. "This may come as a surprise, but if you ever wanted a career change, the force could use someone with your skills. My force, I mean."

"But I'm a maid. My work is to polish guest rooms to perfection. To clean up all the messes people leave behind."

"Is that so different from what I do? I try to leave the world a cleaner place than I found it," Stark says.

I see the similarities, I do. And yet I've never imagined myself being anything other than what I am now.

"It's impossible, Detective," I say. "Changing my profession would mean retraining, going back to school."

"Well, yes. So what?"

"I was never good at school. Actually, I was an abject failure, below my peers in every way, incapable of meeting the bar."

"Maybe the bar was set in the wrong place. Maybe the school was the wrong kind. Maybe the teachers made the same mistake I made—focusing on your weaknesses instead of your strengths."

"Do you know, you sound just like my gran?"

A memory returns with such startling force that the room starts to spin. I grip my hands to my stomach. It's the moment after Gran's death. Gran is in our apartment, dead in her bed, and I'm right beside her, holding her serenity pillow, clutching it to my chest as a wave of grief engulfs me, threatening to drown me and take me under forever.

I think of that pillow now, where it sits on the chair by the front door of the apartment I share with my beloved Juan Manuel. I see that pillow every day. Gran embroidered every stitch of wisdom into it. Why did she choose those words? Why that prayer?

It occurs to me only now, the permanence of her message, meant to resonate with me *in perpetuum:*

God grant me the serenity to accept the things I cannot change, the courage to change the things I can, and the wisdom to know the difference.

What is it I need to accept?

I am who I am. Molly. Molly with all my weaknesses and foibles. And all my strengths, too.

Maybe it's time I accept myself, because there's not a thing I can do to change it.

Am I a maid or am I just employed as one? Is that something I want to change? Is it something I *can* change? Moreover, do I have the wisdom to know the difference?

"We better go," says Detective Stark. "We should get out front and make sure Beulah makes it into my cruiser. I have a feeling the lobby is about to get very crowded."

"You're right," I say. "The snoops have probably already arrived."

The detective puts the lid back on the banker's box. It makes a satisfying sound as it closes.

"Come on," says Stark as she heads for the door. Together, we leave the tearoom, nodding at Angela and Lily, who are standing guard by the door. We thread our way through the corridors until we reach the glorious front lobby of the Regency Grand. Oh, how I love this lobby. How I'd miss it if I didn't see it almost every day—the grand staircase winding to the opulent balcony, the Italian marble floors, the tang of lemon polish that perfumes the air, the receptionists, dressed in black and white like neat little penguins. They're checking in new guests as I watch from afar. On the jewel-toned settees, guests sit in tight huddles, gossiping and people-watching, exchanging confidences and secrets that become steeped into the fabric of everything.

I observe the guests, noting their expressions. Some faces are so clear to me, transparent and open, but most are as locked as the doors of their rooms upstairs. It's just as Gran always said: people are a mystery that can never be solved.

"Hey, you." I feel a tap on the arm. "You work here, don't you?

Do you know anything about what's happening outside on the steps?"

"Me?" I ask, turning to the reporter in front of me. "Why would I know anything? I'm just a maid."

"Oh. Right. Sorry," he replies as he trots off in search of someone more important.

"Let's go, Molly," Detective Stark says as she leads me toward the gleaming revolving doors. We pass through them and find ourselves delivered onto the red-carpeted landing outside.

The entrance is packed. The LAMBS are jammed up on one side of the staircase, nattering and chattering about how they always suspected Beulah was unhinged. Beulah is halfway down the stairs, struggling against the officers who have a firm hold on her hand-cuffed wrists. Detective Stark heads down the stairs to help them.

"This is insane! Can't you see that I've done the world a favor?" Beulah calls out. "I've rid the world of a monster! You should be thanking me, not arresting me!"

There it is—she's just admitted it in front of a crowd.

I spot fuchsia-haired Birdy jostling to get close to Beulah. "How could you?" she yells at her. "How could you poison a literary genius?"

"He was no genius. He was a fraud!" Beulah yells back. "And a predator!"

"You're the fraud, Beulah Barnes! You're also a killer!" curly-haired Gladys bellows as she brandishes her red flag like a sword. "You're barred from the LAMBS forever!"

The reporters and other lookie-loos are arriving now in full force, blocking the stairs, recording videos on their phones, and shouting out questions to Beulah.

"Hey, did you really kill him? Why did you do it?"

"Do you work here? Are you his number-one fan?"

"Did you have help? Or did you do it on your own?"

Mr. Preston pushes back the crowd until he's standing right in front of Beulah.

"Keep your hands on her, boys," Detective Stark orders as Beulah gnashes and struggles against the officers.

"Easy now, Ms. Barnes," Mr. Preston says. "No point thrashing about. Is that how a biographer of your stature behaves?"

Suddenly, Beulah goes still. It's as though Mr. Preston has flipped a switch in her. She stares at him like he's the only person in the world who matters.

"Will you allow me to take your arm, madam?" Mr. Preston asks.

"Stand back, everyone! Let the doorman approach," Detective Stark calls out.

Her officers don't release their grip on Beulah's wrists, but they permit Mr. Preston to take Beulah's elbow. The throng on the stairs watches in silence.

"I don't understand," Beulah says to Mr. Preston. "I uncovered the truth. The world is a better place without Grimthorpe in it."

"On that last point, we agree," Mr. Preston replies.

"Don't let them throw away my research," Beulah begs. "Please, my biography must see the light of day. And will you make sure someone takes care of my cats at home? They don't deserve to suffer."

"I'll do what I can," Mr. Preston replies.

As she leans on Mr. Preston, Beulah steps lightly down the stairs, as though she's a princess being delivered to a royal carriage rather than a lonely, disturbed woman who murdered a famous man. Mr. Preston guides her all the way to the bottom of the stairs, where Mr. Snow is standing by the police car.

Stark opens the door of her cruiser.

"Easy now, madam," Mr. Preston says as he releases Beulah's

elbow. He protects her head as Stark's officers put her into the back seat, closing the door behind her.

"Take her to the station," Stark orders. "I'll be there soon enough." One of the men grabs the detective's keys, then gets into the car.

The crowd surges forward, and Mr. Preston and the valets hold them back as the car departs. The last thing I see is Beulah's face of confusion as she stares out of the fogging window wondering how on earth it came to this.

Once the car is gone, Detective Stark trots up the stairs, blazing a trail until she's standing tall behind the doorman's podium on the landing.

"Ladies and gentlemen!" she calls out in a firm and authoritative voice. "If you have questions—be they burning, inappropriate, or just plain dumb—would you be so kind as to direct them to me? The workers at this hotel have suffered enough harassment in the last few days. For the record, they are not, *nor have they ever been*, to blame for any of this."

The crowd surrounds her at the podium, but Detective Stark isn't paying attention to them. She's looking at me.

I curtsy, stepping one foot back and bowing my head exactly as my gran taught me to do so many years ago. When I look up again, Detective Stark has disappeared behind a relentless horde of guests, reporters, and hotel employees.

I suddenly feel quite dizzy. I can't catch my breath. I hold on to the brass railing for fear I might pass out right here on the steps of the Regency Grand.

I feel a hand on my arm.

"Are you quite all right?"

It's Mr. Preston. He's always had a way of finding me in my moment of need. Of propping me up. Whatever would I do without him?

"I'll be fine," I say.

I'm staring out into the street, observing the black skid marks left behind by the cruiser. "I should clean those," I say.

"Clean what?" he asks.

"The tire marks. On the road."

"Goodness me, Molly. We've got bigger messes to clean," he says. "Did she really do it, that Beulah woman? I've spoken to her many times. She always said she was Grimthorpe's biographer and number-one fan."

"I'm afraid she's also his killer, Mr. Preston."

I expect him to say something respectful about the dead, but he doesn't. He remains silent.

"Do you remember how I told you about a guest room Lily and I cleaned that was so filled with junk it looked like a rat's nest?" I ask.

"Of course," Mr. Preston replies. "You regaled Juan and me with that doozy just last week."

"That room was Beulah's. It was filled with detritus, hoards of miniature shampoos . . . and a poisoned silver honey pot."

Mr. Preston shakes his head. "Loneliness and emptiness, hoarding to fill the void. A terrible affliction with a simple cure."

"Which is?" I ask.

"Kindness. A patient ear. A loving arm. If she'd had any of those things, maybe it wouldn't have come to this."

It strikes me how right he is.

"Molly? Are you sure you're all right?"

"Yes," I say. "It's actually a relief to get some closure. Maybe things will go back to normal around here."

"Let's hope so. All's well that ends well," Mr. Preston says. "Molly, I was wondering. Do you think you can spare a moment sometime soon for us to have our chat? I really do need to speak with you."

I nod. But then another thought occurs to me. A terrible thought. I can't believe it never occurred to me before.

I clasp Mr. Preston's hands in mine. "You aren't sick, are you? Please tell me you aren't dying."

Mr. Preston chuckles. "My dear girl, even as a child, you had the most overactive imagination. And a tendency to jump to conclusions. I am not ill, Molly. I'm in perfectly good health, for a doddering old man, at least."

I breathe a sigh of relief. "In that case," I say, "I need time to rest and recover. It's been quite a day, quite a week, in fact. Can it wait until Juan Manuel returns?"

Mr. Preston pats my arm. "Of course it can. After all, it's waited this long. I don't see that a little longer will make much difference."

One Week Later

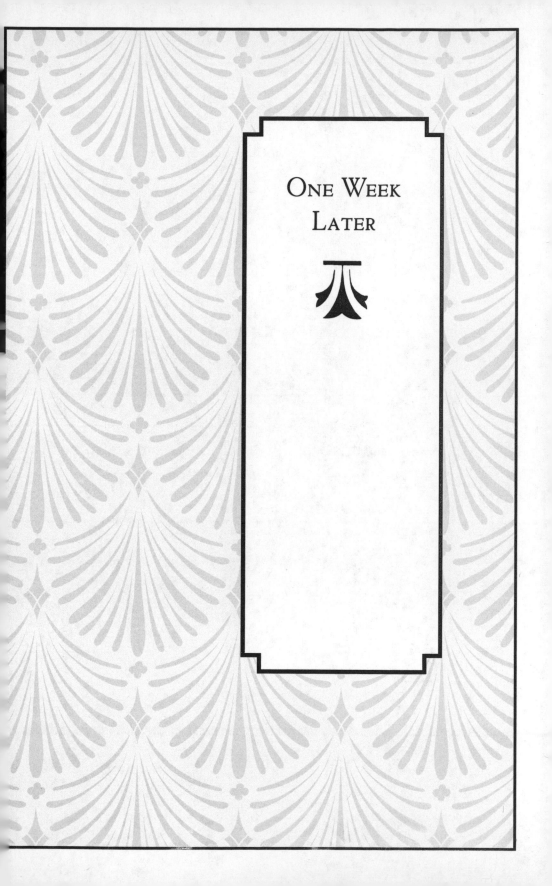

Chapter 28

As a maid in a hotel, I experience a fair number of déjà vu moments. Sometimes, when I'm cleaning Room 401, I'd swear on the Oxford dictionary I'm in Room 201. In my dreams at night, the corridors morph and blend, dirty sheets mixing with clean ones, but eventually I sort it all out. I make the beds in record time, tucking hospital corners tight, topping pillows with turn-down chocolates, and leaving everything in a pinnacle state of cleanliness.

I'm having a déjà vu moment right now. I'm standing in the Regency Grand Tearoom surveying it one final time before today's big event, just as I did a little over a week ago on the day of Mr. Grimthorpe's big announcement, an announcement he never got to make.

I have laid the tables with crisp white linens, pleated every napkin into a rosebud fold, and arranged the polished Regency Grand silver for each place setting. Now, I'm admiring the result—a splendid sight indeed. Let's just hope that today no one drops dead on the tearoom floor, thereby upsetting the perfect order of things and tarnishing the sterling reputation of our five-star boutique hotel.

Today we have a chance at resurrection—of the Regency Grand, I mean, not of Mr. Grimthorpe. Mr. Grimthorpe will never breathe again.

I've been working tirelessly to arrive at this moment, but I'm not alone. I've had plenty of help. This morning, as I entered the hotel, I stopped on the stairs to greet Mr. Preston.

"The big day has arrived," he said.

"Yes," I replied. "The announcement is at ten sharp."

"Oh," Mr. Preston says as he clears his throat. "That's not what I meant. I meant it's the day of our chat."

Amidst all the preparations for the press conference, I'd forgotten that I agreed to have Mr. Preston over to my apartment for tea. I suggested we could have our long-awaited talk and then both be there this afternoon to greet Juan upon his return from his trip. Mr. Preston readily agreed to this plan.

Mr. Preston thinks it's some big surprise, but I know what he will tell me—that he's retiring from his job as a doorman at the Regency Grand. He thinks this news will upset my fragile equilibrium, but it won't. I'm stronger than everyone thinks. Good eggs don't crack so easily.

I will miss him terribly, of course, but I will carry on. And we'll still have our Sunday dinners.

"Good luck in there today," Mr. Preston had said earlier this morning. "I'm here if you need anything."

"You always are," I replied. "And for that I'm grateful."

He tipped his hat. Then I raced up the stairs and pushed through the gleaming revolving doors into the Regency Grand. The enormous gilt-framed sign in the lobby advertised the day's big event.

Today
VIP Press Conference
TOPIC: J. D. GRIMTHORPE
Deceased Mystery Author
10:00 A.M.
Regency Grand Tearoom

I hurried past the sign and rushed downstairs to the housekeeping change rooms, where Lily had arrived early for her shift. We donned our uniforms. I placed my Head Maid pin adroitly above my heart, but I surprised her by saying, "Hold on a moment. Give me your pin."

Lily looked at me in confusion as she placed her Maid-in-Training pin in my open hand. I then exchanged it with what I had concealed in my other palm—a fresh new pin, black with shiny gold letters. It said:

LILY
Maid

She gasped as she took it from my palm. "Really?" she asked as she held proof of her promotion in her own hands.

"You've earned it. Put it on," I replied.

She turned to the mirror and affixed it right above her heart.

"Lily," I said, "do you think you can serve the tea to our VIP guest, just as you did last week?"

She shook her head, her eyes wide with shock.

"I don't mean that literally. I assure you the end result of today's tea service won't be an untimely death. Can you manage, Lily? Tell me if you can't."

"I can do it," she said in her new, confident voice. "A good maid has a can-do attitude," she added. "You taught me that."

"I best be off," I said. "Please get the VIP tea cart ready. You can roll it into the tearoom at five to the hour."

Lily curtsied, then left.

I heard the familiar sound of feet flopping down the hallway. It could be only one person.

"Good morning, Cheryl," I said as she entered the change room. Miracles are possible, and the proof was on the wall clock. Cheryl was early for her shift!

"To what do I owe the pleasure of your punctuality?" I asked her.

"Dunno," she replied with a shrug. "Doesn't it say something about the wisdom of early birds in that annoying handbook of yours?"

I gritted my teeth but said nothing. After all, her punctuality was a sign of improvement, and that's exactly what I've been hoping for.

After a rather impassioned debate between Mr. Snow and me a week ago, it was decided that despite Cheryl's flagrant theft and mischief, we would not fire her. I wanted to give her one last chance to redeem herself as a maid.

I made it expressly clear that animalistic behavior of all kinds would not be tolerated. "In other words, you are not to behave like a thieving rat or a trash panda," I explained. I placed her on a PIP explaining that I had "Great Expectations" for her in the future. Naturally, she didn't understand my witty references to Charles Dickens's novel, so I explained that PIP was short for "Professional Improvement Plan," meaning Cheryl's employment was subject to strict adherence to every chapter, rule, and verse of *A Maid's Guide & Handbook*. It also meant she would retrain as a maid, working right by my side, where I could watch her every move—and I have been watching her every single day.

I do believe Cheryl is grateful for my clemency, not that she has expressed it in words. But she shows it in other ways. A few days ago, she sneezed and was about to wipe her nose on her sleeve, but I stopped her. "Ah, ah, ah," I said. "Tissue for your issue." I handed her one right from her own trolley.

Yesterday, I caught her about to use her toilet cloth on a guest's washroom sink. "Ah, ah, ah," I said. "What's the rule?"

"Please be neat when you sterilize the seat," she replied with only the faintest trace of sarcasm.

So you see: we're making progress.

"Earth to Molly. Are you with us?"

I shake off my reverie to find Angela and Detective Stark standing outside the maroon cordon by the entrance to the tearoom. Angela holds up the cordon, and they both duck under and come my way.

"Detective Stark," I say. "I didn't know you were coming today."

"Neither did I," says Stark. "But the LAMBS showed up at the station yesterday and dropped off this lanyard for me."

I look at the VIP event pass hanging around her neck. "I couldn't help myself," she says. "Curiosity killed the cat and all of that."

"Here's hoping no feline, or anyone else, is killed in today's proceedings," I reply.

"How are preparations for the court case going?" Angela asks.

"Beulah pled guilty," says the detective. "So there won't be a trial. Just a sentencing. And you'll never believe what she admitted."

"Do tell!" says Angela as she rubs her hands together with glee.

"The maid she tracked down, the one who used to work for the Grimthorpes ages ago," Stark says. "Turns out, that maid knew all about the ghostwriter in the mansion, said she figured out long before she was fired what Grimthorpe's personal secretary really did for him."

"Have you talked to the maid?" I ask.

"Nope. She told Beulah everything but demanded anonymity,

said she had good reasons for remaining invisible. And when Beulah realized she'd devoted her life to a fraud, she devised a plan."

"To kill Mr. Grimthorpe," I say.

"Not quite," Stark replies. "She decided to give him the benefit of the doubt. She rewrote her biography, turning it into a searing exposé. So now she had two versions—her original flattering portrait, and the second, which was completely damning."

"But why?" I ask. "Why would she write the biography two ways?"

"Because she wanted to ask him herself if he really was a fraud and a predator. Which version she published depended entirely on his answer."

"But when she met Grimthorpe outside his hotel room the day before the big announcement, he refused to answer her troubling questions," I say. "Beulah wrote something about that in her ledger."

"Uh-huh," Stark says. "He also rejected her as his official biographer, even under threat of having an exposé published."

"And he slammed the door in her face," I add.

"So after that encounter, she decided to kill him," Angela says with somber finality. "The triple whammy sent Beulah into a quiet murderous rage."

"And as it turns out," Stark says, "the tea cart in this tearoom wasn't the only one Beulah poisoned. She poisoned every honey pot on every tea cart left outside his hotel room, from the day before the big event to the morning of it."

"Which explains why he died so quickly," I say. "He'd been drinking poisoned tea for over twenty-four hours."

"Well, holy shih tzu," says Angela. "It's just like the plot of his novel *Poison & Punishment*. What a kick-ass podcast this would make."

"Maybe you should make it," says Stark.

Angela's eyes go wide. "You really think I could?"

"Yeah, I do," Stark replies.

Before Angela can contemplate this further, Mr. Snow enters the tearoom. He's dressed in an emerald-green waistcoat and a paisley bow tie.

"My, my," says Detective Stark. "Someone's dressed to impress."

"Good to see you, Detective," he says. He grabs his pocket square and mops the excess sweat collecting along his brow. "Is everything ready? The guests are lined up outside. Shall I let them through?"

"Release the hounds, Mr. Snow," Angela says.

"And the LAMBS," I add.

He heads to the tearoom entrance, and a few moments later, crowds of VIP guests pour into the well-appointed room. Many of them are recognizable as LAMBS, their faces and gray hair familiar. But there are only two that stand out in particular—Birdy, the tiny treasurer with pink highlights, and Gladys, their tall, curly-haired, flag-bearing leader.

Detective Stark takes a seat in front of the stage as the LAMBS swarm her, hurling questions about Beulah and if there will be a trial while squabbling about who gets to sit next to the lead detective.

Meanwhile, reporters rush to the back of the room, shouting directives to one another as they ready their cameras and phones, focusing their attention on the spotlighted podium at center stage.

My own phone buzzes in my pocket. I take it out. It's a text from my beloved Juan Manuel.

Five minutes to boarding the ✈. Can't wait to BWUBH!

BWUBH? I text back.

Be With U Back Home.

I can't wait either! I reply. And it's true. I've missed him so much. Life will be better the moment he walks through our apartment door. I have just one niggling concern: How will I ever explain to him everything that's happened during the time he's been away? Will he ever forgive me for keeping it all a secret? But I can't think about that. Not yet.

One step at a time. It's the only way to get anywhere in this life.

I check the time on my phone. Five to ten. Right on cue, Lily arrives with her VIP tea cart in tow. She wheels it over to the side of the stage and nods my way as she gets into position.

The guests are sipping their tea and enjoying their finger sandwiches, an anticipatory buzz filling the room.

Mr. Snow enters carrying a teacup and a spoon. He heads straight up the stage stairs to the podium and switches on the microphone.

"Good morning, everyone," he says, tapping the silver spoon against the Regency Grand cup to get the crowd's attention—such a delightful tinkling sound.

"It is my distinct pleasure to introduce our VIP speaker who will be making an important announcement regarding the recently deceased, internationally renowned master of mystery, Mr. J. D. Grimthorpe. Please welcome a charming young lady of unusual poise and distinction, formerly Mr. Grimthorpe's personal secretary, the lovely Serena Sharpe."

The hidden stage door in the wood paneling opens as the crowd goes silent. Ms. Sharpe, dressed elegantly in a tailored blue dress suit, takes the stage.

She stands behind the podium holding cue cards in her trembling hands. She clears her throat, then begins to speak. "A week ago, a man who claimed to be the solo creator of *The Maid in the Mansion*, one of the top-selling mysteries ever written, along with countless other bestselling titles, graced this very stage to make an announcement. As you all know, that announcement was never made."

The entire room is pin-drop silent. All eyes are on Ms. Sharpe.

"Today, I'll tell you the secret he never lived to tell. It is this: J. D. Grimthorpe was not the author of his books. They were in fact written by my deceased mother, his former personal secretary."

The silence is broken by murmurs and whispers, passed person to person throughout the room.

"For over thirty years," Ms. Sharpe continues, "my mother wrote all of his novels, helping him shape his scrambled ideas into clear and compelling story lines. She was paid a modest wage as his personal secretary when in fact she was his ghostwriter."

Ms. Sharpe waits for the whispers to cease before continuing. "I intimidated Mr. Grimthorpe into holding last week's press conference, during which he was supposed to divulge the truth to the world his way—meaning semitruthfully, elliptically, and narcissistically. I have no doubt he would have found a way to subtly diminish my mother's work, but I didn't care because in return for my silence, I would receive a lump-sum fee and one hundred percent of his book royalties going forward.

"As it turns out, justice really is possible," Serena says, "at least sometimes. Last week, Mr. Grimthorpe's publisher contacted my lawyers to inform me they've begun legal proceedings to restore both credit and royalties to the rightful author of Grimthorpe's books, meaning my mother. All I ever wanted was for her to be properly acknowledged. J. D. Grimthorpe was a fraud, not a master of mystery. The real magic behind his work was my mother, Abigail Sharpe. Now, it is her name that will go down in literary history—*in perpetuum*. Thank you."

Ms. Serena Sharpe puts down her cue cards, steps off the stage, and heads toward the tearoom door. When the crowd realizes she's leaving, they jump to their feet, hurling questions at her in rapid succession.

"Ms. Sharpe! Where are you going? There are things we need to know!"

"Tell us more about your mother! What was Abigail like?"

"Where did she get her ideas?"

"Was she inspired by real life?"

"Ms. Sharpe, will you write her authorized biography?"

"Will there be a sequel to *The Maid in the Mansion?*"

Ms. Sharpe makes it out of the tearoom, but not without a train of VIPs and LAMBS and journalists trailing after her. Their volley of questions echoes all the way down the corridor.

After a minute or two, only a few stragglers remain in the tearoom, including me and one imposing detective.

I approach Stark where she sits alone at her table in front of the stage.

She grabs a shortbread biscuit from a platter. "Well, that's that," she says as she takes a bite.

"Indeed," I say.

"Wow. These are good."

"Made right in the kitchen downstairs."

Detective Stark turns her laser-eyed focus on me. "Molly, I'm serious about what I said the other day, that you'd make a great detective." She takes another bite of biscuit, chews mindfully, then swallows. "And just so you know, there are uniforms in my profession. I prefer to work in plain clothes, but that doesn't mean you'd have to."

She passes the platter of cookies to me. I grab one between two fingers.

"There's a badge as well," she adds. "You could pin it right above your heart, just like you do now."

I take a bite of the shortbread and try to imagine it—me, in a police uniform, DETECTIVE GRAY on a badge above my heart.

"Does the police station handle dry cleaning?" I ask. "Are the uniforms sanitized daily and wrapped in clingy plastic?"

Stark's eyes squint in a funny way. "Why is it that I never quite know what's about to come out of your mouth?" she asks. "As for dry cleaning, I suppose clingy plastic could be arranged, for the right employee. I must warn you, though, an officer's hours are long. Criminals never take days off. They work harder than most."

"Harder than maids?" I ask.

"You have a point there." And with that, she stands suddenly and heads for the tearoom door. At the threshold, she stops and turns my way one more time. "Will you give what I said serious consideration?" she asks.

She waits as I take another bite of the shortbread biscuit, chew it twenty times, then swallow. "I'll consider it," I reply.

"Good," she says. "See you around, Molly Gray."

What she does next completely surprises me. She puts her right foot behind her left and performs a slow, deep curtsy. Then she nods and leaves the room.

—

Epilogue

N *ever fear a new beginning. One chapter must end for another to begin.*

I'm standing in front of Gran's curio cabinet in the apartment I used to share with her and will soon share once more with my beloved Juan Manuel, who is returning from his trip in just a short time.

In one hand, I hold a cloth. In my other hand, I hold an ornamental egg. The Fabergé has not been cleaned in well over a decade. I'm certain I was the last to clean it, getting in trouble for wiping the patina of age away, for restoring the tarnished jewels and gold to a perfectly polished shine.

I don't care if my cleaning it makes the egg less valuable. I don't even know if this egg is a rare treasure as Mrs. Grimthorpe suggested it was all those years ago. That's not what matters—not to me. What I behold is a thing so radiant and enchanting, it takes my breath away every time I look at it. I give it one final buff and polish, then place it on top of Gran's cabinet right beside the photo of my mother as a young girl. Maggie, the stranger at my door. Maggie, who said she had once worked with my gran as a maid. Is that true? Did she, too, work in that loveless mansion, polishing silver and suffering Mr. Grimthorpe's abuse? Three years after her mysterious appearance at our door that day, Gran told me my mother died. And yet, even so, I sometimes have visions of her appearing in my life out of nowhere, knocking on my door again the way she did all those years ago. But she hasn't yet. And I suppose I must accept that she never will.

As soon as I think it, there's a knock on the door, which makes me gasp and jolt. I look out the fish-eye peephole and am relieved to see Mr. Preston, right on time, wearing his plain clothes rather than a doorman's cap and coat. He shifts from one foot to the other.

I open the door. "Mr. Preston, do come in," I say. "I have our tea ready. We have just enough time for a chat before Juan Manuel arrives."

"Wonderful," he says as he steps inside. He passes me a box.

"Raisin bran muffins," he says. "Your favorite," he adds with a wink.

"How very thoughtful. I'll add them to our tea service," I say as I take them to the kitchen.

Mr. Preston removes his shoes, wipes the bottoms with the cleaning cloth in the closet, then neatly slips them onto the mat inside.

"How did the rest of today go, Mr. Preston?" I ask.

"I survived," he replies. "When the press conference let out, the valets and I were mobbed on the stairs. I practically had to beat the crowd off as poor Ms. Sharpe made her escape in a taxi."

"Did you know her when she was a child?" I ask.

"No," he replies. "Unlike your grandmother, Abigail Sharpe never brought her daughter to the mansion. You were the only child around—our bright spot of hope amidst all that dreary dark-ness."

The kettle boils. I transfer water into a proper teapot on Gran's thrift-store silver tray and bring it to the living room along with two porcelain cups.

Mr. Preston takes a seat on the sofa, but he's clearly unsettled. He fidgets and shifts in his place.

"Juan will be here in a bit," I say. "He's landed. But we have time for a spot of tea now."

"Lovely," says Mr. Preston. I pour tea into my favorite cup, the one with pretty white-and-yellow daisies on it, and I pass it to him. I fill Gran's country cottage cup for myself.

"I better get to it, then," he says as he takes a sip, then puts the cup down on its saucer. "There's no easy way to say this, Molly, though I suspect you've known what I'm about to say for some time."

"I'll admit I do know, Mr. Preston. And it's okay. It's perfectly reasonable for you to retire. You deserve to enjoy your time off. No one can work forever."

Mr. Preston stares at me with a look I can't quite read. After a moment, he says, "Molly, I'm your grandfather."

At first, I'm certain I'm hearing things. But then I realize what's really going on. Poor Mr. Preston is older than I think and is losing touch with reality. Goodness me, his mind is starting to curdle like warm milk.

But when Mr. Preston repeats it—"Molly, did you hear me? I really am your grandfather"—I put down my teacup. The world begins to spin. Fabergés and muffins and Gran's thrift-store silver dance before my eyes.

"Molly. Please don't faint. Here," he says, picking up my cup from the table and putting it in my hands. "Tea cures all ills."

"My gran used to say that," I say between long, unsteady breaths.

"I know," he replies.

I look at him as the spinning world slows to a standstill. "Mr. Preston, are you of sound mind?" I ask.

"What? Of course I am," he replies.

I wait for him to say more.

"Molly, years ago, when your gran and I were young and in love, her parents were desperate to keep us apart. Once upon a time, your gran had money. Her parents were very well-to-do. She was upper crust, and in her parents' eyes, I was just a poor, useless crumb. But, you see, her parents failed to keep us apart."

"Failed how?" I ask.

Mr. Preston takes a sip of tea. "I mean it literally, not figuratively." He clears his throat and squirms in his seat.

It takes me a moment. "Oh," I say. "I see."

"Molly, when I found out your grandmother was pregnant, I wasn't upset. Not at all. I told Flora it was the best thing that had ever happened to me. I wanted to elope and live happily ever after. We made a plan to do it, but it never happened."

"Why not?" I ask.

"On the day we'd planned to run away together, I went to her home, a posh three-story mansion in a neighborhood far from my own. I knocked on the door, but I wasn't allowed in. Her parents didn't even have the nerve to speak to me themselves. It was the butler who told me she was long gone."

"She'd run away?" I ask.

"No. She was shipped away against her will. By her parents. They sent her to a home for unwed mothers, the kind where they take the baby away from its mother once it's born."

"But they didn't take the baby away," I say, my eyes turning to the photo on the curio cabinet. "Gran kept her. She raised my mother."

"Yes, because she ran away from that loveless place. She escaped. She came back to the city. She showed up on her parents' doorstep begging for forgiveness, but her parents disowned her. She was eight months pregnant, Molly. She accepted a job as a domestic maid, working for a very wealthy family. When her time came, she took a few days off to have her baby, and then she kept working with the infant bundled on her hip."

"But why didn't she come back to you? Why didn't you help her?" I ask.

"She wanted nothing to do with me. Her parents had filled her with shame, told her she was a failure and a good-for-nothing who never understood the reality of things until it was too late. For years, your gran refused to see me. She rented this very apartment, Molly, and she lived here until the day she died. Did you know any of this?"

"No," I say.

"I tried many times to help her. She wouldn't let me. She wouldn't let me see my child either. Eventually, I gave up trying. I met my wife, Mary, and we married, had our daughter, Charlotte. And we were very happy. But I never forgot Flora. And I never forgot your mother either," he says.

"Maggie," I say.

"So your gran told you her name."

"No," I say. "She didn't."

"After a lot of pressure, Flora eventually let me back into her life. I'd told Mary everything, of course. My beloved wife knew the whole story, that I'd fathered a child with Flora out of wedlock. My Mary was a good woman. She and your gran formed a lovely friendship over the years. When your gran struggled, all on her own like that, it was Mary who convinced her to accept our help. We did what we could when we could."

"The rent money," I say. "You gave it to us."

NITA PROSE

"Yes. And later when your mother got mixed up with that . . . that . . ."

"Fly-by-night?" I offer.

"I was going to say 'thieving drug dealer,' but you've always been more polite than I am." He looks at me, his eyes brimming with tears. "I'm sorry I didn't tell you any of this before. I tried, but I couldn't find the words. I worried the shock would undo you."

"It hasn't," I say. "It won't."

"No. You've always been stronger than anyone gives you credit for."

I turn my eyes to Gran's teacup in my lap. "I never had a mother. And I never had a father either. I lost my gran," I say. I look up at the man before me. "Mr. Preston, I can't believe it. I've never been happier than I am in this moment. It's like magic. I've gotten a piece of my family back."

I feel a warm hand on my arm, and it's hard to see Mr. Preston through my own tears. "I don't know what to call you anymore. Mr. Preston doesn't seem quite right," I say.

"What about Gran-dad?" he offers.

I reach for my cup and take a sip of warm tea. "Yes," I say, resting the cup on the saucer. "Gran-dad. I like that very much."

Just then, there's a sound at the door, a key turning in the lock. The door opens and Juan Manuel appears, rolling in a large suitcase behind him. I jump up from my seat and rush to the door.

"*Mi amor!*" he says as he takes me into his arms. "How I've missed you . . ."

It feels so good to have him back. I hold on tight and don't want to let go. I do so only when I realize I've left Mr. Preston on the sofa all alone.

"Mr. Preston," Juan says as he walks over and gives him a pat on the back. "Are you well?"

"I am," my gran-dad replies. "I'm better than ever."

"Good," says Juan, flashing his beautiful, bright smile. "First, let me tell you that my family says hello. If I forget to mention that, I'll be in big trouble. My mother sends her love. My nephew sends his report card. He wants to brag about how well he's doing in school. He also wants a dog, but my sister is against it. He'll convince her, though, I'm sure of it. Here, look, this is a photo of everyone sending me off at the airport."

Juan calls up a photo on his phone—his giant family, all gathered at Departures, grinning and holding up a banner that says HASTA PRONTO—see you soon. There are so many of them, they barely fit in the frame.

As Juan chatters on, taking a seat beside Mr. Preston, I go to the kitchen and bring out an extra cup and a plate of treats, setting them down on the coffee table.

"Molly, look at this one," Juan says as he shows us another photo. "See? My mother, she wrote you a card in English." She's holding it, pointing proudly. He zooms in on the open card: *To my daughter-in-law*, it says. *I miss you and love you. Visit us soon.*

"But I'm not her daughter-in-law," I say.

"Not yet," Juan replies, but before I can ask what he means, he starts to chirp again like a little bird, going on about how much he missed me and how nice it was to see his family but how great it is to be home.

Suddenly, he goes quiet. "I am rude," he says. "I haven't even asked you both how you are. I'm so sorry. You know how I talk and talk and talk when I'm excited."

"Oh yes, we know," my gran-dad replies with a chuckle.

"So? How are you?" Juan asks. "Everything good?"

I pour him a cup of tea, hoping that I won't have to answer that.

"All's well that ends well," says my grandfather. "But it's been . . ." He pauses, searching for the right word.

"A tumultuous time," I say.

"Tumultuous?" Juan asks.

"Meaning: stormy, volatile, intense," I explain. "Let's just say that we had to contend with some very unusual vermin."

"*What?*" he asks. "In our apartment?"

"No," says my gran-dad, "in the hotel."

"Did you get rid of them? Did you lay traps?" Juan asks.

"We most certainly did," I say with a smile.

"In fact," says my grandfather, "Molly is the one who caught the rat."

Juan turns to me, beaming from ear to ear. "That's my Molly. Fear never stops her. In fact, nothing stops her."

"You're so right," my gran-dad replies. "Do you know, she's been like that ever since she was a child."

"Really?" Juan replies. "Tell me more."

As the two of them converse, my gran-dad sets the stage for the seismic revelations, about both the murder that happened in the hotel while Juan was away and the fact that he is not just Mr. Preston, the doorman, but in fact is my relation. My flesh and blood.

I sit across from them, listening, waiting, and sipping tea from Gran's favorite cup.

She's not here with us, my gran. She's not sitting on the sofa between my beloved and her own, nor is she humming her little tune in the kitchen. But I know she's here nonetheless because she always has been. She is the key to everything. The outline of my entire life gives her presence every single day.

I know she's watching. I can hear her in my head even now:

Wonders never cease, Molly.

What doesn't kill you makes you stronger.

Good things come to those who wait.

ACKNOWLEDGMENTS

It takes a village to publish a book. It really does.

When I wrote *The Maid*, I wrote it in secrecy because I was scared of failure. What if it didn't meet the bar? What if people hated what I put out there?

Let's just say I couldn't keep *The Mystery Guest* quite as secret as *The Maid*. The good news? As I wrote it, I had the best support team a writer could ever ask for. They championed and guided me in the background as I toiled away on that most difficult of ventures—the dreaded Book Two.

Madeleine Milburn, you don't realize how extraordinary you are. It's an act of superhuman generosity to give so much to so many writers. Huge thanks, too, to the amazing team at Madeleine Milburn Literary, TV & Film Agency—Rachel Yeoh, Liane-Louise Smith, Valentina Paulmichl, Giles Milburn, Saskia Arthur, Amanda Carungi, Georgina Simmonds, Georgia McVeigh, and Hannah Ladds.

What's the perfect editorial shape? A triangle. My three ingenious editors form a triad so powerful that it points me in the right direction every time. Thank you, Nicole Winstanley at Penguin Random House Canada, Hilary Teeman at Ballantine US, and Charlotte Brabbin at HarperFiction UK. And thanks, too, to the amazing teams in all of your houses, with special thanks to Dan French,

Bonnie Maitland, Beth Cockeram, Meredith Pal, and Kristin Cochrane in Canada; Michelle Jasmine, Caroline Weishuhn, Taylor Noel, Megan Whalen, Jennifer Garza, Quinne Rogers, Kara Welsh, Kim "Blue Type" Hovey, Jennifer Hershey, Hope Hathcock, Diane McKiernan, Elena Giavaldi, Pamela Alders, Cindy Berman, and Sandra Sjursen in the US; Kimberley Young, Lynne Drew, Sarah Shea, Maddy Marshall, Emilie Chambeyron, Alice Gomer, and Bethan Moore in the UK.

My silver-screen cheerleaders include Chris Goldberg, brilliant writer and producer at Winterlight Pictures; the indefatigably positive Josh McLaughlin at Wink Pictures; and the savvy and charming Josie Freedman at ICM.

Friends, writers, and publishing people—you know who you are. If I wrote down all of your names, I might cause another paper shortage. Adria Iwasutiak, Sarah St. Pierre, Janie Yoon, Felicia Quon, Sarah Gibson, Jessica Scott, Adriana Pitesa, and Carolina Testa—you remind me what passion in publishing looks like. Aileen Umali, Eric Rist, Ryan Wilson, Sandy Gabriele, Roberto Verdecchia, Sarah Fulton, Jorge Gidi, Martin Ortuzar, Jimena Ortuzar, Ingrid Nasager, Ellen Keith, Matthew Lawson, Zoe Maslow, Liz Nugent, Dan Mallory, Amy Stuart, Nina de Gramont, and Ashley Audrain—you keep me sane (well, you try your best anyhow). Thanks also to Arlyn Miller-Lachmann for her wise comments and thoughts.

I must apologize for having the best brother in the world, Dan Pronovost (sorry to the rest of you who have other brothers; they just can't compare). I also have the gift of his family, my wonderful sister-in-law, Patty; my niece, Joane; and my nephew, Devin. You make me laugh, and I'm grateful that you laugh *at me,* too. If that doesn't deserve acknowledging, I don't know what does. Freddie and Pat—long may we raise margaritas. *Ma tante Suzanne et ma cousine Louise,* you're in these pages and forever in my DNA. And my beloved Tony, I don't know how or why you put up with me, but I'm so glad you do.

Readers, you are wonderful. You make the world a better place. Thank you for your support.

Dad, you were the first reader of this book. It's okay that you're not with us anymore because I hear your voice every time I call you in my head. Thank you for answering.

NITA PROSE is the author of *The Maid*, which has sold over one million copies worldwide and was published in more than forty countries. A #1 *New York Times* bestseller and a *Good Morning America* Book Club pick, *The Maid* won the Ned Kelly Award for International Crime Fiction, the Fingerprint Award for Debut Novel of the Year, the Anthony Award for Best First Novel, and the Barry Award for Best First Mystery. *The Maid* was also an Edgar Award finalist for Best Novel. Nita lives in Toronto, Canada, in a house that is only moderately clean. She would love to hear from you at **nitaprose.com.**

Twitter and Instagram: @NitaProse

This book was set in Albertina, a typeface created by Dutch calligrapher and designer Chris Brand (1921–98). Brand's original drawings, based on calligraphic principles, were modified considerably to conform to the technological limitations of typesetting in the early 1960s. The development of digital technology later allowed Frank E. Blokland (b. 1959) of the Dutch Type Library to restore the typeface to its creator's original intentions.